## IT TAKES TWO TO UNTANGLE....

The next day, instead of going back into the game, he decided to spend his time on the outside, thinking about the clue. He looked at it from every angle and replaced every move. He Googled the name Fawn Liebowitz, even though he knew exactly where the programmer had taken it from, and even though the fact that she was known only for dying in a kiln explosion would do him no good at all.

And then he realized the one piece he hadn't played with yet. She was a student. That was the key. There had to be some secret code that only students knew, some special way to talk to them. That would make sense, since most of the game's audience would be college kids desperate for an excuse not to study.

The only trouble was Shawn had never been to college. He hadn't been a student since he'd graduated from high school, and while he had talked to a lot of college girls, the subject of their studies somehow never came up.

But that wasn't a problem. Because Gus had actually been to college. And in his years there, he had spent some time in every major they had on offer. For all Shawn knew he might have even spent some time in this so-called library science, if such a thing really existed. If there was anything to know about college life, Gus would know it. Shawn grabbed for the phone and started to dial.

And then he remembered. Gus didn't work for Psych anymore.

And Gus would never work for Psych again.

## THE PSYCH SERIES

# Psych

## MIND-ALTERING MURDER

William Rabkin

AN OBSIDIAN MYSTERY

OBSIDIAN

Published by New American Library, a division of
Penguin Group (USA) Inc., 375 Hudson Street,
New York, New York 10014, USA

Penguin Group (Canada), 90 Eglinton Avenue East, Suite 700, Toronto,
Ontario M4P 2Y3, Canada (a division of Pearson Penguin Canada Inc.)
Penguin Books Ltd., 80 Strand, London WC2R 0RL, England
Penguin Ireland, 25 St. Stephen's Green, Dublin 2,
Ireland (a division of Penguin Books Ltd.)
Penguin Group (Australia), 250 Camberwell Road, Camberwell, Victoria 3124,
Australia (a division of Pearson Australia Group Pty. Ltd.)
Penguin Books India Pvt. Ltd., 11 Community Centre, Panchsheel Park,
New Delhi - 110 017, India
Penguin Group (NZ), 67 Apollo Drive, Rosedale, North Shore 0632,
New Zealand (a division of Pearson New Zealand Ltd.)
Penguin Books (South Africa) (Pty.) Ltd., 24 Sturdee Avenue,
Rosebank, Johannesburg 2196, South Africa

Penguin Books Ltd., Registered Offices:
80 Strand, London WC2R 0RL, England

First published by Obsidian, an imprint of New American Library,
a division of Penguin Group (USA) Inc.

First Printing, February 2011
10  9  8  7  6  5  4  3  2  1

PUBLISHER'S NOTE

This is a work of fiction. Names, characters, places, and incidents either are the
product of the author's imagination or are used fictitiously, and any resemblance
to actual persons, living or dead, business establishments, events, or locales is
entirely coincidental.

The publisher does not have any control over and does not assume any responsibility for author or third-party Web sites or their content.

*Simply, for Carrie*

# Prologue

*1990*

Santa Barbara police detective Henry Spencer stared down at the red mark on the paper. It was good, he had to admit. He'd been working on a big forgery case for the past few weeks, and nothing he'd come across there had looked as authentic as this.

Henry drew his thumb across the paper, pressing down hard as he tried to smudge the red ink. It didn't smear. It had been on the page long enough to set.

That didn't mean the mark was genuine. Henry's prey was crafty and thorough. He would have taken the time to prepare his forgery well in advance. But no matter how good he was, the felon must have made a mistake somewhere.

Henry pulled a magnifying glass out of his desk drawer and peered at the red mark through it. He knew where he'd find the telltale signs of tampering—there would be an extra line added to the mark's right side, or its bottom curve would have been erased and a new slash drawn through the middle.

But no matter how long Henry stared at the symbol, he

could find no evidence that this was anything but the original mark. Which meant the impossible had happened.

Shawn had gotten an A on his book report.

Of course, that was only impossible if Shawn had actually written the report himself. The handwriting was his, but that had been true when he'd copied an essay out of the back of the teacher's edition, too. Henry quickly skimmed the first page. It read like the work of a twelve-year-old, not of a doctoral candidate hacking out sample compositions to help make his student-loan payments.

That still left the question of which twelve-year-old had done the work. And before Henry broke out the ice cream to celebrate his son's unprecedented academic triumph, he needed an answer.

He took the steps two at a time and threw open the door to Shawn's bedroom as if he expected to catch him in the middle of an act of plagiarism.

Shawn barely looked up from his Hot Wheels. "It's real, Dad," he said. "I got an A."

"Someone got an A," Henry said. He turned his fiercest gaze on Gus, who had picked up a toy car and was studying it so intently he might have been working up a repair estimate for an insurance company. "The question is who?"

"It was Shawn," Gus said, never looking up from the car's undercarriage.

"All on his own?" Henry said, staring down at Gus.

"Don't you have any faith in me, Dad?" Shawn said.

"Way too much to fall for this," Henry said, still not taking his eyes off Gus. That kid would crack soon; Henry could tell by the nervous way he was spinning the car's wheels. "So what did Shawn do, son? Did he copy off your paper?"

"Dad!"

Henry ignored him. "You can tell me, Gus," he said in his most fatherly voice, the one he reserved for children who were not actually related to him. "Did Shawn copy your paper?"

"No, sir," Gus said.

"Then I don't suppose you'd mind letting me look at your book report," Henry said. Before either of the boys could move, he snatched Gus' backpack off the chair where it was hanging and pulled out a three-ring binder neatly arranged by subject and date. He flipped to the section marked "English" and then to this week's assignment.

"Dad, that's none of your business," Shawn said.

"It is if his report is identical to yours," Henry said. He turned a page and saw a book report with the same date as Shawn's.

"See, Mr. Spencer?" Gus said. "They're not identical."

They weren't. Not in any aspect. The subjects were different. The sentences were different. And most of all, the grades were different.

"You got a C minus?" Henry said, amazed. "You've never done worse than a B plus in your life."

Gus stared down at the orange-plastic track. "Apparently my thoughts were ill formed, my grammar was sloppy, and my vocabulary didn't rise to grade level," he said.

"That doesn't sound like the Gus I know," Henry said.

"Well, it is," Shawn said. "Your own son scored an A, and all you can do is whine about how bad Gus did. Way to encourage me to work hard in school, Dad."

The anger in Shawn's voice made Henry take a step back. Was he right? Did Henry reflexively discount his own son's accomplishments? Was he actively sabotaging Shawn? He replayed Shawn's sentence in his head. And then he knew he was being played again.

"That's an interesting thought, Shawn," Henry said. "Not particularly well formed, though. And it's not grammatical to say 'how bad Gus did.' The adverbial form is 'badly.' Oh, and a vocabulary at your grade level would lead you to say, 'Way to encourage academic excellence,' not 'to work hard in school.'"

Shawn glared at him, caught. "What's your point?"

"I understand why you copied Gus' paper and turned it in as your own," Henry said. "What I can't figure out is why Gus would claim yours."

Gus seemed to be finding worlds of wonder in that orange track, because he refused to look up from it.

"It's shameful enough to get a C minus when you're capable of A work," Henry said. "But if you don't confess right now, I'll take this to your principal and then you'll both get an F."

"But then Shawn will be held back!" Gus said.

Shawn slapped his forehead in frustration. "Falls for it every time."

Henry ignored Shawn. He got down on his knees in front of Gus. "You helped Shawn with his homework so you'd both be in the same grade next year?"

Gus nodded solemnly.

"That's very thoughtful of you," Henry said. "It's wrong, but I can appreciate the sentiment. But why didn't you just write two book reports and give one to Shawn? Why turn in his own lousy work as your own?"

Gus sniffled back a tear. "If I got another A, they were going to promote me to the advanced class."

"That's wonderful, Gus," Henry said. "Congratulations." And then he realized. "But then you and Shawn wouldn't be in the same class anymore."

"He said if I turned in his work, there's no way they'd let me go to nerd school."

Henry had been mad at Shawn before. Sometimes he felt that he'd gotten angry the moment his son was delivered and hadn't calmed down since. But this was different. Shawn had betrayed his own best friend, used Gus' love and trust against him. Henry had to force himself to keep his hands down for fear he might grab his son and throw him out the window.

"How could you do that to your best friend?" Henry said.

"Do what?"

"Trick him so he wouldn't qualify for the advanced class," Henry said.

"I didn't trick him," Shawn said. "He wanted to stay in the normal class with me."

"That's true," Gus said.

"You may have just stolen his future," Henry said.

"Gus doesn't need a future," Shawn said. "He can share mine."

"That's right," Gus said. "I can share Shawn's."

Henry took a deep breath. Counted to ten. Recited the alphabet. Then, fighting to keep a calm smile on his face, he turned to Gus.

"I think it's time for you to run along home now, Gus," Henry said.

"Can't I stay a little longer?" Gus said. "My mom's still got her bridge friends over, and that house is nowhere for a boy when they're there."

"I think you need to leave now," Henry said, ushering him toward the door. "Because Shawn's immediate future is something you really don't want to share."

# Chapter One

As a store it wasn't much. Fifteen feet deep, maybe half that wide, a long counter running down the middle. Behind the counter the wall was covered with liquor bottles, and the liquor bottles were covered with dust. The only ones that weren't encased in grime were the strong, vile brews favored by those with deep thirsts but shallow pockets. The cheap corn whiskeys, the Bulgarian fortified wines, and the "malt beverages" made from grain alcohol sweetened with Kool-Aid twinkled brightly from a shelf the man behind the counter could reach without having to turn his back on the customer.

Not that he looked like he had any intention of turning his back on his customer. He stared across the counter at Gus, his ancient face crumpled into a permanent squint, one hand holding on to the tarnished register, either to keep it from walking out the door or to keep his knees from buckling, and the other just out of sight under the counter, undoubtedly fingering the shotgun hidden down there.

"You want something?" The owner's voice was as cragged as his face.

This was the moment Gus had been dreading. The

clues he'd been following had brought him here as surely
as the Yellow Brick Road took Dorothy to Oz. But like
that lemon-colored highway, this path held dangers at
every turn. And so far not one of them had been as be-
nign as the Scarecrow or the Lion. The only person he'd
met who acted at all welcoming was a young woman in
hot pants and a halter top, who'd offered to party with
Gus in an adjacent alley for a mere forty dollars. Gus
wouldn't have been tempted to accept her offer even if
he hadn't seen the shadowy figure lurking just inside the
alley's mouth.

That danger recognized easily, he moved on as quickly
as he could, stopping only to pick up a brick and smash the
window of a Porsche Cayenne that someone had left at the
curb. A note on the driver's seat gave the address of this
liquor store, and he ran here as fast as he could.

But now that he faced the withered shopkeeper across
the grimy countertop, he wasn't sure what he should do
next. His first instinct was, as always, to be as friendly as
possible and simply ask for help. But he'd already tried that
once in the emergency room. It made him sick to think of
what had happened next.

"It's a store, not a damn museum," the owner croaked,
the sagging skin of his left arm twitching as his hand
clutched the shotgun. "You want to buy something or you
want to get out."

Gus scanned the shelves of bottles, trying to make out
a label underneath the grime. Nothing looked right to him.
He had to bring something back to Morton; that was the
only way he could prove he was trustworthy. At least that
was how the dead guy who used to own that Cayenne was
supposed to prove his worth. Since Morton had never seen
either of them, all Gus had to do to win a place in the Organization was show up with the proper token.

It occurred to Gus that he should probably say something. The old guy might have been expecting Cayenne and would know to turn over the right item to him. If only there had been something on the note besides this address.

*Maybe it's not what was on the note,* Gus thought. *Maybe it's the note itself.* That didn't seem likely. It was just a scrap off a yellow legal pad, nothing on it but this address scrawled diagonally across one side. The back was blank. But as soon as the thought crossed his mind Gus was certain he needed to show the note to the shopkeeper.

"You want to buy something or you want to get out," the old man croaked again, and this time Gus was sure he could see dust rising out of his mouth.

Gus dug in the pockets of his silk suit and pulled out the scrap of paper. He unfolded it carefully, then slid it across the counter to the proprietor.

The old man didn't even glance down at the paper. He stared at Gus. "You want to buy something or you want to get out," he said.

"I'll buy something," Gus said, desperately trying to figure out what it was he needed. He glanced away from the shelves of bottles and studied the other side of the store. There was a rack of tattered magazines, their covers featuring naked women or motorcycles or naked women on motorcycles. A locked case held cans of what Gus could only assume was chewing tobacco, although it had never occurred to him that there could be so many brands of something no one he'd met had ever used. Against the wall were bare shelves littered with a few items that might once have been intended to be eaten—packaged snack cakes, their pink marshmallow and coconut shells turning brown and shriveling with age to reveal the permanently moist chocolate crumb underneath; cardboard tubes reportedly filled with chips made from "at least thirty-two percent real potato"; a cloudy plastic bucket containing soggy sticks of jerked something. There was nothing here that Morton could possibly have wanted to allow into his immaculate penthouse, even as an identification marker.

Gus turned back to the owner, who was still staring directly at him. "You ready to buy something?"

"Sure," Gus said. "Let me have . . ." Desperately he scanned the shelves behind the old man. There wasn't a hint of what he was supposed to purchase, just row after row of filthy bottles.

Then he saw something. A glint of light. It came from one of the upper shelves. Gus peered up and saw that there was one bottle that wasn't dirty at all. It looked like it had just been placed there. "I'll have that bottle of Glen Graggenlogan," he said, hoping he was reading the label correctly from this distance.

The old man stared at him for a moment, then gave Gus an almost imperceptible wink. "Think you can handle it, junior?" he said.

Was this some kind of test, or was the old man really trying to warn him away for his own good? Gus couldn't tell. "Is there something I should know?"

The shopkeeper didn't answer, just kept staring. There wasn't going to be any help coming from him. "Just give me the bottle," Gus said.

The old man pulled his hand out from under the counter and turned slowly to a rickety library ladder attached at the top to a railing that ran parallel to the ceiling. Sliding it slowly into position, he managed to lift one leg up to the bottom rung, where he rested as if waiting for the strength to continue.

Gus checked his watch, then checked it again. Time was flying past. Morton wasn't going to wait forever.

"Can I help you with that?" Gus said, if only to keep himself from screaming at the old man to hurry the hell up.

"Don't need no help," the shopkeeper said. "Not from a punk like you."

Was that a deliberate provocation? Once again Gus

wished he knew more about the old man's role in his task. If he was in on it, if he was reporting back to Morton, it wouldn't sound good that Gus was willing to take this kind of insult from him. Cayenne wouldn't have. He'd have shaken the rickety ladder until the rungs broke free and the geezer fell to his death. But if he wasn't, if he was just naturally unpleasant, then all that mattered to Gus was getting the bottle and getting out.

"Sure this is the one you want?"

Gus looked up to see that somehow the old man had reached the top of the ladder and grabbed one of the dusty bottles with the hand that wasn't clutching the guide rail.

Gus's first instinct was to thank him, then point out that he was close to the proper bottle. But now he was seized by the suspicion that this was some kind of test, and that he wouldn't pass it with a demonstration of graciousness. "You blind, deaf, or just stupid?" he snarled. "I said the Glen Graggenlogan, not whatever swill you're trying to pawn off on me."

If the shopkeeper was unused to this level of rudeness, he didn't show it. He thrust the dusty bottle back into its place on the shelf, nearly sending the entire row crashing down onto the floor, then extended his arm as far as it would go, his fingers barely brushing the bottle Gus had demanded.

Gus couldn't look. He knew what was going to happen. The old man was going to nudge the bottle again and he was going to knock it off the shelf. The only thing he'd be able to bring Morton would be the broken neck, which was undoubtedly what Morton would give him in return.

A buzz sounded behind him. The door alarm. Gus started to turn. Before he could see who had come in, two shots blasted through the air.

The old man flew off the ladder, smashing into the wall of bottles, then crashed to the floor in a rain of broken glass and cheap scotch.

Gus stared over the counter at the shopkeeper's bloody corpse. "Why did you do that?"

Shawn stepped up to him, thrusting the .44 Magnum into the pocket of his leather duster.

"The question," Shawn said, "is, why didn't you?"

# Chapter Two

"Why didn't I what?" Gus said. "Murder an old man who was trying to help me?"

"Is that what you call it?" Shawn said.

"Murder is what the law calls it," Gus said. "It's what the Bible calls it. It's what everyone in the world calls it."

"I could be wrong about this, but I seem to recall hearing that in different countries they have different words for things," Shawn said as he stepped over to the shelves of snack foods and gave an exploratory squeeze to a package of Twinkies with a pull date from before the turn of the millennium.

Gus couldn't pull his eyes away from the dead man lying on the floor in a pool of blood and whiskey. "Why did you kill him?"

Shawn put down the Twinkies and turned his attention to the freezer chest loaded with ice-cream bars. Or, as he discovered when he tried to take one out, loaded with a single ice-cream bar, as all the smaller units had melted and refrozen into a cube six feet on each side.

"Because it was him or you." Shawn took two running steps, then leaped over the counter, landing in a crouch next to the body, his duster sending waves through the puddle spreading across the floor.

"What was he going to do?" Gus said. "Throw the bottle at me?"

"Worse. He was going to give it to you." Shawn pulled the bottle of Glen Graggenlogan from the shopkeeper's cold, dead hands and looked it over carefully. Then he pulled out the cork and turned it upside down. There was a rattle of metal on glass, and a small olive-colored device fell into Shawn's hand.

"What is that?" Gus said.

"Doesn't matter what it is now. What matters is what it would be if you walked out the door with it," Shawn said.

"And what is that?"

"The ultimate theft-protection device," Shawn said. He jumped back over the counter, opened the door, and tossed the device out onto the street. The thing bounced twice on the asphalt and then exploded into a fireball that took out two cars and the area's last remaining pay phone.

It took a few seconds for Gus' ears to stop ringing. He spent the time staring at the crater in the center of the road and trying to figure out how far his body parts might be separated by now if Shawn hadn't stopped him from taking the bottle.

"I thought that was the thing I was supposed to bring Morton," Gus said finally.

"Apparently you were supposed to think that."

Gus looked around the liquor store in despair. "So what is the object?" he said. "What is it we're supposed to collect here? Because I haven't seen it."

"That's where you're wrong," Shawn said. "You were staring at it all along."

"I wasn't staring at anything all along," Gus said, then realized he wasn't completely right. "Except . . ."

Shawn nodded. "Except." He jumped back over the

counter and fished around under it in the area the old man had kept his hand, then came up with a machete.

"Morton's people would never allow us into his lobby carrying a weapon like that, let alone into his penthouse," Gus said.

"The machete isn't going anywhere," Shawn said. "Except through a couple of vertebrae."

It took Gus a moment to realize what he was hearing. By that time Shawn had already raised the machete high over his head and was beginning to bring it down toward the old man's body.

"Stop!" Gus shouted.

Shawn froze, the machete poised in midair. "You want to do this?"

"Of course not," Gus said.

"Then what's the problem?" Shawn said. "You can kill a couple of cops when we leave here. Then we'll be even."

"I don't want to kill anybody," Gus said.

"You're no fun," Shawn said.

"I am fun," Gus said. "I am huge amounts of fun. Entire barrels of monkeys spend their lives yearning to be as fun as I am. What isn't fun is shooting unarmed people and cutting off their heads."

Gus reached up and grabbed his own ears. He gave them a hard tug, as if he was trying to pull his head off his shoulders.

"He had a grenade in one hand and a machete under the counter, which strongly suggests he wasn't entirely unarmed," Shawn said.

Despite his best efforts Gus' ears remained stubbornly in place. "What about the little old lady you gunned down in the park?"

"She had that dog," Shawn said.

"A bichon frise," Gus said. "A Muppet would have been more of a threat. That didn't stop you from putting three bullets in her."

"I admit I got a little overeager there," Shawn said. "But I paid the price for that. The cops came down pretty hard on me."

"Until you ran them all over with your Hummer," Gus said.

"Which dented the fender and put the car out of commission," Shawn said. "Why do you think you were able to get here first?"

Gus gave his ears another yank, then grabbed his nose with one fist and twisted fiercely. "I wish I hadn't. I wish we had never started this in the first place."

"But we did," Shawn said. "And now we have to finish."

"I am finished," Gus said. He squeezed his temples between his hands, then twisted his head furiously. The last thing he heard was the crack of his neck snapping.

# Chapter Three

Gus blinked against the sudden harsh light, then turned to see the cyclops next to him. It wore Shawn's traditional khakis, along with a plaid shirt open over a white tee, but its head was a solid sphere of white plastic. It stumbled through the empty room, waving its arms in front of it like a small child playing zombie.

Gus grabbed the cyclops by the shoulders, then pulled the globe off its neck. Freed from the helmet, Shawn glared at him.

"You're never supposed to pull someone out of an immersive reality like that," Shawn said. "You could have destroyed my brain."

"The only thing destroying your brain is that stupid game," Gus said.

Shawn stared at him. "Sorry, Dad. I didn't recognize you with all that hair and the new tan," he said finally.

"I am not some grumpy old man trying to unplug the computer because you've been playing *Monkey Island* for sixteen hours straight," Gus said. "Although I'm beginning to see his point."

"What, that people shouldn't be allowed to have fun?" Shawn said.

Gus put the two helmets into their slots on a low shelf that ran along one side of the handball court–sized room. As soon as they were back in place, there was an electronic click and the door set into one wall sprang open.

"Now look what you've done," Shawn said. "I hope this game saves itself automatically, or we're going to have to start all over again. And I don't know about you, but I don't feel like hijacking another bus full of schoolkids."

"You didn't have to hijack the first one," Gus said. "You didn't get anything out of it."

"I got major street cred," Shawn said. "Especially after I threw the driver off the bridge, then landed the bus on top of him."

"Listen to yourself," Gus said. "You sound like a maniac."

"Desperate times call for desperate measures," Shawn said.

"Your measures aren't desperate. They're stupid," Gus said.

"The whole point of the game is to take over Morton's crime syndicate, and you can't do that unless you can win his trust and get close to him," Shawn said. "So first thing, you've got to establish yourself as the new face of crime in Darksyde City so he'll invite you to join his organization. And you call that stupid?"

"It is when we have a job in the real world," Gus said. "Gaining street cred with a fictional mobster in a computer game isn't bringing us any closer to finding Macklin Tanner."

That was one thing the events of the game had in common with those of the real world. Nothing they had done before entering the virtual world had offered a clue to the whereabouts of the man they'd been hired to find.

Macklin Tanner, founder and CEO of VirtuActive Software—one of the biggest computer-game companies in the country—had disappeared mysteriously a week before. The police had done some investigating and found no traces of foul play; in fact, they'd found a note on his computer saying he was going on vacation for a few weeks. That closed their investigation.

But when the company's president, Brenda Varda, came to the Psych offices, it was clear she didn't believe a word of it. Although her manner was cool and professional, they could tell she was seriously troubled. She had the seemingly effortless beauty that often came with a multimillion-dollar salary, but there was a haunted look in her eyes as she explained the problem.

"We've been working on this new game for years," she said as she stared across the desk, pleading for help from Shawn and Gus. "It's Mack's dream, a completely interactive three-D action game with an entirely new interface. It's going to change the world of gaming. It may even change the rest of the world. And there's no way he'd leave just before the launch."

"Unless the stress got to him," Gus suggested. "People do strange things when they're under that much pressure."

Brenda sighed and picked her purse up off the floor. Before she could get up, Shawn jumped to his feet.

"Excellent work, Gus," Shawn said. "You knew exactly what the police told her and you were able to repeat it word for word."

Brenda turned her cool green eyes on Gus. "Is that what you were doing?"

"Sure," Gus said. "It couldn't possibly be true."

Shawn took one of Brenda's hands in his own and looked at her. And he *saw*. Saw the sheen under her eyes where she'd put on cream to reduce tear-induced swelling. Saw the faint pale shadow on her ring finger.

Shawn closed his eyes and put his fingers to his temples. "I see him," Shawn said.

"You do?" she said. "Is he all right?"

"He's on an altar," Shawn said. "It's some kind of bizarre ritual."

"Oh, my God," Brenda said. "Are they going to sacrifice him?"

"No, wait," Shawn said. "He's not *on* an altar. He's in front of it. And you're there next to him."

Brenda let out a gasp. "No one knows about that," she said. "We were only married for days back in college. Then we realized we were made to be best friends, not lovers, and we had it annulled."

"I'm sensing a greater love than that," Shawn said. "At least from you."

She blushed. "He's still the only man I've loved completely," she said. "And I guess he likes me, too. We still go on vacations together twice a year as man and wife. Which is the other reason I know he didn't just wander off on his own without telling me."

That might actually be another reason why he did, Gus realized. Maybe he'd met someone and didn't want to hurt her feelings.

But if that thought occurred to Shawn, he didn't share it with Brenda Varda. Instead he promised they would find Tanner.

The only trouble was that there were no clues. Or, worse, there were clues, but they all pointed to the same conclusion the police had already reached. A couple of Tanner's suitcases were missing, his favorite of his eight cars—a restored candy apple red 1964 Impala—was gone from his garage, and his closets had gaps where a couple weeks' worth of resort wear might have hung.

With no physical evidence to follow and no real reason to believe anything had happened to Tanner, Gus suggested they check air- and cruise-line manifests to see which exotic vacation he'd chosen. Shawn had a different idea: They should hunt for Tanner in the game itself.

"Maybe we should start our search in 1995," Gus had

said. "That's the last time anyone thought the idea of a guy being sucked into a computer game was halfway interesting. And that was only because no one knew enough about Russell Crowe to be annoyed by him yet."

"No one got sucked into a game in *Virtuosity*," Shawn said. "In fact, it was just the opposite. The killer escaped from the game to stalk the mean streets of reality. Which would be an interesting twist if we could prove it happened here."

"Yes, searching for a character from a computer game set loose in real-life Santa Barbara sounds like a much better use of our time than trying to figure out where Tanner actually went," Gus said.

"I'm not the one who brought up the idea," Shawn said. "I said I thought we should look for clues inside the game."

"Why would there be clues inside the game?" Gus said.

"It's called *Criminal Genius*," Shawn said.

"So?"

"Whoever planned Tanner's disappearance is clearly intelligent," Shawn said. "Can we agree on that much?"

"Since I'm working on the assumption that Tanner did it himself, yes, we can," Gus said.

"The crime was perfect. There wasn't a single clue left behind," Shawn said. "No one could pull off that kind of job and not want to boast about it somewhere. And having that game sitting out there, the irony would be too great to resist."

"What if the guy who did it doesn't think he's a criminal genius?" Gus said. "What if someone killed Tanner in a moment of panic or passion, and then threw some clothes in a suitcase to cover it up?"

"It doesn't matter what the intent was," Shawn said. "The loser who sticks up a 7-Eleven considers himself an evil mastermind if he gets away with it. All crooks do."

"And you know this how?" Gus said.

"The same way I know there isn't a man on Earth who

thinks he's a bad father, or a woman who believes she's a lousy driver," Shawn said. "Every crook needs to boast about how smart he is, and the smarter the crook, the bigger the boast. He left a clue in that game."

"What if he didn't work on the game?" Gus said.

For the next twenty-five minutes, Shawn refused to acknowledge Gus' existence. That was fine with Gus. He used the time to discover that Tanner's name wasn't listed on any flights, trains, or ships within three days of his disappearance. Of course, since his car was also missing, that wasn't tremendously helpful, except as a way of ruling out various avenues to investigate. Finally Gus agreed to take an exploratory trip through the game, if only because he couldn't think of any other place to start and a dumb idea seemed better than no idea.

At least that's what he'd told Shawn. As he said the words he could hear their falseness so clearly he began to suspect his voice and lip movements might have fallen out of synch. He couldn't believe that Shawn would fall for his obvious untruth.

But Shawn did. And that disturbed Gus more than anything else. He tried to look at the situation generously: They'd been best friends for so long Shawn had no reason to doubt anything Gus told him.

That wouldn't stop the nagging feeling in the back of Gus' mind that Shawn accepted what Gus had to say only because it matched up with what he wanted to hear. That he was incapable of listening to anything that contradicted his prejudices.

That was why Gus wouldn't tell Shawn what he was really thinking. Not only about this case, but about the agency and about their profession. About his future.

Gus knew he had some serious decisions to make in the next couple of days. And whichever choice he made, it was going to change his life forever.

# Chapter Four

Oh, to be flying again, legs bare in the warm breeze, blond hair streaming against the blue, crowd noise Dopplering to a pulsing beat. To cast off the shackles of gravity and soar, higher each time before the Earth's gentle hand reached up to pull her softly down to that tender embrace of skin and bone and sweat.

This was Juliet O'Hara's dream, the one that recurred too rarely and left her humming all day when it did. The memories of her days on the squad remained with her always, part of her pool of experiences. But the sensation of it, the joyous floating freedom, she could regain only in her sleep.

This was something she never talked about. It was hardly a secret that she'd been a cheerleader in college, and those who didn't know assumed it based on her looks. If anyone ever asked what those days had been like, she made a joke about dating the quarterback or chanted a halfhearted victory call.

It wasn't that she was ashamed of her cheering days. Although the trajectory from pep leader to cop inevitably led to Buffy the Homicide Detective jokes, she'd been making them longer than anyone. And if the stereotype of the cheerleader was round-heeled and airheaded, she was secure enough in her self-knowledge that she never let other people's prejudices bother her. Let them think she was dumb—she'd find a way to use that to her own advantage.

It wasn't even the difficulty of persuading a noncheerleader that there was a spiritual aspect to the art. She'd never been shy about standing up for anything she believed in, no matter how obscure or unpopular.

But that sensation, that moment of floating—that was private. It belonged to her alone, and she wouldn't share it if she knew how. Every once in a while she'd catch the eye of another former flyer and an understanding would pass silently between them. They were a sisterhood of the flight, and they had something the rest of the world lacked—a memory of peace, a sense that there was always the possibility of transcendence in the world.

Which was why the tableau into which she had stepped made so little sense.

She and her partner, Head Detective Carlton Lassiter, had picked up the call as they'd returned to their unmarked car after a fruitless morning searching for witnesses in the previous night's hit-and-run death of a wino on State Street. Possible 187 on Lasuen Road.

Lasuen Road was one of Santa Barbara's most beautiful streets, a curving line of ocean-view houses leading up to the El Encanto Hotel. But no neighborhood was safe from crime, not as long as there were people in it. And if she'd had any doubt about that the flashing lights of the three police cruisers outside the rambling Spanish house would have put them to rest.

As Lassiter pulled the sedan into the long driveway, O'Hara gave the scene a quick once-over. The house looked small from the front, but she knew that like many of its neighbors it was built down the steep hillside, and might have as many as three stories below the ones visible from the street. There was a tiled walkway cutting through a lush lawn toward the heavy oak front door.

A woman was standing in front of that door, staring into space as if she were trying to figure out how she'd gotten here. She was sheathed in a gray St. John Knits suit that brought out the blue in her striking eyes even from this distance. Long blond hair framed a face that might have looked thirty just moments ago. Shock and grief had undone in a second all the work of Santa Barbara's top plastic surgeons, and there was no hiding the fifty-five years she'd been on the Earth.

O'Hara waited for Lassiter to meet her on the passenger's side of the car, and they fell into lockstep as they walked toward the woman. Before they'd made it halfway across the grass, a uniformed officer stepped between them and the woman.

"DB's down this way," the officer said, attempting to steer them toward a concrete path that ran from the driveway down the hill along the side of the house.

"That's funny," Lassiter said, whipping off his sunglasses so he could aim his most terrifying glare at the officer. "I don't remember asking for directions. Do you, Detective O'Hara?"

The officer, who looked like he might have graduated from the academy that morning, turned pale. "I didn't mean to—"

"To tell us how to investigate a crime scene?" Lassiter finished for him. "To determine the order in which we collect our information? Maybe you could save us all a lot of time and just let us know who killed the victim."

The rookie's throat muscles throbbed as if he were fighting to keep his lunch from coming up. He'd seriously overstepped and he knew it. O'Hara might have joined Lassiter in torturing the kid, until she noticed the dark, wet patch on his uniform shirt just above his badge, and a small beige smudge next to it. Then she understood.

"Tears don't stain unless you let them, Officer Randall," she said, reading his nameplate. "But foundation is a bitch to get out of blues. That's the mother?"

The officer's face went from white to red like litmus paper dunked in lemon juice. "She asked me," the officer started. "That is, she's upset. Understandably upset, since it was her daughter and—"

"Unless she was understandably upset because she killed her daughter," Lassiter snapped.

"I didn't think—"

"We're well aware of that, Officer Randall," Lassiter said.

O'Hara could see a real danger that the rookie's tears would soon be joining those of the grieving mother on his shirt. "It's all right, Officer," O'Hara said. "Comforting grieving survivors is part of the job. Just make sure to keep in mind what the most important part of the job is. Now, where's the body?"

O'Hara could sense Lassiter's irritation without glancing over at him. He wasn't done hazing the rookie yet. But something about this scene was troubling her, and she couldn't figure out what it was. There was nothing new to her about tragedy striking in the best neighborhoods, at the most fortunate people, on the most beautiful of days. Still, ever since they got the call she'd had a rumbling in the back of her mind that this was going to be bad, and she needed to find out just how much.

"Follow this path down the stairs," the officer said quickly, before she could change her mind. "At the end of the house turn right onto the deck. There's a sliding door to the laundry room. She's inside."

"Thank you, Officer," Lassiter said with exaggerated politeness. "You may go back to comforting the bereaved. But do us one favor. If she should happen to say something—anything—jot it down with a little note about the time, would you?"

Without waiting for an answer, Lassiter turned and headed toward the stairs. O'Hara considered saying something reassuring to the kid, but really, what was the point? He had screwed up, and he deserved everything her partner had said to him, along with several of the things he'd wanted to but didn't.

O'Hara followed Lassiter down a steep, narrow flight of concrete steps that plunged down the hill alongside the white stucco wall. Halfway to the garden there was a door set into the side of the house. Out of habit Lassiter jiggled the knob and found it locked, then continued down.

At the bottom of the hill the path led onto a small, flat parcel of garden surrounded by a high hedge of cypresses. The space had clearly been landscaped by pros some time ago, but since then it had been allowed to go wild. A patch of roses was overrun by weeds, while the gate to the caged vegetable garden had been left open and deer had eaten everything inside down to the roots. Something had gone wrong in this household even before today's tragedy, and O'Hara made a mental note to check whether it was financial or medical or something else that might concern their investigation.

"This way," Lassiter said, gesturing to the wooden deck that came off the path. She followed him to a sliding glass door that had been left open and stepped through.

She hadn't thought much about what she was walking into. A basement converted into a laundry room or a hobby den, most likely. If she'd asked above she might have learned that the house's lowest level had been converted into a apartment for the owner's daughter.

But whatever she might have learned would have done her no good once she stepped through the door. She might as well have plunged down the rabbit hole or passed through the mirror.

What Juliet O'Hara saw was herself, flying. There was the long blond hair, the blue-and-gold cheerleader's sweater and short pleated skirt revealing the toned tan legs floating effortlessly above the tiled floor.

She blinked hard and forced away the sensation of flight. Blinked hard and forced herself back to the now.

It was remarkable how strongly the young woman resembled O'Hara. It wasn't just the hair and the cheerleader's uniform; her face was the same Kewpie-doll oval and her eyes that piercing blue. She was a few years younger than the detective, but it was hard to tell by how many because of the way her eyes were bulging from their sockets and her mouth was twisted into an agonized grimace.

The cheerleader was flying, but gravity's gentle hand could not bring her down. There was a rope around her neck, tied to a pipe that ran across the ceiling, and it held her a foot above the ground.

# Chapter Five

Gus glanced at his watch, then looked down at the orange chicken congealing on the plate in front of him. When the kid in the paper hat with a panda on it had dropped it on his table forty-seven minutes ago, Gus had picked up the plastic fork and made an attempt to eat a little of it. Even after two tines snapped off somewhere between the outer layer of citrus-flavored goo and the inner shell of deep-fried chicken skin, he still thought he might nibble at a couple of the smaller pieces. But before he could yank a chunk of chicken out of the rapidly hardening sauce, his stomach growled a warning and sent a tendril of bile into the back of his throat. If he tried to swallow anything from this plate, he'd have reason to regret it.

It wasn't the quality of the food that was turning Gus' stomach. He'd eaten at several Chop Them Sticks outlets since they started popping up a few years back, and the Orange You Glad You Ordered the Chicken was always exactly the same—hardened nuggets of dubious poultry in a sauce that tasted like double-strength orange Jell-O. That was fine with Gus, who had long believed that an entrée that doubled as dessert saved both time and money.

Gus looked back at his watch just in time to see the larger hand slide over the four. In ten minutes it would be twelve thirty, and in ten more his flight would start boarding. He'd timed the walk from the strip of fast-food restaurants to the terminal and he knew it wouldn't take him more than five minutes. Security wouldn't add more than another five. The Burbank airport's main midweek function was as a commuter portal, and since even the most laid-back techie tried to get to work no later than noon, the lines were rarely long this time of day.

Better yet, Gus was leaving from the smaller of the two terminals. He'd decided to fly into San Francisco, even though it would cost half as much to land in Oakland. It wasn't simply the convenience of being able to hop on a BART train at SFO that would take him to his ultimate destination—for the difference in ticket price Gus could have hired a limo in Oakland and still had money left over for a substantially better lunch than the one in front of him.

It was, in fact, the ridiculously higher ticket price that convinced Gus to fly from Burbank to San Francisco. He didn't think he'd left any clues about his trip, even making his plane reservations from what might have been Santa Barbara's last pay phone. If he'd been careless, though, he didn't want to make it easy for Shawn to track him down. That meant doing the opposite of what his friend would know he'd normally do. Which was, of course, to take the easiest flight or the cheapest, those two rarely occurring together.

If he'd cared about cost, he would have flown out of LAX, where competition between airlines served to keep prices low. If convenience had been the key, there were frequent, if ludicrously costly, flights from Santa Barbara International to the Bay Area. Driving eighty miles down the always jammed 101 to Burbank only to spend as much as he would on a ticket from Santa Barbara was the dumbest thing he could have done.

He thought he'd made it out of Santa Barbara without being noticed. Shawn had scheduled himself for another immersion in *Criminal Genius* and was without a doubt completely occupied in burning down a police station or looting an orphanage when Gus slid behind the wheel of the Echo and headed out of town. But if Shawn had begun to suspect that Gus was trying to slip away unnoticed, he might try to track down his flight. With a limited amount of time before his plane took off, Shawn would have to prioritize his search, and terminal two at Burbank would barely kiss the bottom of the list.

Gus' stomach released a fresh flare of acid and he thought he could feel a piece of the lining burn away. This was all so absurd. He was sneaking around as if he were cheating on his spouse, and it was tearing his insides apart. What he should have done was just tell Shawn he was heading up to San Francisco for the afternoon, and on the off chance that there were any follow-up questions, simply told him the truth.

Except if he did that, he'd have to take the consequences. If he lied, if he snuck around, then he could put off that moment for just a little bit longer.

It didn't matter if his stomach felt like a face hugger had planted an egg in him and it was about to burst out. Once Shawn learned the truth, their entire lives as they knew them would be over. To postpone that, he'd take a little pain.

Gus looked at his watch again. The minute hand had moved ahead a couple of clicks. It was time to start moving. He checked all the tables in the restaurant, in case Shawn had slipped behind one while he was staring at his food, but he was the only customer. Shawn was clever enough to go undercover behind the counter, but unless he was also clever enough to have become Chinese over the past couple of hours, Gus was safe from all three members of the Chop Them Sticks team.

Gus slid out along his bench, then grabbed his tray and deposited his uneaten lunch in the trash. Normally he would have felt guilty about throwing away so much perfectly good food when there were hungry people all over the world, but he had more pressing things to feel guilty about right now, so this would have to wait. Besides, judging by the number of similarly full trays in the bin, this might not have counted as "perfectly good."

The air outside the restaurant was hot and dry; it stank of jet fuel and deep-fry oil. The sun blasted down through a cloudless sky and the heat waves radiating up from the asphalt made it feel like there hadn't been a breeze in days. Gus longed to be back in Santa Barbara, hanging out at the pier with Shawn, feeling the soft salt spray on his face. Instead he quickened his step and crossed the street to where a narrow concrete sidewalk snaked along the lanes of the airport entrance.

As he'd expected, the airport was practically deserted. Gus made a left at the Southwest counter and walked quickly through the narrow corridor that connected the two terminals. Fishing his driver's license out of his pocket, he stepped up to the United counter.

The ticket agent glanced at Gus' license, then typed his name into the system. "Looks like we're up for a quick trip today, Mr. Guster," he said. "We have you booked on the nine o'clock return flight tonight."

"That's right," Gus said.

"Must be business, then," the agent said, printing out Gus' boarding pass. "If you were going to San Francisco for pleasure, there's no way you'd be coming back in only six hours."

"Business," Gus agreed, feeling a sudden urge to confess everything to the complete stranger who was beaming across the counter at him. To explain everything he'd been feeling over the past couple of months and why what he was doing wasn't really a betrayal. Instead he scooped up his driver's license and boarding pass and walked toward the gate.

# Chapter Six

Shawn glanced at his watch, then looked down at the pop-corn shrimp and clam strips the waiter had just deposited on his table. The smell of perfectly fried seafood filled his senses and made his stomach growl. That was something he hadn't expected. He'd taken a seat in the Yankee Pier only because it gave him a clear view of gate one, and he'd ordered only because there were other people waiting for his table. He'd chosen the first thing he saw on the menu and didn't expect to eat any of it, having polished off a fast-food burger and fries at the Santa Barbara airport before catching his flight to SFO. But now that the food was here, there was no way he was going to leave a speck of it behind. He'd never known you could actually get good food in an airport. If it was going to happen anywhere, he figured, it would happen in San Francisco.

If this turned out to be today's only surprise, that would have been okay with Shawn. United flight 6396 was already approaching the runway. Five minutes after its wheels touched down the gate doors would open and the Burbank passengers would spill out. He'd sit here and watch them all as they deplaned, and if none of them looked the slightest bit familiar he'd be nothing but happy. He'd already bought a ticket for his return flight just in case, and it would start boarding in half an hour.

But he didn't expect to be on that plane. Not if Gus had been on this one. Because there was only one reason Gus would have taken the most expensive, least convenient flight he could have found, and that was to hide his trip from his best friend. That was why Shawn hadn't bothered checking out any of the cheaper or easier flights. If Gus had taken one of them, Shawn would have known not to worry. Sure, it would have been strange that Gus had flown to San Francisco without telling him, but there could have been an innocent explanation for that. The most likely, in fact, was that Gus had told him at one of those moments when Shawn hadn't been paying attention. Or that Gus had told him and he'd completely forgotten all about it, like he did most things that had no immediate impact on his own life. But for Gus to take this flight was a screaming admission that he was deliberately trying to hide the trip.

Even that wouldn't have seemed so disturbing if it had been the only strange behavior Gus had demonstrated in the last few weeks. But Gus had been acting so oddly that Shawn frequently found himself checking the back of Gus' neck to see if the Martian invaders had been tinkering with his brain.

It all started around the time they were hired to find Macklin Tanner. To Shawn this was the greatest case they'd ever landed. It was, in fact, the very case he'd had in mind when he first decided to become a private detective. In order to solve the crime he and Gus would have to live in a completely virtual world that no one had ever seen before. They were going to be paid to play and win the coolest computer game ever invented.

And yet when Brenda Varda came to them for help, Gus hadn't wanted to take the case. Instead he kept muttering about how the police had already looked into it and the guy had probably taken off on his own.

That had sparked their first real argument since they had given up trying to agree on whether or not it was right for George Lucas to digitally "upgrade" the original *Star Wars* movies. Shawn's point had been simple and, to his mind, obvious—if Tanner had gone for an unannounced vacation, then the case was guaranteed to have a happy ending. If, on the other hand, something had happened to him, then Shawn and Gus were the only ones who could help him. Either way they were going to get paid a lot of money for an experience most people could only dream about.

Gus finally agreed to help on the case, but Shawn could tell his heart wasn't in it. And once they were actually inside Darksyde City, the game's fictional locale, Gus managed to be no fun at all. The first two days, he hardly killed anyone, even when a good bit of mayhem might have moved him up a level. It was like he couldn't wait to get out of the virtual world.

Even when he was back on real ground, Gus seemed distracted, moody, and distant. Shawn tried to ask him if something was wrong, but Gus insisted everything was fine. Then he went back to being a grump.

This was not the Gus Shawn had known for so many years. Yes, he'd always had a tendency toward the judgmental and there was frequently an undercurrent of unnecessary seriousness running through him, but Shawn had never seen him in such a mood for longer than a day or so. Something was wrong.

Then it got worse. For the first time in as long as Shawn had known him, Gus started to become unreliable. He'd come into the office an hour late, claiming that his alarm hadn't gone off or that he'd been stuck in traffic. And once he got there he'd disappear for hours at a time. When he came back he'd give only the vaguest of excuses, claiming that there was some kind of problem at the pharmaceuticals company where he still maintained a second job as a sales rep.

This behavior presented Shawn with two immediate problems. The first was obvious—a small firm like Psych couldn't afford to have two partners who were both unreliable, and this had been Shawn's role since the firm's founding. It was a position he prized, and he didn't plan to give it up just because Gus was in a bad mood.

But the second problem was much more serious. Shawn recognized all the excuses Gus was giving him because Shawn had used them himself, over and over again. So he knew these were not only lies, but lazy lies. They were the lies of someone who doesn't care if anyone believes them. They were the lies of a man who'd moved on.

Shawn had spent a lot of time trying to figure out why Gus might not want to be part of Psych anymore, but he couldn't come up with a single reason. They did what they wanted when they wanted, took only the cases that sounded like fun, and managed to avoid almost all sense of adult responsibility. Who could ever find fault with that? Who could ever want anything else?

In general, Shawn didn't like taking on two cases at once. Not since the time he'd gotten mixed up and had accused a suspect in one case of committing the murder in the second. But this was different. One of these cases, as they said on the movie posters, was personal.

So while Shawn continued to search for Macklin Tanner, he was simultaneously going undercover to spy on Gus. Fortunately his cover was strikingly similar to his own persona—in fact, he was going undercover as himself—so he could move back and forth between his two roles without needing to adjust fake mustaches or even change clothes. But while the outside world might see him as a psychic detective hunting for a missing tech genius, secretly he was engaged in spying on his partner.

Gus hadn't made it easy on him. There were no surreptitious phone calls, no mysterious meetings, not even any unexpected e-mails in any of Gus' accounts. If he was hiding something, Gus was playing it cool. Which was, to Shawn, the most suspicious sign yet, since Gus and "cool" were almost never mentioned in the same sentence.

Shawn was beginning to think he might have to consult the army field interrogations manual to find the truth when Gus finally slipped up. They were hanging out at the office when Shawn mentioned he was in the mood for pizza from LaVal's by the Pier, the one place in town that didn't deliver. This wasn't the first time Shawn had mentioned this craving, and usually it led to forty-five minutes of Gus refusing Shawn's offer to wait at the office if Gus wanted to run down and pick up the pie, and then to the inevitable call to Domino's. But this time Gus didn't argue at all. He asked what toppings Shawn wanted.

This was the moment. The only reason for Gus to give in so easily was that he was about to make his move. All Shawn had to do was follow him and see where the trail led.

That would have been a lot easier, of course, if Shawn had had any mode of transportation faster than his own feet. Unfortunately Gus had picked him up from his home that morning so they could share the forty-five-minute ride to VirtuActive's headquarters in Thousand Oaks. If they'd had the foresight to set up a suitcase full of chemicals in the office, Shawn could have hoped for a lightning bolt to spill them all over him, granting him superspeed. But without the proper equipment—or even a cloud in the cool evening sky—chasing Gus' car on foot didn't seem like a profitable enterprise.

But he had to know where Gus was sneaking off to. He couldn't let this chance go to waste.

"Why don't we go together and eat there?" Shawn said.

If Shawn had been hoping for some kind of strong reaction from Gus, he was disappointed. "Fine" was the only answer he got.

During the ride down toward the pier, Gus didn't seem

any more tense than he had over the previous few weeks, so Shawn began to doubt he was trying to make a secret rendezvous. What was he up to, then?

It wasn't until Gus pulled up outside the pizzeria that Shawn figured it out. More precisely, it wasn't until Gus made a big show of fumbling in his pockets for change, then announcing he needed to run across the street to the convenience store to break a dollar for the parking meter.

The excuse was so transparent, Shawn nearly pointed out that the meters had stopped being enforced an hour ago, and that Gus' pockets were so full of change he'd been jingling as they left the office. But he managed to stop himself a second before the words spilled out. He told Gus he'd get a table, then went into the restaurant and spied out through the front window as Gus walked toward the convenience store. But just as Gus approached the entrance, he made a sharp zig to the left and went to the pay phone that stood outside it. He picked up the receiver, dropped in a few coins, then dialed. After a few moments he hung up the phone and headed back toward the car. Shawn didn't stay at the window to see him feed the meter, but he did check on their way out and saw they still had twelve minutes left. If nothing else, he had to admire Gus for being thorough.

The next day, finding out whom Gus had called was easy work, as long as you consider impersonating a police officer work rather than, say, a felony. He called the pay phone company and, after spending twenty minutes being transferred from office to office, gave Detective Carlton Lassiter's name and badge number to a junior vice president for community relations.

Gus had spent 107 seconds on the phone with United Airlines. It should have been quick work to find out if he had booked a ticket and if so to where. But the operator he spoke to would not give out any information without something called a "record locator number," and once Shawn realized this was not a case of privacy protection but simple incompetence on the part of a bureaucracy he gave up trying. He'd have to figure out where Gus was going on his own.

That wasn't hard. If Gus planned to be away overnight he'd need to come up with some excuse, and he hadn't mentioned anything. So it was going to be a day trip. Realistically that ruled out any flight longer than a couple of hours. But which way would he fly? Not south—Gus could drive to LA or even San Diego almost as fast as he could fly, and Tijuana would require a passport, which Gus didn't have. West was out, too, unless Gus was planning to bring scuba tanks. Seattle seemed too far for a day trip, and while Portland was inside the zone, Shawn couldn't imagine why anyone would go there.

That left three good possibilities: Phoenix and Las Vegas to the east and San Francisco up north. Gus had distant relatives in Phoenix, so if he had been planning to go there he would certainly have told Shawn he was going to visit cousin Enid and the kids. Vegas was possible, but it just didn't feel right. That left San Francisco.

Of course even if Shawn was right about the destination, he still didn't know when Gus was going to fly. But since the trip meant Gus was going to be away for most of a day, Shawn just had to wait until he announced he needed to attend an all-day sales meeting at his other job.

As for the flight, that was the easy part. He knew how Gus' mind worked and he knew how Gus would think about how Shawn's mind worked. This was the one that Gus would assume Shawn would find least likely. Which meant it was the one he would pick.

Unless, of course, Gus had taken his logic a step further and realized that Shawn would have figured out what he was thinking, and so changed to a direct flight from Santa Barbara. But Shawn knew that Gus had a strong dislike of that kind of circular thinking. As a child he'd seen too many science fiction movies and TV shows where the hero was able to make an evil supercomputer explode simply by offering it an example of a logical feedback loop, and he was always careful to protect his own brain from that particular danger. So unless Gus had just given up on the whole project, he was going to be on this flight.

As he finished off the plate of fried food Shawn looked over at the gate and saw that the doors were open and passengers were coming out. The first few were middle-aged businessmen in suits and ties. They were followed by what looked like either a start-up's software-development team or a group of escapees from a juvenile mental institution. They were all talking to the air in front of them, but since Shawn couldn't confirm they had Bluetooth headsets attached to their ears he couldn't decide which they were. Most of the remaining passengers were clearly tourists, ambling out of the Jetway with looks on their faces that said, *This airport is already something to see and I'm going to take my time about it.* At the end of the line was one more middle-aged man in a suit and tie. He walked slowly and kept glancing back over his shoulder. Shawn assumed he'd spent the trip flirting with one of the flight attendants, and he was still hoping she might come running after him to thrust her phone number into his hand.

And then the Jetway doors were empty. One of the gate agents peered in to see if anyone else would be deplaning, but that seemed to be it. There was a rush of movement around the gate as passengers waiting to board the plane started to jockey for position.

Shawn was surprised to discover how relieved he felt. After all, the mere fact that Gus wasn't on this plane didn't mean there wasn't something seriously wrong. He could have used a different calculus to choose his flight. Or Shawn could have been completely wrong and Gus could be hailing a cab outside the Las Vegas airport right now. Or Gus could have gotten sick of trying to outgame Shawn's thought process and driven up north.

Whatever the explanation for Gus' failure to deplane from this flight, the underlying problem, whatever it might be, would still be there once Shawn got home. And worse, Shawn would have blown his best shot to figure out what it was.

Intellectually he knew that was all true. But he didn't care. Gus wasn't here, which meant that Gus was not betraying him. At least not in the manner that he'd suspected. There would probably be plenty of things to feel terrible about, but they would come later. For the moment he could relax.

Shawn scrawled his name across the bottom of the credit card slip the waitress must have placed on the table while he was staring across the terminal and stood up. He was going to make that flight home after all.

He was halfway out of the restaurant when he noticed one of the gate agents rushing down gate one's Jetway. He didn't want to wait to find out what was going on. His departure gate was at least half a mile away and it was going to start boarding soon. But something made him stay, frozen, staring at the doors.

For a long moment, the doorway was empty. And then Shawn saw a flash of chrome and he relaxed again. There was a wheelchair coming up the ramp, carrying a woman who looked like she was born when her father was still fighting in the trenches of the Western Front. That was why the gate agent had rushed in—after all the walking passengers had gotten off the plane, he'd brought down a wheelchair for her.

Fighting the urge to whistle a merry tune, Shawn headed down the terminal toward his own homeward gate. If it hadn't been for the bakery case at the Emporio Rulli Gran Caffe, he might have made it back to Santa Barbara in the same good mood.

But as he passed the case his feet came to an involuntary stop. It wasn't that he was hungry. The first lunch had left him full, and the second had had to squeeze into whatever room remained in the odd corners of his stomach. But when he approached the café, it was as if he'd been hit by a tractor beam.

As far as he could tell, the beam was emanating from a slice of cake the label called "Honoré" and described as all-butter puff pastry with Italian pastry cream filling, layered with sponge cake brushed with rum, decorated with chocolate whipped cream and pastry cream and pastry cream–filled cream puffs.

Shawn would be ill if he ate another bite, and while something as spectacular as the Honore might have been worth a spot of nausea, he didn't want to spend his flight home in one of those tiny airplane lavatories.

Mustering all the strength in his body, Shawn stopped his foot midstride as it was about to take another step toward the bakery case. Then he commanded it to turn ninety degrees back toward the way he had come. Pressing his eyelids shut, he brought his other foot around and when he opened his eyes again the café was gone from his sight.

He found himself facing the ancient woman from the Burbank flight, whose wheelchair was just coming through the doors.

And now he wished he had stopped for a piece of cake. Now he wished he'd eaten the entire bakery. Because not only did he see the old woman, he saw the person who had volunteered to push her chair up the ramp.

It was Gus.

# Chapter Seven

The high school had been a dead end. She'd known it would be, even as she made the appointment to talk to the principal. Mandy Jansen had graduated almost ten years earlier. Whatever had led to the moment of her hanging in her mother's basement almost certainly had nothing to do with her years on the cheer squad.

The only reason Juliet O'Hara could find for taking the investigation all the way back to high school was the fact that she was found wearing that uniform. But as a clue that seemed like less than a long shot.

Even as she'd sat waiting outside the principal's office, she knew she was wasting her time. And everyone she'd met over the next two hours seemed to prove her right. The principal had only been in the school for two years, and there had been three others since Mandy's day. He was able to pull up her records on the district's computer, but there was nothing there but the transcript of Mandy's good, not great, grades. Mandy's guidance counselor couldn't place the name; she'd been one of a thousand students over the last decade. Even the coach of the cheerleading squad only remembered Mandy as a "nice girl, legs like springs."

But O'Hara had needed to visit the high school, because

she didn't have anywhere else to turn. All the evidence seemed to suggest—to insist—that Mandy had taken her own life. There had been no signs of an intruder in the basement apartment, no signs that anyone besides Mandy had been down there in weeks.

What evidence they did turn up kept suggesting the same thing: that Mandy was a deeply troubled woman, who was battling depression for reasons no one seemed to understand. She'd apparently left a lucrative career in sales to move back in with her mother, who was undergoing treatment for some kind of rare cancer. Since then she had barely left the house except to take her mother to the doctor or to run to the supermarket or the pharmacy, and while she told her mother, who was too weak to make it down the stairs, that she was taking care of the garden, she'd clearly been letting it go for a long time. Mrs. Jansen thought Mandy had had a girlfriend over a few times, because she'd heard voices through the floor, but she had no idea who it might have been, and O'Hara was never able to find a trace of her.

As soon as they'd walked into the crime scene Lassiter had made the judgment that Mandy's death was suicide, and O'Hara hadn't found anything to suggest he was wrong.

But she couldn't accept that. Wouldn't accept it. When Lassiter showed her a draft of his report, she refused to sign off on it, and insisted they keep the investigation open just for a little while longer.

But that little while had already stretched past its breaking point and unless O'Hara could come up with something fast, she'd have to put her name on the report that would close the case.

If she could just articulate what she felt was wrong about the case Lassiter would have come over to her side. He would have grumbled, because that was what Lassiter did. But he trusted her instincts and he would have followed her lead.

But she had nothing. No suspects, no motives, no evidence. Just a conviction that Mandy Jansen hadn't killed herself. A conviction for which she couldn't find a single fact.

She was so busy trying to figure out her next move as she crossed the visitors' parking lot that at first she didn't hear the man following her. There were so many kids running to their next class that one set of footsteps didn't make much of an impact on her consciousness. But as she got closer to her car, she could hear the steady slap of leather on asphalt and could tell the footsteps belonged to someone who was hoping to catch her before she reached the sedan.

*This could be it,* she thought. Someone who had heard her questions but didn't want to speak up in front of other people. Someone who knew something about Mandy and needed to talk about it, even at great personal risk.

O'Hara slowed down just a little, then turned quickly to see the person who was going to break her case wide-open.

It was her partner.

"Gee, Muffy, didn't mean to startle you," Lassiter said. "I just wanted to know who was taking you to the prom."

"How did you know I was here, Carlton?" she said.

"You had an appointment," Lassiter said. "It was on your scheduler."

"You broke into my computer?" she said, anger rising.

"Let me rephrase that," Lassiter said. "You had an appointment. It was on your scheduler, right under the reminder about the meeting with the Coalition to Help the Homeless."

O'Hara felt her anger melting rapidly into embarrassment. She'd completely forgotten about that. "How bad was it?"

"How bad was it?" Lassiter said. "Let's see—how many times in an hour do you imagine one noble philanthropist could mention that his wife sits on the city council?"

"That clown?" O'Hara said. "About a thousand."

"Sure, he's a clown," Lassiter said. "Only I was the one feeling like I had a red nose and floppy shoes. Because when he wasn't reminding me that he sleeps next to a woman who controls our budget, he was demanding to know what kind of progress we were making solving the hit-and-run of a homeless man on Santa Barbara's busiest street. And what could I tell him? That we hadn't done jack on the case because we were busy trying to prove that an obvious suicide really wasn't?"

"Carlton, I'm sorry I missed the meeting," O'Hara said.

"Don't be sorry. Be right," Lassiter said.

"I don't understand," O'Hara said.

"Find some evidence fast that this cheerleader was actually murdered," Lassiter said. "That way no one can accuse us of ignoring our jobs."

# Chapter Eight

The meeting had gone well. Better, in fact, than Gus had expected. He'd spent much of the previous night memorizing facts and figures, studying company history and trying to game a strategy for dealing with a roomful of skeptical executives.

But to start with, the room hadn't been full. There had only been two people sitting at the conference table. One of them was Armitage, of course. He'd been Gus' contact all through this, and he was exactly as Gus had envisioned him during their multiple phone calls. Maybe the suit was a little more expensive than Gus had imagined, but that was only because his imagination had trouble picturing anyone spending that much money on clothes. His hair was white, but the lines of his face looked like the kind that come from lots of outdoor living, not decay. He had a firm handshake and a broad smile that matched the one Gus had always heard in his voice.

The other man was young enough to be Armitage's grandson, and he was dressed like he'd stopped in to cadge a free lunch out of gramps on the way to a Hacky Sack tournament in the marina. His bright pink polo was wrinkled, his chinos stained at the cuffs by grease from a bicycle chain. While Gus did his best to answer Armitage's questions without sounding like he'd stayed up late rehearsing them, the kid barely looked up from his smartphone, except for one moment when he let out a loud "boo-yah!" that seemed to have more to do with whatever was on his screen than Gus' frank confession that he often put his work obligations over his personal life, even to his own detriment.

In another context Gus might have pulled Armitage aside and suggested they give the kid a handful of quarters and send him to the arcade down the street until their meeting was over. Or he might have gotten so annoyed that he grabbed the punk by his tiny ponytail and dragged him out of the conference room.

But this was Armitage's meeting, and if he wanted his grandson here, then his grandson would be here.

After an hour, Armitage gave him another of his broad smiles. "I think that's everything we need to know," he said, getting to his feet and holding out a hand for Gus to shake. "You'll be hearing from us very soon."

"I'm looking forward to it," Gus said. Only then did he turn toward the kid at the end of the table. "Nice to meet you."

The kid didn't exactly look up from his smartphone, but he did raise a hand to give him half a wave.

As Gus rode back down in the walnut-paneled elevator, he tried to figure out what he'd do next. If the meeting had been a failure, of course, he wouldn't need to make a decision. He'd fly back to Burbank, sweat the traffic up the 101, and in the morning he'd pick up Shawn and accompany him to Darksyde City.

But if he'd read things correctly Gus was about to be facing a serious decision. And this wouldn't be like most of his decisions, which he usually made, unmade, and remade at least a dozen times before he committed to a certain path, and then a dozen more afterward. This one would be final.

The elevator dinged and the doors slid open, letting Gus out into a small lobby of granite walls and marble floors. He slipped the visitor's pass out of his shirt pocket and slid it across the security guard's console, then click-clacked his way across the stone floor to the metal and glass door.

It was amazing what a couple tons of granite can protect you from. Inside the lobby you'd never know this building sat at one of the busiest corners in San Francisco, with thousands of screeching brakes and blaring horns going past every hour. Inside, life seemed sane and calm and peaceful. If only Gus could stay right here for a few hours to think things through. Removed from the noise and bustle and confusion of life, he could surely come to the right decision. If the security guard hadn't started to eye him suspiciously and finger the gun at his waist, Gus might have slid down to the floor and stayed there until he'd made up his mind.

Instead he pushed the door open and let the sounds of the traffic wash over him along with the cool air that was being pushed into the city by the oncoming layer of fog.

*Even out in the noise it isn't bad,* Gus thought. Maybe it wasn't the isolation of the stone lobby that had made him feel so calm and so free. It was simply being away from home.

Gus glanced at his watch. His flight didn't leave for another four hours. Normally he'd already be worried about missing the plane and would spend the next half hour debating whether he should take BART or spring for a taxi. But right now he didn't feel any pressure to get to the airport. He didn't want to go home. He had a strange feeling that whatever decision he made, it would be easier to reach here.

So Gus would stay for a few hours. He'd stroll through

the financial district, maybe toddle down toward the waterfront, where he could watch the ferries come and go. Or he could head over to Chinatown and atone for his lunch by ordering some real Chinese food. Maybe he'd just walk. Walk and think. And if he wasn't done thinking by eight o'clock, he could find a cheap hotel and postpone his return until the morning. Worst-case scenario was he'd get bad news from Armitage after he'd rescheduled his flight and be stuck here for no reason.

Now that the thought of staying overnight had occurred to him, Gus started to like it more and more. He might as well just commit now. He'd call United and change his reservation, then look around for a hotel.

Gus pulled out his cell phone and powered it up—he had, of course, switched it off for the meeting. It went through its usual delaying tactics, showing logo screen after logo screen. Then it told him it was searching for service. Finally a series of four bars appeared at the top of the display. Gus started to dial when the phone rang. It was Shawn.

"Hey, Shawn," Gus said as casually as he could. "Good timing. We've got a short break in the sales conference."

"Good, because I need some advice," Shawn said.

Gus regarded the phone suspiciously. In all the years they'd been first friends, then colleagues, Shawn had never actually asked Gus for advice. Even on those occasions when he knew he needed it, Shawn always found a way to phrase the request so that it sounded like he was doing Gus a great favor.

"About what?" Gus said.

"Remember that guy you killed?" Shawn said. "The one with the Cayenne?"

"You mean the character I killed in the computer game we were playing," Gus said. He didn't know for sure that the government had computers that sifted all cell calls for certain phrases, but if they did "remember that guy you killed" was probably one that sent up a lot of flags.

"That's him," Shawn said. "He was a hit man who was working for Morton, right?"

"He was a fictional hit man whose role in the game was as a soldier for the fictional mobster known as Morton, right," Gus said.

"Let's say I've been following this guy," Shawn said.

Gus felt a flare of irritation. He was on the cusp of making a life-changing decision, and Shawn wanted advice on a move in a computer game. "Why?" Gus said. "He's dead, at least in the fictional scenario we've been discussing in this entire conversation. Because as you pointed out, when I was playing the game, I killed him. In the game."

"Let's say I had to restart the game," Shawn said.

"You had to restart the game?" Gus was doubly glad he'd decided to stay in San Francisco now. He had no desire to relive the terrible events at the petting zoo. The *fictional* terrible events at the petting zoo, he corrected himself, although he doubted that any government agency actually had the technology to pick up stray thoughts.

"Let's say," Shawn said.

"Okay, you've been following Cayenne," Gus said. "So?"

"Let's say I think he's going to lead me to Morton, thus shortcutting me through at least two levels of play," Shawn said.

"Congratulations," Gus said. If he'd thought of that the last time he'd been in the game, it would have saved him from the encounter with the liquor store owner.

"Only when I followed him, he didn't lead me to Morton," Shawn said. "Instead he took me to a part of the city we hadn't seen before. He went to an office building and disappeared inside."

"And?" Gus said, wishing he could finish this call so he could reschedule his flight.

"Let's say I was able to trace the ownership of the building," Shawn said.

"How?" Gus said.

"It's a game," Shawn said. "There are clues built in."

"Okay, fine," Gus said. "So who owns the building?"

"Flint Powers," Shawn said.

Gus tried to remember why that name sounded familiar, at the same time trying to understand why he should care what was happening inside some dumb game. "He's the other mob's boss, right?" Gus said. "Morton's only rival?"

"That's right," Shawn said. "What do you think that means?"

"I assume Cayenne didn't kill Powers," Gus said. "Because you probably would have told me. So I've got to assume the only reason he's going there is because he's actually working for the guy."

There was a long pause on the other end of the line, and Gus was about to check the readout to see if the call had cut out when Shawn's voice came back. "So, you're saying that if I see an employee of one mobster going into the place of business of another mobster, it means that the employee is betraying his boss. Selling him out to his rival behind his back."

"I don't see what else it could be," Gus said.

"That's kind of what I was thinking," Shawn said.

"You didn't need me to tell you this," Gus said. "You've seen as many mob movies as I have."

"Let me try one other thing," Shawn said. "Let's say that Cayenne wasn't a hit man."

"Shawn, my meeting's about to start up again," Gus said.

"Let's say he's actually a private detective," Shawn continued.

"Fine, but let's say that later," Gus said. "I really have to go."

"And let's say he works for one detective agency, but his boss begins to wonder why he's never around, so he tails him one day. And you know where it gets him?"

Gus felt his throat go dry. "Shawn, I—"

Before Gus could come up with a verb, Shawn stepped

around the corner, slipping his cell phone into his pocket. Barely casting a glance at Gus, he rapped on the shining brass sign affixed to the building's granite entrance. The sign that read: RUTLAND ARMITAGE, DISCREET INVESTIGATIONS.

"It gets him right here," Shawn said.

# Chapter Nine

*If you love somebody, set them free.* That was how the song went, anyway. Not that Shawn had any idea what came after that line because every time it came on the radio, Gus insisted on changing the station. There was some grammatical issue in the line that used to drive him crazy for reasons Shawn probably wouldn't understand even if he had bothered to listen.

Even so, he got the basic idea that the song was trying to convey. And he was fine with it. Shawn had never been possessive or jealous. He'd always been secure in the knowledge that he was more fun than anyone else around, so if a girlfriend started acting like she was ready to break it off, he knew he was better off without her. If she couldn't appreciate what he had to offer, then they should go their separate ways.

That was true with friends, too. Even with Gus. Despite the fact that they'd been inseparable for three quarters of their lives, Shawn understood that their paths would have to split off at some point. If that time was now, then so be it.

All of which made it hard to explain to himself exactly why he had followed Gus through the airport to the air train, and then on to BART. He'd waited until Gus had stepped into one silver car, then gone into the next one. Positioning himself at the door between the cars, he'd watched the back of Gus' head through the window, prepared to duck back if Gus ever happened to glance over his shoulder toward him. But Gus seemed to be lost in thought and stared straight ahead for the entire thirty minutes of the trip. When the loudspeaker announced that the next stop was Powell Street, Gus got up and stood by the door, apparently without a thought that someone might be following him.

Even that left Shawn with mixed feelings. On the one hand it was making his job a lot easier. But it also suggested that Gus had forgotten everything Shawn had tried to teach him over the years. If Gus took a stroll through Darksyde City without paying any more attention than this, he'd be chopped into pieces and made into soup by one of the mobs of feral children that roamed the place.

As the train slid to a stop in the tiled subway station, Shawn told himself to be a little more generous with his old friend. He had no idea what was going on here. Maybe Gus was trying to protect him, or was simply concerned about facing his judgment.

Or maybe Gus was waiting to find out if something was seriously wrong before bringing Shawn into it. Something medical, for instance. Maybe Gus had been slipping away all those times to see doctors and he'd come here to visit a specialist. If that was the case, Shawn had promised himself, if Gus led him to a medical building he'd back off and wait for Gus to give him the news when he was ready. And he'd do everything he could to make Gus' life easier until that moment came.

By the time the train doors whooshed open Shawn had almost convinced himself that he should turn around and go straight back to Santa Barbara. If Gus needed a little privacy to deal with a medical crisis, Shawn certainly owed him that much. But since he'd been standing in the doorway when he reached that conclusion, he was pushed out to the platform by a surge of exiting passengers just in time to see Gus heading toward the escalator. He figured he might as well trail his friend for a block or two, if for no other reason than to see how good Gus was at spotting the tail.

He was appallingly bad. By the time they were halfway through the station, Shawn was considering jumping up and down and screaming Gus' name, just to see if he'd notice that. Even when Shawn used the exit turnstile right next to his, Gus didn't look around to see him. If Gus had simply inclined his head a few degrees while he was riding the steep escalator that brought him from the station up to the street, he would have spotted Shawn a dozen steps behind him. But he remained oblivious.

This, to Shawn, suggested strongly that he had indeed figured out the reason for Gus' odd behavior. If you've traveled four hundred miles to ask a complete stranger whether you're going to live or die, you're probably not concerned with much of anything else.

That made Shawn glad he was following Gus. This way when he found the name of the mystery doctor Shawn would check up on him. If the news was good Shawn might leave it alone. But if the doctor gave Gus any prognosis other than seventy more years of happy living Shawn would work night and day to prove he was a fraud. Because Gus was healthy. Shawn knew it. He might not be a medical man, but he did have a sense of the way the universe was supposed to work, and people like Gus did not get serious diseases. That was simply out of the question.

Not that the area above the Powell Street station looked like a medical corridor. Not unless the new government health plan covered postcards, T-shirts, and trinkets. One side of the street was filled with tiny boutiques selling touristy kitsch, which was perhaps not surprising since the sidewalk was jammed with out-of-towners lined up waiting for a cable car.

Gus was already walking up Powell Street alongside the line of waiting tourists. Shawn pushed past an unwashed man who'd stopped in front of him to ask for a quarter, and followed.

If Gus were suffering from some kind of terrible disease it didn't seem to have reached his legs yet. Shawn nearly had to run just to stay twenty feet behind him. After a couple of blocks Gus made a left turn up a side street, then disappeared into a low, gray stone building. Shawn bolted after him just in time to see the door closing behind him. That was when he noticed the sign on the building's wall. RUTLAND ARMITAGE, DISCREET INVESTIGATIONS.

Gus wasn't sick. Gus wasn't dying. Gus was interviewing with another detective agency.

For the first time in his life Shawn understood the impotent fury of the cuckold. He'd been covering for Gus with their client, coming up with excuses for his poor performance. And all this time Gus had been sneaking around behind his back, looking for a job with a bigger agency. One with a fancy stone building and snooty name instead of a beach bungalow and a snazzy brand.

*If you love somebody, set them free.* That was how the song went. But there was a bumper sticker that took that thought a step further. *If you love somebody, set them free. If they don't come back, hunt them down and kill them.*

Shawn had hunted Gus down. Now it was time for step two.

# Chapter Ten

Shawn had no idea how long he'd been waiting outside that building before Gus finally came out. All he remembered was a red haze before his eyes that began to dissipate only when he saw his friend come out of the ornate door and turn on his cell phone. That was when he'd decided to make the call.

Now he stood directly in front of Gus and he still didn't have any idea what he was going to do. He was outraged; he was hurt. But he was still aware enough to realize that he didn't actually have a real cause for complaint. None that wouldn't make him look even more foolish than he already felt, anyway.

He ran through his vast memory of movie scenes, trying to find a role model. But he didn't have a tabletop laser, so the thought of tying Gus down to one seemed terribly impractical. And while the phrase "this matter is best disposed of from a great height—over water" did have a certain ring to it, Shawn's conspicuous lack of a henchman to say it to robbed it of most of its significance.

Finally he decided to simply say nothing. Let Gus come up with some lame excuse. Then he'd know which way to go.

For a long time Gus chose silence, too, which was definitely not helping Shawn's strategy. Finally he broke down.

"This is not what you think it is," Gus said.

Shawn stared at him. "That's the best you can do?"

"It's a classic," Gus said defensively.

"'Let's get out of here. This place gives me the creeps' is a classic," Shawn said. "The kind of line that is so perfect for its setting that it sounds fresh and new in any situation, no matter how many times you've heard half-naked teenagers say it before someone sticks a machete through their neck. 'This is not what you think it is' isn't even a cliché. It's a placeholder. Filler. Because the next line has to be 'Then what is it?' And then comes the real excuse."

"The next line isn't 'Then what is it?'" Gus said. "It's 'What do you think I think it is?'"

"Okay, then," Shawn said. "What do you think I think it is?"

"I know what you think it is," Gus said. "You just told me. You think I'm applying for a job with another detective agency."

"If you already know what I think, why did you ask?" Shawn said.

Gus stared at him helplessly, which made Shawn feel pretty good for a moment. At least he still had the power to twist Gus into knots of logic. He was pretty sure that if he put on just a little more pressure, he could make Gus' head explode just like one of those movie computers. And maybe that was exactly what he deserved for his betrayal.

Shawn fixed Gus with a steely gaze. "W-H-Y. Question mark," he said.

Shawn thought maybe he should duck back behind the corner to miss Gus' brain shrapnel. But the look on Gus' face suggested a level of distress no greater than mild irritation.

"Really?" Gus said. "Haven't we been through this a million times? If you feed a computer a nonspecific question like Why? it won't explode in an existential crisis after pondering the meaning of suffering in the universe. At best it will respond that it needs more information to process the request. Most likely it won't do anything except sit there until you get tired of waiting and start playing solitaire."

Gus' brain had apparently been hardened. No doubt he'd known this was coming. "What if I told you that everything I ever said was a lie, including this?" Shawn said.

"I'd say it was a slight exaggeration," Gus said. "And I'd also say it's pretty harsh for you to be trying to make my brain explode when you're the one who's been following me."

Now it was Shawn who could feel his head threatening to explode, if only at the unfairness of the accusation. "I only followed you because you were hiding something from me."

"Maybe that should have been a hint," Gus said. "If I was hiding something from you, maybe it was because I didn't want you to know about it."

"What kind of person hides things from his best friend?"

"What kind of best friend doesn't respect his best friend's privacy?" Gus said.

This was not going at all the way Shawn had thought it would. Gus should have broken down and begged for forgiveness by now. Instead he seemed as angry as Shawn. Now Shawn wasn't sure where to turn. Escalation was always an option, of course, but he wasn't quite sure how to accomplish that without sounding like a jilted lover. He could try being calm and reasonable, but that approach just didn't appeal at the moment. And he'd already tried to blow up Gus' brain. Maybe, he thought, he should have come up with a plan before he confronted Gus.

But one of Gus' great qualities was his inability to stay mad for long, and the anger was already easing from his face. That old, familiar guilty look was coming on. Which meant that he would be ready to have a civilized conversation about his elaborate betrayal. Better yet, it meant he'd gone soft, and it would be a snap for Shawn to grind him into the sidewalk.

"Look, I'm really sorry about keeping this from you," Gus said before Shawn could raise his boot heel to start the grinding.

"You didn't keep anything from me," Shawn said. "I've known about it all the time. All about it all the time, in fact. As if you could hide anything from me."

Gus didn't look like he'd been ground into anything, let alone the concrete. He didn't even look angry. Shawn studied his face and tried to understand the expression on it. Then he took a step back when he realized it was pity.

"Of course not," Gus said. "And I should thank you for going along with me on this and pretending you didn't know anything about it until now."

Shawn's mouth dropped open, but no words came out. Was it possible that Gus was patronizing him?

"This was always going to be a really hard decision for me," Gus continued, "and it was one I needed to make all by myself. I kind of wish you'd have given me another day alone on this, just so I had all the information I needed, but my mind's pretty much made up by now."

"So you're going to work for another detective agency?" Shawn said. "What are they offering you that's so great? You've already got the best cases, the best offices, and the best work schedule anyone could ever ask for."

At least this wiped the look of pity off Gus' face. And while his bones didn't seem to be cracking under Shawn's heel yet, the expression of surprise was slight improvement.

"Why would I work for another detective agency?" Gus said.

"That was my question," Shawn said. "You're the one who's supposed to give the answer."

"I'm not interviewing for a detective job," Gus said. "I'd never leave Psych for another agency."

Before Shawn could rap the brass nameplate to provide a physical action that would lend a visual underline to his next statement, the heavy door swung open behind Gus and a scrawny punk in dirty khakis and a wrinkled polo grabbed him from behind in a bear hug.

"You are the man, Burton Guster," the punk said, his ponytail bobbing enthusiastically. "I want you to start work tomorrow."

Even though Shawn had figured out exactly what was going on, to hear it confirmed like this stabbed him like an ice pick in the heart. "So you'd never leave Psych for another detective agency," Shawn said, then turned to glare at the punk. And he *saw*. Saw the designer thread count of his khakis through the layer of grime. Saw the full carat twinkling in the stud in his ear. Saw the admissions wristband from Sid's Joint, one of San Francisco's trendiest and most expensive clubs, holding back his ponytail. Saw the folded copy of *Pharm Report* sticking out of his back pocket.

And he knew the truth. "This guy isn't a detective," Shawn said. "He's a high-ranking official in a pharmaceuticals company."

"Hey, that's really impressive," ponytail said, beaming. "How did you know that?"

"I speak to the spirits." Shawn was about to turn back to Gus, but ponytail grabbed his arm.

"That's really cool," he said. "I want to know more about it."

"Some other time," Shawn said.

"Anytime," ponytail said. "Stop by my office whenever you feel like it. I'm Diarmuid Robert Benson, president, CEO and owner of Benson Pharmaceuticals. But to my friends I'm D-Bob, and since you seem to be a friend of my new friend Gus, that makes you my friend, too."

Shawn pulled away from D-Bob's clutch. "Your friend Gus?" Shawn said. "You always make friends this fast, Diarmuid?"

"Only when I can offer them a quarter mil a year, plus housing allowance, hiring bonus, and three weeks' paid vacation," Benson said cheerfully.

Shawn stared at Benson, then turned to Gus. "What's going on here?"

"I told you," Gus said. "Rutland Armitage isn't a detective agency. It's a headhunting firm."

"And Gus is the head they've hunted for me," Benson said. "Burton Guster is Benson Pharmaceuticals' new junior vice president of marketing."

# Chapter Eleven

Carlton Lassiter strode quickly down the marble corridor, forcing Juliet O'Hara to scramble just to keep up with him. It was certainly a change from the way he'd been acting the past couple of weeks. In the month since they'd been called to the scene of Mandy Jansen's death, he'd been dragging his heels every time she wanted to investigate further. Now that they were at Mandy's former workplace, it seemed he couldn't wait to get to their appointment.

"Our meeting isn't for another fifteen minutes, Carlton," she said, as he sprinted for the elevator and pounded his index finger against the already lit button.

"We get in early, we get out early," Lassiter said.

"If Mandy's old boss can see us early," O'Hara said. "And even if that's the case, we're here to get certain information. That's going to take as long as it's going to take."

"You've got sixteen minutes," Lassiter said as the elevator doors slid open. He stepped into the car and jabbed the DOOR CLOSE button, forcing his partner to leap in before the panels slid shut in front of her.

"What's the hurry?" she said.

"It's a little thing called money," Lassiter said. "Maybe

it doesn't mean anything to you, but it certainly does to the department. And I don't feel free just to fritter it away."

"They're paying us the same whether we talk to this guy for five minutes or five hours."

"It's not our salary I'm worried about," Lassiter said. "It's the parking in this building. Fifteen dollars for twenty minutes? If we're going to arrest anyone in this pit of depravity, it should be the guy who runs the garages."

"You could have badged the attendant," O'Hara said.

"As I've mentioned about eight thousand times, we have no jurisdiction in San Francisco," Lassiter said. "Which means we have no right to expect to be treated as if we did. Which would make free parking an illegal emolument."

"Maybe we could get a validation."

"And if there actually is a killer and it turns out to be someone at the company?" Lassiter said. "Tell me then how we're not hideously compromised."

O'Hara flirted briefly with the idea of telling him a lot more than that, but she decided to let it pass. She knew Lassiter had only agreed to this trip because she had begged him. He still believed that Mandy's death was a suicide and saw no reason to investigate further. If he'd stated his opinion firmly to Chief Vick that would have been the end of the case. But instead he gave the chief a passionate argument for keeping it open just a little longer, and even for taking a day trip up north to check out Mandy's former employer.

That didn't mean he was happy about doing it or that he believed they would find anything up here. But partners stick up for each other, he said. If Juliet hadn't been willing to back down—and he could tell she wasn't—then his only choice was to let her lead or put in for a new partner.

They'd spent the first part of the drive up the 101 going over the details of the case. Since there were essentially no details, that took them about as far as Solvang; then they'd ridden the remaining ninety percent of the way in silence.

That was fine with her. She knew if they'd talked Lassiter would have spent most of the time trying to convince her that Mandy's death had been self-inflicted and that they should close the case. That was a conversation she wasn't eager to have again because she still didn't have a substantive response for him. She couldn't say why she refused to believe that Mandy had killed herself. She just did.

She knew it wasn't just because, as Lassiter had hinted several times, she was identifying with the victim. It was true that the sight of a twenty-eight-year-old woman hanging by the neck in her cheerleader's outfit had an immediate emotional resonance with anyone who'd ever called the Rebel Yell or the Tiger Roar or the Duck Quack. You couldn't help but think of that time you were at your lowest ebb, fired from a job or dumped in a relationship or just lost in your life, and you put on the colors "just to see if they still fit."

But she knew there was more to it than that. She wasn't projecting her own psyche onto a suicide victim. She was too good a cop for that. Something about the crime scene was making her crazy. So far she'd just seen little things that didn't make sense for an imminent suicide: a prescription for her mother she'd arranged to pick up the day after her death, a book on caring for ill relatives she'd requested from the library's interbranch loan.

There had to be something bigger. She just couldn't identify it. Whatever it was, it had registered somewhere in the back of her mind and she hadn't been able to bring it forward yet. Usually if she took a quick walk or a long shower she could turn off enough of her conscious brain to allow the subconscious to seep through. But she'd walked and showered and showered and walked and still she was no closer to the solution. She'd hoped the hours in the car, staring out at the scenery, might coax the clue out of hiding, but by the time they cruised past old Candlestick Park and into the city there was still nothing.

That was why this interview with Mandy's supervisor was so important. If she couldn't find a lead here she'd have to admit there really was no case. She was not going to cut it short, no matter if the parking threatened to cost more than the unmarked Crown Vic was worth.

The digital readout on the elevator's control panel flipped to 34 and the car decelerated suddenly. The doors slid open and they stepped out into open space. At least that was what it looked like. The vast lobby was nearly empty, a black slate floor running uninterrupted the entire length and width of the building, so that whichever direction you looked you saw nothing but floor-to-ceiling windows.

Or almost nothing, anyway. A football field's length away from the elevators the slate rose to form some kind of large shelf, and behind that a wide spiral staircase led up to what Juliet assumed was the thirty-fifth floor. As they walked toward the eruption they saw a pair of tanned legs coming down the stairs, and by the time they were halfway there the legs had been joined by a torso and finally a head. The body parts belonged to an athletic young blond woman in a dress so short a professional tennis player might think twice about wearing it at Wimbledon. She seated herself behind the shelf and gave them a gleaming smile as they approached.

"May I help you?" she said.

"We have an appointment with Sam Masterson," O'Hara said.

The blond woman's smile faltered. "May I ask what this is about?"

"You can, but it won't do you any good," Lassiter said. "Take it from someone who's been asking for weeks."

"I'm Detective Juliet O'Hara with the Santa Barbara Police Department," she said. "This is my partner, Detective Lassiter. We scheduled this appointment with Mr. Masterson to talk about one of his former employees, Mandy Jansen."

"In that case, you'd better follow me," the blond woman said. "I'm Chanterelle, by the way."

"That's a pretty name," O'Hara said.

"It's a mushroom," Lassiter said.

"It's a pretty mushroom," Chanterelle said.

The woman named for a fungus got up from behind the desk and started up the spiral staircase. O'Hara looked up to see where they were going and found herself wondering why any woman who knew she'd be going up and down steep stairs all day would wear such a short dress, unless she was hoping to save money on visits to her gynecologist. Staring straight ahead she followed the sound of the receptionist's footsteps until both of her own feet were on level floor. Then she looked around.

They stood in a much smaller lobby, which was only the size of the entire Santa Barbara police station. Corridors led off in either direction and they were dotted with doors spaced far enough apart that Juliet was certain the offices behind them must be enormous.

Chanterelle waited until Lassiter had stepped up next to O'Hara—his sense of chivalry had kept him from mounting the first stair until the hem of the receptionist's dress had disappeared through the hole in the ceiling—and then pointed to a double door. "I'm going to put you in conference room B."

"Are you going to put this Masterson in there with us?" Lassiter said. "Because we'd prefer not to bankrupt our city government."

The receptionist smiled broadly, apparently choosing to ignore whatever she couldn't understand, and walked to the double doors. She gave a gentle knock on one of them and then threw it open.

As Chanterelle headed back down to her station, O'Hara led Lassiter to the door. Inside, the room seemed to stretch the length of the building and it contained a polished granite table that ran from one end to the other.

Enough leather chairs were clustered around it to seat a joint session of Congress. All the way at the far end of the table Juliet could make out the form of a man.

"Mr. Masterson?" Juliet said, hoping she could make her voice carry over such a distance without shouting.

"Please come in," the man said. His voice was muffled by the distance, but Juliet thought there was something familiar about it.

O'Hara and Lassiter came into the conference room and started down the length of the table.

"Mr. Masterson, we talked briefly on the phone," O'Hara said as they began to get close enough to make out the figure sitting at the end of the table.

"I'm afraid Sam Masterson isn't with us anymore," the man said.

"I just talked to him a few days ago," O'Hara said. "He didn't mention he was leaving the company."

"I'm sure if he had left the company he would have contacted you first," the man said. "Sam was really good about things like that."

"Was?" O'Hara said.

"He took a personal day on Monday and zipped up to Tahoe with a girlfriend to get in a little skiing," the man said. "Hit a tree at sixty miles an hour. At least he didn't suffer."

"And you are?" O'Hara said.

She took another step forward and now she knew why he had looked so familiar. And from the shocked gasp in her ear, she could tell Lassiter had recognized him, too.

"Really glad to see you," Gus said. "Seems like it's been forever."

# Chapter Twelve

The girl was holding something back. Shawn knew it. She tried to come across as an innocent college student—majoring in library sciences, no less—but he was convinced she was the key to finding Macklin Tanner.

He had first become suspicious when he'd spotted her ducking out of a jewelry store he'd been trying to break into. The safe inside contained a diamond the size of a large house cat, and if Shawn could steal it, he'd almost certainly be invited to join Morton's crew on a heist they were planning. But every time he'd tried sticking the place up, he'd been killed by a team of well-armed security guards. There was no way he was going to get that gem when anyone was looking.

Not that breaking in promised to be much easier. What looked like a normal storefront during the day became an impenetrable fortress at night, all four walls covered by thick steel slabs that slammed down once the doors were locked. And even if Shawn found a way into the building, he was pretty sure the diamond wouldn't just be lying around on a counter. He'd still have to break into the safe.

There was only one answer to both these problems—he'd have to use some kind of explosive. Since he hadn't come across any dynamite in the game, Shawn had to check his inventory to see what other incendiaries he might have earned along the way. At first nothing jumped out at him. He had an arsenal of machine guns, pistols, and shotguns; he had switchblades, machetes, and stilettos—both the knife and the shoes; he had stacks of cash, piles of gold, and heaps of jewels. He'd been doing well for himself lately, picking up trophies at every encounter. But he didn't have anything that looked like it might explode.

Shawn dug deeper in his inventory, searching through the things he'd been given that seemed to have no use at all. There was a spare tire from a boat hauler, the skeleton of a fish, an empty can of pork and beans, a broken floor lamp with no bulb. And then there was the poo.

That was the first thing Shawn had won in the game. Just after he'd logged in he was attacked by a pack of rabid dogs. They killed him. Three times in a row they killed him seconds after he materialized in the city. The fourth time he was ready for them. Just before his third death he had noticed a wrench lying in the gutter by a fire hydrant. The fourth time he stepped onto the mean streets he didn't waste any time reaching for the single revolver his avatar started with. He dived to the ground and rolled over to the hydrant. As soon as he touched it the dogs stopped in their tracks, then trotted docilely over to him. He waited until they were lined up right in front of him, then used the wrench to open the hydrant and sent the hellhounds tumbling away in a torrent of water.

His reward for that bit of ingenuity was a massive heap of dog poo in his inventory. He'd tried to get rid of it, but there didn't seem to be a way. He supposed it was a message from the game's creators: You may think you're clever for figuring this one out, but it's the most basic of all the puzzles so don't get cocky.

But over the course of his sessions, Shawn had learned a lot about the logic of this world. There was never anything in the inventory that couldn't be used in some way, but the mode of employ was rarely what a normal person would expect. It was like that with the gas can he'd acquired a few levels back: When he tried to fill the tank of his car with it, the auto exploded into flames. This gasoline was intended only for external combustion.

Shawn knew that in the real world there were very few uses for dog poo. Sure, you could scoop it into a bag, then put it on a grumpy neighbor's doorstep and set it on fire, so that he'd stomp on the bag and get it all over his shoe. But if you tried that with anyone in Darksyde City, he'd shoot you or stab you or blow you up, which took much of the fun out of the prank.

The logic of the game world worked differently from our own. There was a lot of metaphor involved, as Gus had said early on. And Shawn knew that in the real world people made bombs out of fertilizer—in the virtual one dog poo would probably perform the same function.

Shawn stole an SUV from a parking lot and filled the passenger's compartment with the poo. He drove it into the alley behind the jewelry store, noticing that the car's keyless remote had grown a new button, one illustrated with a cartoon explosion. Apparently Shawn was on the right track. He was about to push the detonator button when he saw the girl casually strolling out of a side exit. He didn't think to grab her then—it seemed more important to make sure she was free of the blast zone, since he'd finally figured out that the game tended to penalize the player for indiscriminate killings of innocent civilians. He watched her walk out of the alley, then put her out of his mind.

At least he did until the next time he was inside the game. The explosion had worked spectacularly—too spectacularly, as it turned out. Not only did the car bomb blast through the steel walls, it wiped out the entire city block, vaporizing Shawn's avatar into pixels that swirled for minutes before resolving into the "game over" screen.

Clearly, Shawn realized, he had used too big a vehicle, and once he had the game restarted, he grabbed a ten-speed that some bike messenger had left outside an office building and filled its courier pouch with the poo, then rode it back to the alley. Fortunately the SUV's keyless remote was still in his inventory. More promisingly, its detonator button had shrunk down to half its previous size. Shawn assumed that meant the explosion, too, had been right-sized.

He was about to use the remote to detonate the bicycle when a small door in one of the steel walls swung open and the same girl came out. She was carrying a small bag, as if she'd just made a purchase from a store that had closed hours ago.

That was when Shawn realized the girl was more than a misplaced bunch of pixels. She was a major clue. Shawn started to chase after her, but before he could close the distance between them he tripped over a crack in the asphalt and landed on his remote, triggering the explosion and killing himself. He quickly restarted the game, rehijacked the bicycle, and rode back to the alley. But no matter how long he waited, she never reappeared. Worse, the keyless remote had disappeared from his inventory, and he had no way to set off the explosion.

That night he was able to report for the first time to Brenda Varda that he'd found a major clue in the game and would be following it up in the morning. Not that he had any idea how he'd be doing it.

By the time he reentered the game he had come up with one. She'd shown up every time he came up with a new way into the jewelry store. So he had to plan one.

Shawn had no idea if the jackhammer he stole from the Darksyde City work crew could actually penetrate the steel walls, and he didn't really care. As long as the game thought he was trying, he figured that would be enough. And as soon as he pressed the blade to steel, he was proved right. The girl stepped through the suddenly appearing door in the wall and headed down the street.

Shawn ran as fast as he could—which was a lot faster in the virtual world than in the real one—and caught up with her quickly. According to game logic he probably should have kidnapped her right there, hauled her back to an abandoned warehouse, and worked her over until she talked. But even though he had given himself almost entirely over to the virtual way of life when he played this game, there were still some things that he couldn't bring himself to do. Blowing up a building wasn't a problem for him. Even driving that bus off the bridge caused him no pain, any more than the moment in a disaster movie when a bunch of extras were knocked off.

But he found himself pulling back when confronted with the prospect of committing the kind of interrogation that any civilized nation would consider a war crime, especially on a pretty young woman. So he tried talking to her instead. She pulled out a gun and pumped eighteen bullets into him.

After he'd restarted the game and tried a new way into the building, this one involving a bulldozer, she appeared again. This time he grabbed her and hauled her through a manhole into the sewer. That was where she informed him that her name was Fawn Liebowitz and she had a bomb strapped to her back. Before he could check out the claim, the sewer exploded and Shawn was out of the game again.

It had taken several more tries before Shawn could get any more information out of the young woman, and each time he ended up feeling a little less compassion for her. But no matter what methods he tried, he couldn't get her to say anything except that her name was Fawn Liebowitz, that she was a student at Darksyde U, and that she was majoring in the most ridiculous, phony subject whoever invented her character could come up with, something they called library science. Whatever he did next ended up with her dying or him dying or both of them dying or, in one spectacular bit of game play, the entire human race dying, and none of it was advancing his cause any.

The next day, instead of going back into the game, he decided to spend his time on the outside, thinking about the clue. He looked at it from every angle and replayed every move. He Googled the name Fawn Liebowitz, even though he knew exactly where the programmer had taken it from, and even though the fact that she was known only for dying in a kiln explosion would do him no good at all.

And then he realized the one piece he hadn't played with yet. She was a student. That was the key. There had to be some secret code that only students knew, some special way to talk to them. That would make sense, since most of the game's audience would be college kids desperate for an excuse not to study.

The only trouble was Shawn had never been to college. He hadn't been a student since he'd graduated from high school, and while he had talked to a lot of college girls, the subject of their studies somehow never came up

But that wasn't a problem. Because Gus had actually been to college. And in his years there, he had spent some time in every major they had on offer. For all Shawn knew he might have even spent some time in this so-called library science, if such a thing really existed. If there was anything to know about college life, Gus would know it. Shawn grabbed for the phone and started to dial.

And then he remembered. Gus didn't work for Psych anymore.

And Gus would never work for Psych again.

# Chapter Thirteen

When he thought back on that day in San Francisco, Shawn was still surprised at the way it had turned out.

Not so much at Gus' choice. By the time you start tracking your partner through airports and subways to find out whom he's going to see, you can pretty much assume the best days of the relationship are over.

What surprised Shawn was his own choice. He had let Gus go.

Not that there was anything he could have done to make Gus stay. It wasn't like he'd signed a contract with Psych, or that Shawn had people who'd break the legs of anyone who crossed him

But Shawn understood Gus. Understood how he thought. Understood him so well that nine times out of ten he could predict what Gus would do or say in just about any situation. And because he knew what Gus was going to do before Gus did, he also had a pretty good idea of how to make what he did match up with what Shawn wanted him to do.

Not always, of course. Gus wasn't just Shawn's puppet. He had a will and a mind of his own, which is what had made him such a valuable partner as well as a friend. But if they were trying to decide what movie to see or where to eat or who should drive, Shawn was generally able to lead Gus to his preferred choice and do it in a way that Gus thought it had been his own idea.

When Shawn learned that Gus was not interviewing with another detective agency but was instead talking to a pharmaceuticals company about an executive position, his first instinct was to beat him around the head and neck. But once that first instinct faded he started working out his strategy for bringing Gus back into Psych.

Once D-Bob had skipped off down the street—at least Shawn remembered him as having skipped—Shawn began to put his plot into action. The first step was easy.

"I'm hungry," Shawn had said. "Is there any place to eat in this town?"

Using their unique detective prowess, they managed to track down a '50s-style diner with a sign proudly advertising HOT DOGS AS BIG AS YOUR HEAD AND BURGERS THAT MAKE THEM LOOK SMALL. Once they were seated in a red-vinyl booth and the waitress had done a quick check of their hat size to make sure their food would live up to its billing, Shawn launched into step two.

"So," he said, "pharmaceuticals."

It wasn't much of a second step, but it was more than he'd planned for the next one. Shawn hadn't actually come up with a step three. Or, rather, he'd planned several possibilities. It all depended on how Gus reacted. If Gus seemed angry about Shawn spying on him, Shawn would have to be hurt by his friend's lack of trust in him. If Gus claimed he was actually working undercover on a case and that the interview was part of his investigation, Shawn would keep pumping him for details until the lie fell apart under its own weight. If Gus claimed that he had no idea what he was doing in San Francisco and that all he remembered

was going to sleep in his own bed last night and waking up
on that street corner and being hugged by D-Bob, Shawn
would insist that Gus check himself in for observation at
the nearest mental hospital and refuse to leave him alone
until he did.

But what Gus actually did was something that even
Shawn had never thought to prepare for. As soon as the
waitress had departed with their order, he leaned across
the table and gave Shawn a warm smile.

"I can't tell you how happy I am you followed me today,"
Gus said. "Thank you."

Shawn studied Gus' words as closely as he studied the
face across from him. Now matter which way he looked at
them, they made no sense.

"You're thanking me for spying on you?" Shawn said
finally.

"Yes," Gus said.

"For violating your privacy, breaking your confidence,
and basically being a complete jerk?"

"Yes," Gus said.

Now Shawn understood. His face tightened. "Because
that just makes it easier for you to tell me to go to hell,"
Shawn said. "It's one thing to screw over a friend and colleague. But to do it to a creep—no big deal, right?"

Gus looked more surprised than hurt. "Because I've
been looking for a way to tell you about this for weeks," he
said. "I never had the nerve. But you took the kind of bold
action I was too chicken to try, and now everything is out
in the open. Which just goes to show why you're the best
friend anyone has ever had."

Shawn ran through his catalog of response scenarios,
and none of them fit the situation. Even his ultimate fall-
back of sticking a fork into Gus' eye and running away
didn't seem to be appropriate. Although he'd thought he'd
gamed this out in every possible way, he had completely

overlooked the idea that Gus might use simple honesty. Shawn was crossing unknown territory here and he had to work his way through it with extreme caution.

"I'm such a good friend you couldn't tell me you were interviewing for another job?" he said finally. It was more of a stall than a move, but he thought it might buy him a little time until he could see the board more clearly.

"Exactly," Gus said. "Do you have any idea how hard it was to get this terrific, exciting news and not be able to share it with my best friend? There were times I thought my head was going to explode from the pressure of keeping a secret from you."

That made Shawn think of his own attempt to blow up Gus' head with logic and he suddenly felt ashamed. But he hadn't gotten where he was in life by paying attention to useless emotions like shame or guilt.

"So you want me to feel sorry for you?" Shawn said.

"I want you to be happy for me," Gus said. "Until just a few minutes ago I didn't know what I was going to do if they offered me this job. When I was first contacted by Rutland Armitage, I didn't even think I'd answer the e-mail. I had two jobs already—why would I be interested in a third one? But to ignore it seemed rude, so I e-mailed him back and asked for more details. I figured I'd see what he had to say, then politely decline, having given the appearance of considering it seriously."

"You've always been thoughtful toward strangers." Shawn congratulated himself for that response. On its surface it was complimentary, but it could easily be spun into an attack with addition of a single phrase like "too bad you don't care about your friends," if that looked like the way to go.

"I wasn't even sure I was going to open Armitage's follow-up e-mail," Gus said, apparently oblivious to the conversational trap Shawn had just set for him. "I glanced at it to be polite. And then I looked at it again. It was all about Benson Pharmaceuticals. They're an old company, but they're under new management and it's like an entirely new world. They don't work like other companies. They're small, fast, vital; able to maneuver like a shark where the big firms move like dead whales. The entire executive staff seems to be under thirty-five, starting with the chairman and CEO—but you met D-Bob already."

"Oh, yes," Shawn said. "D-Bob."

"There's almost infinite room for growth," Gus said. "The promotion track is incredibly fast. And they wanted me to come in as a junior vice president. Vice President Guster. Pretty incredible, isn't it?"

"Incredible," Shawn said.

"I still wasn't convinced I wanted to make a move," Gus said, his enthusiasm growing with every sentence. "But I agreed to meet with Armitage and then with some of the other executives. That's why I've been so unreliable lately—all these meetings. I wanted to tell you what was going on, but I think I was kind of afraid to."

"You were afraid of me?" Shawn said.

"I wasn't ready to admit to myself that I wanted this," Gus said. "If I told you about it I knew I'd have to make that decision. So I kept it secret, thinking that way I could always drop out at any time. But the further in I got the less I wanted to drop out."

"And Psych?" Shawn said. "You wanted to drop out of Psych?"

The smile left Gus' face. He looked down at the table. He picked up his fork and bounced it on his napkin.

"You did want to leave," Shawn said, realization flooding through him. "It wasn't just about being an executive at some new company. You were looking for a way out."

"I wasn't," Gus said, still staring down at the table. "Not until . . ."

"Until?"

"I think it was when we started looking for Macklin Tanner," Gus said.

"You mean you didn't want to leave Psych until we started on the greatest case that any private detective has ever had?" Shawn said. He was too astonished even to be angry.

"It was when we got into the game," Gus said.

"I know, the virtual world was so vivid and exciting it made our own reality seem dull by comparison," Shawn said. "That's why we stopped at BurgerZone after every session—to remind ourselves that there are some things that can't be duplicated in pixels. Yet."

"It was vivid," Gus conceded. "And the characters in it seemed completely real at first. But as we got killed those first few times and had to restart the game at the beginning, those characters always said and did exactly the same things."

"Not exactly," Shawn said. "Look at the mailman. One time he shot you in the head. Another time he sprayed acid at you."

"That's actually my point," Gus said.

Shawn knew what he wanted to say. He wanted to say *No, it's not. Spraying acid in the face isn't anything like getting shot in the head except that the head is attached to the face.* And then they could debate all the ways that the two modes of death were different or similar and by the time they were done the food would have come and for a long while they wouldn't say anything because their mouths were full and then they'd be full and happy and nobody would want to leave Santa Barbara and be a junior vice president of anything and they'd go home together and everything would be the way it always used to be. But one look at Gus' face told him that it wouldn't work.

"It is?" Shawn said.

"The game is filled with all these well-defined, incredibly lifelike characters who seem to be acting with free will," Gus said. "But once you look a little more closely you see that their range of options for movement is limited to two or three minor variations on the same small set of actions."

"They are just characters in a computer game," Shawn said.

"But we're not," Gus said. "And I've been feeling like I am. That I keep doing the same things over and over. The same things I've been doing for years. I feel stuck. Stuck in place, stuck in time, stuck in life. I need to unstick myself. I need to move on."

This was Shawn's moment. He could see it so clearly he could practically touch it. Gus had let all of his defenses drop away. He was speaking from the heart now, baring his soul. And there's not much in the world that was more vulnerable than a bare soul.

Shawn saw exactly how to play the next few moves. He'd have to act sympathetic at first, maybe even agree that they'd been stuck in a rut for a while. Even though it was an insane lie—the last few months had seen them stranded on the top of a mountain with a deranged killer and kidnapped to England by a lunatic, and it was difficult for Shawn to see that as any kind of routine. But it was the way Gus felt about things, and he'd have to pretend to go along with it.

Then he'd slip into a reminiscence of one of Gus' favorites of their coolest earlier cases—maybe the spelling bee—and how great everything used to be.

Once Gus was suitably softened up by sentimentality Shawn would start talking about the future. No, not the future—*their* future. How they could build Psych into a real business. How they could spend less time acting like kids and more being the adults they'd become. He might even thank Gus for bringing up a thought that had been bothering Shawn, too. It was time to put away fun and join the serious world.

Before he was halfway through Gus would be in tears.

He'd beg Shawn to stop. He didn't want to join some corporation; all he wanted was to go back to the way things were supposed to be.

There were only two problems with that plan. The first and more easily ignored was that it might not hold for long. Although there had been times over the years when Gus had expressed dissatisfaction with their eternal adolescence, he'd never really seemed to mean it. Usually it just meant he'd struck out with a cute girl who was in the market for someone with bigger earning potential.

But this didn't seem to be one of those passing moods. He'd clearly been thinking about it for a long time. Even if Shawn's nostalgia trip managed to persuade him to pass on this opportunity, the feelings would come back sooner or later. They'd be dealing with this again soon.

Still, soon was a lot better than now and a temporary fix was better than no fix at all. Now that Shawn knew what the issue was, he could put some real thought in how to deal with it.

It was the second problem that was keeping Shawn from moving forward with his plan.

He didn't want to do it.

Gus thought this move would make him happy. And for all that Shawn hated having to think of anyone's happiness but his own, he realized that he wanted the same thing Gus did. He didn't understand it, but he didn't need to.

For the first time since he'd boarded his flight in Santa Barbara, Shawn smiled. "If this is what you really want, you should go for it."

# Chapter Fourteen

66 **I** don't know what kind of sick game you think you're playing, Guster, but this is our case," Lassiter said. "You are not welcome here."

*At least that's something,* O'Hara thought. *Lassiter has actually started thinking of this as his case—or as a case at all.*

"Are you here about Mandy, Gus?" O'Hara said as she finally got close enough to speak without feeling the need for a megaphone.

"I'm sorry to say I don't know anything about anyone named Mandy," Gus said. "I've only been here for a couple of weeks."

Lassiter snorted with disgust. "You've been on this case for a couple of weeks and you still don't know the victim's name?"

"I'm not on a case, Lassie," Gus said. "I'm *here*."

Juliet realized why it had taken her so long to recognize him. The Gus she knew always dressed nicely, in pressed khakis and button-down shirts, but now he was in a tailored suit. It looked like a Zegna. The tie alone must have cost more than the entire outfit she was used to seeing him in.

"You work at Benson Pharmaceuticals?" she said.

"Junior vice president of marketing," Gus said, then corrected himself. "Sorry, senior vice president. They promoted me to Sam's level after he passed away."

"Don't tell me you're trying to do undercover work, Guster," Lassiter said. "You're not going to fool anyone, least of all me."

"I'm not under anything," Gus said. "Except thirty-five. As in the Five Hundred Most Promising Executives Under Thirty-Five, as judged by *San Francisco Business* magazine." By some strange coincidence, there happened to be a copy on the conference table and it was open to a page where a tiny picture of Gus was placed next to a large red number 467. "I was going to be four hundred ninety-two, but Benson's PR people were able to let them know about my promotion just before they went to press."

"So you and Shawn aren't working together anymore?" O'Hara said. She tried to remember the last time she'd run into them on a case, or in the station as they tried to cadge a case from the chief. She realized it had been weeks. "Did something happen?"

"If you knocked him off and buried the body, we won't tell anyone," Lassiter said. "Just let us know where the unmarked grave is in case we feel like dancing."

"We're still friends," Gus said. "Best friends. That's forever. But we're getting older and our interests started pulling us in different directions. When this opportunity presented itself, we had a long talk about where we wanted to go in the next few years and we agreed that we should part ways professionally. Not to say we won't be working together again in the future, but for the moment we're both doing what we want to do. So what brings you guys up north?"

O'Hara studied Gus closely. In all the time she'd known him, he and Shawn had been inseparable. Even on those few occasions when they'd been fighting, they stuck together. She'd imagined them ending up together in an old folks' home years from now, bickering about which Corey had squandered more potential in his later acting career. If someone had told her that he and Shawn had gone their separate ways she would have assumed they'd both be devastated—particularly Gus, who always seemed to be the junior man in the relationship.

But if Gus was devastated he was hiding it well. And she had never known Gus to be particularly skilled at hiding anything, least of all his emotions. He looked happy and successful. He looked good.

"I wish we'd known about this before you left," she said finally. "At least we could have bought you a cupcake."

"It's not like I moved to Shanghai," Gus said. "Although there is a spot opening up in our Asian office and I'm thinking about tossing my hat into that ring. But unless that happens, I plan to be going back to Santa Barbara all the time. It's still my home."

"When you come back don't feel obligated to say hello," Lassiter said. "I'm sure you're busy these days."

"Indeed I am," Gus said. "So, what can I do for you?"

Juliet glanced over at Lassiter. It was so odd to be asking Gus for information. "We're investigating the death of a Benson Pharmaceuticals employee named Mandy Jensen."

"Was she murdered?" Gus said.

"No," Lassiter said. "We just drove three hundred fifty miles on a whim because we feel some misplaced sense of connection with a dead woman."

"That's funny," Gus said. "Generally when you use sarcasm, you try to overemphasize the emotion or interest in words that are so obvious they shouldn't carry any extra emotion or interest. That way the listener understands that while you seem to be answering the question, you're actually expressing contempt for the person who asked it."

"Imagine that," Lassiter drawled.

"Now *that's* better," Gus said.

"Mandy Jensen was found hanging by her neck in her

mother's basement," O'Hara said. "She had apparently put on her old college cheerleader's uniform, then tied a rope around a water pipe that ran across the ceiling and made a noose on the other end. She put the noose around her neck, then jumped off a chair."

"Sounds like she must have been very unhappy," Gus said.

"We haven't found any reason to think so," O'Hara said. "That's why we wanted to speak to Sam Masterson, to see if he knew whether she would have had any reason to kill herself. But if you can think of anyone else here who might have known her, that would be a place for us to start."

"We are a dynamic and growing company," Gus said. "Half the employees here seem to have started after me. But let me check her file."

O'Hara expected Gus to get up and leave the room or at least to pick up a phone to buzz a secretary to bring the file. Instead he waved his hand through a beam of light that shone down from the ceiling and a small square hatch slid open in what she had thought was a seamless piece of wood, revealing a computer monitor. He touched the screen in a couple of places and a virtual filing cabinet slid open. Gus waved his fingers over the image and files flew by until he found the one he wanted. Then he tapped the screen again and the image of the file opened. Gus leafed through the pages quickly.

"Okay, it looks like she joined Benson three years ago as an assistant in our sales department. She was promoted twice within her first six months and then given a small sales route in our Midwestern region. When she exceeded all expectations, the company gave her the choice of any route in the country. She asked for central California specifically so that she could move back to Santa Barbara, where her mother lived. In the year she worked that territory our sales were up thirty-six percent. Apparently there was serious talk about bringing her back into corporate and giving her—" He stopped, looking surprised, then started again. "Well, giving her my job. My old job, that is."

"They were going to make her the sidekick to a phony psychic detective?" Lassiter said.

Gus smiled. "I'm impressed, Lassie. It was just seconds ago that I had to explain how sarcasm worked, and now you're practically a master at the stuff." He turned back to Juliet. "They offered her a position of junior vice president of marketing. She declined. She sent a letter saying she had decided to end her career in pharmaceuticals sales, thanked the company for the opportunity, and said good-bye."

"When did all this happen?" O'Hara said.

Gus glanced down at the screen again. "Looks like it was a little over a month ago. Just before they made me the offer."

"Maybe Guster killed her," Lassiter said hopefully. "Got her out of the way so he could steal her job. Sure, it's a long shot, but we've got to exhaust every possibility."

"We'll get right on that, Carlton," O'Hara said wearily.

Gus slapped a hand down on the table. "Now, that's what I call sarcasm," he said.

"Is there anything else you can tell us about Mandy?" O'Hara said.

"I'm e-mailing you her entire file right now, but I don't think you're going to find anything in here," Gus said, already entering her e-mail address into the SEND box. "She was doing fine on her own, but then she suddenly felt a desire to return home to live with her mother. Then she quit her job for no reason. It sounds like some kind of downward spiral to me. Maybe she started sampling the product—it happens sometimes. Or maybe she was always fighting depression and it finally got the better of her. Either way, if it were my case I'd have to think it was suicide."

"If Guster thinks it's suicide, then I've finally got a reason to believe the poor girl was actually murdered," Lassiter said.

"How I've missed your zany zingers," Gus said, getting up out of his chair. "It makes me wonder how I could ever leave my old career to take this job. Then I remember I get paid three times as much as you and it all becomes clear."

"There are more important things in life than money, Guster," Lassiter said. "We do this because we want to make a difference in the world."

"Well, people always seem happier after you leave a room, so I guess that's working out for you," Gus said. "And speaking of leaving the room, I've got a conference call. If there's nothing else?"

"You mean in addition to the volumes of help you've provided?" Lassiter said. "No, I can't think of anything else."

"I have a couple more questions," O'Hara said. "Please, Gus. It will just take a second."

"I can let London and Mumbai talk to each other for a bit," Gus said. "I usually can't understand a word either of them says, anyway."

"Ticktock, Detective," Lassiter said. "Not to mention ka-ching, ka-ching."

"If you go now, you can get the car out before there's another twenty minutes on the clock," O'Hara said. "I'll meet you down on the street."

"If there was street parking, we wouldn't have this problem," Lassiter said.

"Drive around the block," O'Hara said. "I'll pay for the extra gas."

Lassiter looked like he wanted to argue, but before he could open his mouth, an alarm on his wristwatch chimed. "I'm going around the block twice," he said as he headed for the door. "Then I'm heading back to Santa Barbara without you."

He disappeared through the conference room door.

"I don't think you have to worry too much," Gus said. "This is San Francisco. With all the dead ends and one-way streets and crazy bicyclists, a single trip around this block is going to take longer than the drive back to Santa Barbara."

"I don't need that much time," O'Hara said. "I just wanted to ask about you and Shawn."

"No, you didn't," Gus said, giving her a look that was meant to be filled with compassion but instead seemed to be the product of eating day-old sushi for breakfast.

"Okay, you caught me," O'Hara said, blushing just a little. "I can see you're fine. How's Shawn doing?"

"How is he always?" Gus said. "He's great."

"Really?" O'Hara said.

"Really."

She thought that over for a bit, then nodded. "Okay, thanks." She turned toward the door, then back to Gus. "It's just that he seems like someone who needs . . . who isn't himself without . . ."

"An audience?" Gus said with a smile.

She colored a little more deeply this time. "Pretty much, yeah."

"I talked to him last night," Gus said. "He's doing great. He's got a whole virtual universe filled with people to virtually talk to."

O'Hara felt an odd mix of emotions she couldn't quite identify, so she chose to ignore them all. "That's good to know," she said. "Next time you talk to him, say hello for me."

"I have a better idea," Gus said. "Since you're both in Santa Barbara, why don't you say hello to him yourself? I'm sure he'd be happy for the company."

"I'm sure I'll run into him on a case," she said.

"Then you can say hello for me," Gus said. "Now if you'll excuse me, I really need to jump on this call."

# Chapter Fifteen

When Gus was little, he had been astonished by the idea of a long-distance phone call. It seemed so miraculous that you could pick up the receiver and talk to someone who was hundreds or even thousands of miles away.

Now Gus found himself astonished by the concept all over again. But it wasn't because he was able to talk to people in London and Mumbai at the same time. It was because no matter how many times he tried to get off the call, it would never end. Apparently the Indian sales team had some complaint about the British marketing department concerning the rollout of a slightly reformulated version of Nitrozine, Benson's hugely profitable cold-and-allergy medication, and the Brits were refusing to take them seriously.

That immediately put Gus on their side because he was having trouble taking the whole thing seriously. As far as he could tell the entire squabble would be over if the Brits would change one word in their marketing campaign, or if the Indians would make a slight alteration in their sales plan, but both sides had dug in and neither one was willing to move at all. The angry voices had been blasting out of the speakerphone for more than an hour and Gus still had no idea what anyone wanted him to do.

What he wanted to do was to get off this call. He'd only been in this job for a few weeks and he already had ideas for ways to improve the company. He'd started putting together a presentation for D-Bob on a major alteration to the product mix and even some changes to the firm's mission statement, which he felt would make them a much more public-oriented business. And the great thing about working here was that he knew his ideas would get a fair hearing and no matter how radical they might seem they'd be taken seriously. Even if D-Bob ended up hating all of them he'd assured Gus that they would still be welcome. Good ideas come out of bad ideas, D-Bob liked to say, and nothing comes out of no ideas. There was no risk to being wrong at Benson and no penalties for thinking outside the box.

The only trouble was finding time to take that step outside the box. From the first moment Gus sat behind his new desk, the phone hadn't stopped ringing and the memos hadn't stopped flowing. And that was only the beginning. There were also instant messages, video chats, and tweets, all of which needed to be answered faster than immediately. Gus had found an apartment within easy walking distance of the office, but he frequently found himself wishing he'd moved farther away so that he could catch a quick nap on the BART train, apparently the only place in the city where his cell phone couldn't find any service bars.

It was so different from all the years he'd spent at Psych. There, his time had been his own—or at least he'd only had to share it with Shawn. Technically it was a job, even a career, but looking back it seemed more like a long vacation. Some mornings when the phone started ringing before his alarm went off, he wondered why he had agreed to leave in the first place.

Until the Benson offer came up, he'd never really thought about it. He assumed that he and Shawn would be together forever. Sometimes, when he was mad at Shawn for some reason, he'd imagine a dramatic breakup for the team—they'd have a huge fight over a case and Gus would leave to set up a competing agency; they'd come to blows over a woman they both loved; Gus would inherit a fortune, but to collect it he'd have to live in an ancient castle in Scotland with distant relatives. But every one of those scenarios eventually led to a reconciliation, just as a TV show's season-ending cliff-hanger would always be resolved in the first episode of the fall.

But his decision hadn't been like that at all. He still wasn't sure exactly when he had decided to leave Psych. It was a thought that had been growing in him for some time, but he couldn't say when it had changed from a vague idea into a concrete plan. If anything, it was like the point in his life when he'd stopped reading comic books. There had never been a moment when he threw down a particularly badly written issue of *Superman* and vowed he was done with the form forever. Instead there had been a long period when he kept buying all the new comics, but let them stack up on his shelf without reading most of them. It was only after months of this that he'd realized he was hopelessly out of date on all the story lines in all his favorites—and that he didn't care enough to catch up.

He supposed this must mean he'd been unhappy at Psych for a while, although he couldn't put his finger on the moment when it had stopped being fun. Not without devoting more time and effort to the question than he had to spare. Besides, just thinking about the subject made him tired. More than tired; whenever the thought crossed his mind, he could feels his palms begin to sweat and his pulse race. It felt like he was waking up from a nightmare he couldn't remember. He didn't understand why this was, and he didn't have any real desire to. There were far too many other things that were wearing him out now.

There was a faint knocking at the open door. Gus looked up from his desk and saw a head peering in. It had thick gray hair and a broad smile. The slightly stooped body attached to the head was wearing a cheap blue coat and striped tie over a white shirt and gray slacks, but the whole package gave the sense that Gus' visitor was actually wearing a green hat and smoking an upside-down pipe. There was just something about him that strongly suggested he'd recently escaped from the Old Leprechauns' Home.

"Mail call," he whispered.

The aging pixie tiptoed in and placed a stack of envelopes on Gus' desk, then started to sneak out again. Before he reached the door the speaker erupted in a blast of Hindi that was unmistakably some kind of expletive. Even though he had no idea what the words meant, Gus found himself blushing.

"Sounds like Sanjay is declaring the Mutiny all over again," the leprechaun whispered.

Gus hit the microphone mute button on his phone. "Do you know him?"

"Never met the man, but I've seen his effect on people around here," the older man said. "If I ever start wishing I were in the executive ranks instead of the mail room, all it takes is one word from Sanjay and I remember why I'm happy where I am."

"Do you know how the other executives dealt with him?" Gus said, then felt himself blushing all over again. "No, I'm sorry. I shouldn't be bothering you with my problems. Thanks for the mail."

He reached to hit the microphone button.

"Is he talking to London?" the older man said.

Gus pulled his finger back. "Yeah. To Simon Birnbaum in marketing."

"That's when he's at his worst," the man said. "He's got a real colonial subject's mentality, even though the colony was gone decades before he was born. And it doesn't help that most of the folks in the London office think nothing's gone right on the subcontinent since the queen pulled out."

"So Sanjay thinks he's being oppressed, and Simon thinks Sanjay's not being oppressed enough," Gus said. "Has anyone ever gotten them to work together?"

"Seems to me they did when Bobby handled this account personally."

"Bobby?" Gus said. "Does he still work here?"

"Don't know how much work he does, but the sign on his door says he runs the place," the older man said with a grin. "Calls himself D-Bob now, but I remember when the old man was in charge and young Bobby would tear off his clothes and run through the offices naked."

"Naked?"

"Completely." The older man laughed. "Of course, he was only two years old at the time."

"How long have you been with the company?" Gus said.

"It's like birthdays," the older man said. "After you hit a certain number, you stop counting. But it's been seven years since I got my daughter Chanterelle that job at the front desk, and that feels like a small portion of my tenure here. My name's Jerry Fellows. Everyone calls me Jerry."

Gus reached across the desk to offer a hand, which Fellows took and shook heartily. "Burton Guster, but people call me Gus."

"Pleasure to meet you, Gus," Fellows said. "May your time here be happy and prosperous."

"Thanks," Gus said. "I'd be happy if I could just get these two to stop shouting at each other."

"Only one thing I know can get two people who hate each other to work together," Fellows said with a wink.

"What's that?"

"Someone they both hate more." Fellows gave Gus a

friendly wave and went out to the corridor, where his mail cart was waiting for him. He pushed it down the hall, its wheels squeaking musically.

Gus watched him go, thinking over what he'd said. Then he pressed the microphone button on the phone and waited for a moment when both combatants would have to pause their battle to take a breath.

"Okay," Gus said. "I've listened to you both and I realize there are deep and substantive differences between you that can't be bridged."

"That's what I've been trying to tell corporate for a month," Simon Birnbaum's plummy accent drawled over the speaker.

"Yes, these people have no idea what will work in India," Sanjay said.

"The English have always known what works in India," Birnbaum said. "And that is whatever is run by the English. Whenever the job gets handed off to your lot, it all falls apart."

"That's exactly the attitude that's caused Nitrozine sales to plummet here," Sanjay said.

"Yes, it was my attitude," Birnbaum said. "It has nothing to do with a sales force that sleeps half the day and drinks the other half. Or the fact that no product left the warehouse for a week because some cow had decided to lie down in the middle of the road and no one could bring themselves to disturb it."

Gus cut in before Sanjay could respond. "There's no need for recriminations," he said. "I understand that you can't work together. So instead of wasting time trying to apportion blame, I'm simply going to give both sales and marketing in the Indian region to our Paris branch."

For the first time in what seemed like hours there was nothing but silence coming from the speaker. Gus started to count slowly to ten. By the time he reached four, Birnbaum's voice came over the phone.

"You know, I've been giving Sanjay's ideas a good bit of thought and I have to say he's got a point," Birnbaum said. "Perhaps our understanding of the local argot is not quite as complete as the natives'."

"I must say that we in Mumbai are in awe of the brilliant work performed by our counterparts in London," Sanjay said. "The wit, the humor, the sheer force of creativity. Perhaps we fail to understand the impact of the whole when we focus on such tiny details."

"No, no," Birnbaum said quickly. "The whole is only as good as the details that go into it. You were completely right to focus on the little things."

"So you two think you can work this out on your own?" Gus said. "Because I'd hate to burden Paris with more work if it isn't necessary."

"Consider it done," Birnbaum said.

"Without a doubt," Sanjay said.

"Good," Gus said with a smile. "I'll be looking forward to next month's sales figures."

Before either continent could say anything more, Gus hung up. *That should keep them quiet for at least a couple of days,* he thought, as he reached into his desk to pull out his file of new ideas. *Now if everyone else would leave me alone, I could actually get some real work done.*

Gus reread the first few pages of his notes and was pleased to see that even though he'd scrawled many of them down just before he was falling asleep, they presented a clear, precise plan. D-Bob was going to be impressed.

At least he was if Gus was ever able to get the damn thing done. But it seemed like every time he managed to get his file open there was some kind of interruption. If it wasn't an urgent conference call or a crucial meeting, it was a celebration for an office birthday—D-Bob insisted that everyone attend for singing and cake cutting, no matter what kind of business had to be put on hold—or one of

D-Bob's impromptu pep rallies, which happened at least three times every week.

*Maybe this time will be the exception that finally lets me finish*, Gus thought as he picked up a pen and started to make notes in the margins of his paper. But before he could complete a thought he heard shouts from the other end of the floor and heavy footsteps running down the corridor.

At first Gus thought he'd stay at his desk and work on his project. If he was needed someone would call him. God knew his phone worked.

But then he got a whiff of roasting meat from the spacious kitchen down the hall. This must be one of D-Bob's surprise bonding lunches, for which he routinely brought in some of San Francisco's most famous chefs. Gus hadn't had the opportunity to experience one yet, but everyone he talked to was still buzzing about the last time, when the entire cast of the current *Top Chef* season prepared tasting menus for all the employees. There was no way Gus was going to miss that.

He shoved his papers back into his drawer, making a silent vow not to go to bed that night until he had finished, and then wandered out into the corridor.

As soon as he stepped through his office door Gus was nearly knocked over by a sales executive who was racing toward the kitchen.

"It can't be that good," Gus said jovially. But as soon as the words were out of his mouth he looked at the faces of the people who were running down the corridor. None of them looked like they were anticipating a once-in-a-lifetime dining experience.

They looked scared.

And then he saw Chanterelle coming out of the kitchen. In all the times he'd entered or exited the building, the receptionist had always been wearing two things—a skirt that barely covered her pelvic bone and a smile so appealing he barely noticed her legs. But now she wasn't smiling. She was crying.

Gus ran toward the kitchen as fast as he could, slaloming around the other employees like a teenager skateboarding through a packed Walmart. There was a crowd clustered in the doorway, but he pushed through them as if they weren't there.

Once he was inside the kitchen the smell of roasting meat was overwhelming. But it wasn't coming from the Viking ovens that lined one wall. It seemed to emanate from the coffeemaker.

More precisely, it came from the coffeemaker's power cord, which was still spitting sparks where it was plugged into the wall.

Gus followed the sparks down as they landed gently on the still-twitching form of Jim Macoby, Benson Pharmaceuticals' executive vice president of worldwide sales and the man who was directly above him on the corporate ladder. At least he had been before thousands of volts had coursed through his body. Now, as the smells wafting throughout the building proclaimed, he was meat.

# Chapter Sixteen

Detective Juliet O'Hara was only concerned with the work of the Santa Barbara Police Department when she pulled up in her cruiser outside the beachside bungalow that housed the offices of the city's premier psychic detective agency. Shawn and Gus had helped them out on dozens of cases, and the local prison was filled with murderers who might have gotten away with their crimes if not for them. But since the team had broken up, Shawn hadn't stopped by the station once. She needed to assure him on behalf of the chief that he was still welcome even if he was on his own.

Not that the chief had asked her to check up on him. Or even, as far as she could tell, noticed that Shawn and Gus hadn't been around lately. But the chief was in the middle of negotiations with the city council over the department's budget for the next fiscal year and she might not have noticed if Montecito slid into the ocean.

*So this isn't an official visit,* she thought as she walked up to the bungalow's front door. It's not like Shawn and Gus had always had a reason when they came to the station. Sometimes they were looking for a gig, it was true, but it was pretty clear that other times they showed up because they were bored and felt like talking to someone.

Not that that was what she was doing here. This was not a social call. She did have some business she needed to talk to Shawn about.

It was the Mandy Jansen case. She still hadn't been able to bring herself to close it. She just couldn't sign off on the idea that this young woman had taken her own life. But she also couldn't find any evidence that suggested anything other than suicide. So the case stayed on her desk, an open file staring up at her every time she came into the station.

She would have to close it soon. Mandy's mother had already called her twice, asking if she'd found anything new. The poor woman needed to let her little girl go, and she couldn't until she knew the truth. Every day Juliet kept the case open was one more day of doubt and fear for Mrs. Jansen.

O'Hara hadn't been authorized to hire Shawn to consult on the case. If she'd tried to suggest it to the chief in the middle of budgeting she'd be lucky if she was only fired. But she and Shawn had always had fun working together and she was pretty sure he'd be willing to take a look at things as a favor to her.

*That's why I'm here,* she told herself as she rapped on the bungalow's green door. Just to get closure on the case. No other reason at all.

She waited for a moment, then knocked on the door again. Still no answer. No one home. She should have called first. Would have, if she'd been willing to admit to herself that this was where she was going when she left the station.

She was turning back toward her car when she heard a heavy footstep from inside. After a moment the door swung open and Shawn stood in front of her.

Actually, to say he stood was something of an exaggeration. Shawn slouched, holding on to the doorframe for support. He looked like he might tumble to the floor if he let go.

O'Hara stared at him, stunned. She was sure it had only been a few weeks since she'd last seen Shawn, but he looked like he'd been living on the streets through an entire winter. And not a Santa Barbara winter, but an East Coast one. His face had gone pale, at least the part of it that was visible through the heavy beard stubble. His eyes were bloodshot and half closed, and his limbs seemed to have lost all their strength.

"Jules," he croaked in a craggy whisper. "Thank God you're here. We've got to go."

"Right now," she said, and took his arm. He let go of the doorframe and nearly fell into her arms before righting himself. She pulled the office door closed behind them, shook the knob to make sure it was locked, and half led, half carried him to her waiting sedan.

"We don't have a lot of time," Shawn said.

"There's plenty of time," O'Hara said, trying to keep the worry out of her voice. "You'll be just fine."

She loaded Shawn into the passenger's seat and wrapped the seat belt around him, then ran to her own door and got in, jamming the key into the ignition. She took a quick glance in the rearview, then slammed the car into gear and squealed out.

"Hey, the freeway's back there," Shawn said, as she made a screaming left turn toward the city's center.

"And the emergency room is this way," O'Hara said.

"I'm sorry. If you need help on a case, I'm usually there for you," Shawn said. "But I'm in the middle of my own, and I don't have any time to spare."

"I don't have a case at the emergency room," she said, trying to follow his logic. "I'm taking you there because you look like you're about to die."

"I'm fine," Shawn said.

"You could barely stand up when I came to your door," O'Hara said.

"So I'm a little tired," Shawn said. "I haven't been sleeping a lot lately."

"Or eating?"

"I went to BurgerZone just, um . . ." His voice trailed off as he tried to remember exactly when that had been. "They don't allow food in the Imaginarium, and by the time I get out everything is closed. Besides, when you've spent the entire night trying to cut through steel plate with a butter knife, it's hard to work up an appetite."

"Shawn, listen to yourself," she said. "You're hallucinating."

"I'm not."

O'Hara had wondered what the breakup with Gus might have done to Shawn. Gus had always been his anchor, the one who kept him from flying off into flights of fantasy. But she couldn't bring herself to believe that this might have been literally the truth. That without Gus, Shawn would actually spiral down into insanity. Something else was going on.

"I'm going to get you to the hospital," O'Hara said. "You're exhausted, probably dehydrated. A little rest, some IV fluids, and you won't believe how much better you'll feel."

"There's only one thing that's going to make me feel better and that's to make that scrawny college girl talk to me," Shawn said.

Was it possible that this was the problem? Shawn was in love and the object of his affection had shut him out of her life? If so, this was a side of Shawn she'd never seen. He'd been with women before, one of whom was a regular—or at least regularly recurring—for a good twenty-six weeks before he'd allowed her to be written out of his life. But he'd never acted obsessed like this.

"If you'd like me to talk to her, I can do that," O'Hara said carefully. "Just as soon as we get you to the hospital."

Shawn brightened, and for the first time since he'd opened the door she saw a little of his usual cockiness.

"You could talk to her," Shawn said. "You can probably speak her language."

"What language is that?"

"Student," Shawn said. "You went to college, right? You must have known women like this. Turn right here and get on the freeway."

"Hospital first," O'Hara said.

"I don't need a hospital. I need a translator," Shawn said. "There's a man missing out there, and if I don't find him he might die. And I can't do anything about it if that girl won't tell me what she knows."

O'Hara knew she should slam her foot down on the accelerator and get Shawn to the emergency room as fast as possible. But before she could put that plan into action, she made one mistake—she looked over at him. And what she saw was not the hollow, shambling mockery of a man who had answered the door, but a pale, shaky version of her old friend. The light was back in his eye and the grin on his face.

"I'll give it half an hour," she said. "And then I'm taking you to the hospital."

# Chapter Seventeen

"**W**hat the hell are you doing?" Juliet O'Hara backed away from Shawn, but not fast enough. She could feel the bullet whizzing past her ear.

"The guard was reaching for his gun," Shawn said, wheeling around to level his shotgun at the other security guard, who was cowering under a desk.

"So you killed three hostages to teach him a lesson?" she said, pointing at the bodies lying on the jewelry store's marble floor.

"Oh, no," Shawn said. "That's going to cost me a chunk of my inventory. We'd better check their pockets to see if there's anything we can use."

O'Hara looked around the jewelry store in disgust. She'd been at hundreds of crime scenes in her career, and seen more than one hostage situation go bad. But she'd never actually been one of the hostage takers before, and even though the victims were all virtual, she wanted to throw up.

"People do this for *fun*?" she said, practically spitting the last word.

"Not yet they don't," Shawn said. "I'm the only outsider who's been allowed to play the game. Except for Gus, of course, and he left before he got anywhere near level seven."

"At least I can see why you were looking so bad when I picked you up," she said. "This can't be good for you."

"It's just a game, Jules," Shawn said. "Don't take it so seriously."

If she had been taking this seriously, O'Hara thought, she would have pulled off her helmet after thirty seconds and called Judge Sanderson to get a warrant to shut the entire company down. She wasn't sure what law this game violated, but there had to be something. And if there wasn't, she'd run for Congress so she could write one.

It wasn't that O'Hara had anything against computer games. She'd grown up playing *Zork* and *Myst*, and even wasted some time at her previous jobs blowing away Nazi soldiers in *Castle Wolfenstein*.

But *Criminal Genius* wasn't just a game. It was an entire world, completely immersive and realistic in almost every way. And it wasn't just sights and sounds. Thanks to the full-body virtual suits, the game also provided a sense of touch. When you picked up a virtual object you could feel its weight, its texture. O'Hara had to admit that when Shawn first led her into Darksyde City she had been astonished. This was an entirely new art form, and one that could bring marvels to life.

Unfortunately, the designers of *Criminal Genius* apparently had no interest in bring marvels—or anything else—to life. Every bit of technological and artistic wizardry that had gone into the game had only one purpose: to teach the player how to be a successful criminal. And the more vicious, the better.

This wasn't a computer game—it was a training program for incipient psychopaths. And as she looked at Shawn aiming his gun at the trembling hostages, she saw the virtual world's effect on him. He was enjoying this, committing hideous acts of virtual violence even when he didn't need to in order to advance the plot. What kind of impact would this have on him in the real world?

"I'm not the one who's taking it too seriously, Shawn," she said. "You dragged me in here to help you solve a crime, remember?"

"Of course I remember," Shawn said. "We need to find Fawn Liebowitz."

"I thought you said she'd show up when you tried to steal the diamond," O'Hara said. "Where is she?"

"It has to be a new attempt," Shawn said. "I've tried this approach before."

She stared at him in horror. "You mean you did this for nothing?"

"You needed to get a feel for how the game works," Shawn said. "You don't want to find yourself in a gunfight if you don't know what it's like when people start dying in here."

"I don't want to find myself in a gunfight at all," O'Hara said. "I just want to get out of here and take a long, hot shower."

She reached up to pull off her helmet, but Shawn put a hand on her arm to stop her. "Jules, just try to relax a little."

"This room is bathed in blood," O'Hara said.

"Hardly bathed. Maybe a little shower," Shawn said, then seemed to realize how upset she was becoming. "It's pixels. No one actually gets hurt. Geez, when did you become such an old lady?"

"I'm an old lady?" O'Hara said, feeling the veins in her temples throbbing. "I'm an old lady?"

"You're sure acting like one," Shawn said. "Lighten up. Play the game. Have some fun."

She dropped her hand away from the helmet. "You want me to play the game?"

"That's kind of the point."

"You want me to have some fun?"

"Ideally," Shawn said.

"Okay, then," O'Hara said.

Shawn broke into a wide smile. "You're really going to enjoy this, Jules. I bet you're going to—"

Shawn's lips finished the sentence, but no sound came out of his mouth. Which wasn't surprising since his head was no longer attached to his neck.

O'Hara dropped her still-smoking shotgun to the floor. It hit just as Shawn's body crumpled down beside it.

"You were right, Shawn," O'Hara said. "This game can be fun if you give it a chance."

She reached up and gave her ears a sharp twist, then lifted her own head off her shoulders. The jewelry story dissolved around her and the last thing she saw before everything went black was Shawn's body, twitching slightly on the floor.

# Chapter Eighteen

Shawn blinked against the harsh white light of the Imaginarium. O'Hara had already put her helmet back in the rack and was heading for the door.

"Wait, Jules," Shawn said.

"Don't bother, Shawn," she said. "I was going to take you to the emergency room, but it's pretty clear that Santa Barbara General isn't the kind of hospital you need."

"I'm not crazy," Shawn said. "I'm sorry if I came across that way. I've been playing this game so much lately that I've gotten used to the world. Believe me, seeing it through your eyes reminds me how horrified I was the first time I put on the helmet."

That, of course, was a lie. The first time Shawn had entered Darksyde City he'd hijacked a car and run down pedestrians until a fleet of police cars forced him into the side of a building, killing him and ending the game. But there was some truth to the statement. After all, Gus had been pretty repulsed by the whole thing, and since they'd still been partners when they first played the game Shawn felt he was entitled to claim fifty percent of his reactions.

Besides, even if it was a lie it seemed to be working.

O'Hara was still standing by the door but she hadn't taken another step.

"Look at yourself, Shawn," she said. "You haven't eaten. You haven't slept. God knows when you last changed your clothes. You've become obsessed with this game. And now that I see what it is that has you under its spell, I'm really worried about your mental health."

"I don't keep coming back here because I enjoy playing this sick, twisted game," Shawn said, knowing that if he tried lying this blatantly inside Darksyde City his nose would grow at least fifteen inches.

But without the contradictory evidence of an expanding organ, he had apparently managed to strike the right note of sincerity and contrition. She actually moved away from the door a little. "Then why?"

"It's about finding Macklin Tanner," Shawn said. "We may disapprove of his work, but there's no denying that the man is a genius. And somebody has kidnapped him."

"The SBPD looked into the disappearance weeks ago," O'Hara said. "Detectives Bookins and Danner found no evidence of foul play."

"If it had been Detectives O'Hara and Lassiter, maybe I'd be a little less concerned," Shawn said. "Well, maybe not Lassie so much. The point is, the fact that there was no evidence makes this even worse."

"Because if he was kidnapped it was by someone who really knew what he was doing," O'Hara conceded. "But who and why?"

"I don't know why," Shawn said. "Maybe there's some kind of entity out there that needed his expertise and couldn't get it legally so they were willing to pay huge amounts of money to anyone who'd deliver Tanner to them. As for who, I'm convinced it was someone inside this company. And I'm equally convinced that person left a clue in this game so that the world could admire his genius."

"And you think this Fawn Liebowitz is that clue?"

"I think she holds it," Shawn said. "The rules of the game may seem random when you first enter Darksyde City, but they are real and they are consistent. They have to be to make the game play satisfying. She's the only thing I've come across that doesn't fit."

"How many times have you tried to make her talk?"

Shawn thought back on his encounters with the student and all the knives, guns, bombs, and poison-gas grenades she'd used to kill him. "At least thirty," he said. "Maybe more."

"What seems to be the problem?"

"I don't know how to talk to her," Shawn said. "There's clearly something I'm supposed to say or do to make her open up, but nothing has worked."

"Well, what have you tried?" O'Hara said.

"I tried being nice to her," Shawn said. "She cut my throat. I accused her of kidnapping Tanner and she blew us both up. I got tough a bunch of times, but she kept finding ways to turn whatever I was using on her against me."

Shawn noticed that look of disgust creeping back onto O'Hara's face. He moved on quickly. "I tried romance a few different ways. I brought her flowers. I offered her jewelry. I even proposed marriage."

"And none of that worked?" O'Hara said, a smile replacing the look of horror. "What kind of game is this?"

"I'm out of ideas," Shawn said. "That's why I was so excited when you came to my door. Because maybe you can get through to her. I'm thinking she speaks a language that only college students understand."

"I don't think so," O'Hara said.

"Sorry I dragged you out here for nothing, then," Shawn said.

But O'Hara still wasn't moving toward the door.

"I don't think it's a matter of speaking a language only students can understand," O'Hara said. "I think you need to speak like a woman."

# Chapter Nineteen

Shawn was on his best behavior. When the streetwalker came up to them and asked if they wanted to party, Shawn knew that the correct response—the one that would add several rounds of ammunition to his cache—was to steal her money at gunpoint. Instead he politely declined and led O'Hara down the street.

Not that she was acting as squeamish as she had been the first time they'd entered the game together. She seemed to have accepted Shawn's reasoning, and instead of being repulsed by what she saw, she took it all as a necessary part of his investigation. She still had qualms about committing the kinds of criminal acts needed to get ahead in Darksyde City, but Shawn was pretty sure that he'd seen a smile on her face when the pustulating wino tried to mug her and she blew him away with a blast from her semiautomatic rifle.

The first real test came when Shawn laid out his plan to lure Fawn Liebowitz to them. He'd acquired a pile of dynamite on an earlier level, and he was going to use it on the dam that held in the local reservoir. The ensuing flood would wipe out a whole neighborhood, but it was the one thing he hadn't tried to get into that jewelry store vault.

When he pitched her the idea Shawn studied O'Hara's face closely—at least he studied the face of her avatar, but since the insides of the helmets were lined with tiny cameras to record and mimic the players' facial expressions, he knew it was an accurate gauge of her mood—and she took it calmly.

But even when they were actually laying the dynamite at the foot of the dam, Shawn wasn't sure he'd won her over to his side. As Shawn taped three sticks to the concrete and set their fuses burning, a man's voice shouted, "Stop there!"

Shawn turned slowly to see a security guard emerging from the darkness, pointing an enormous pistol at him. Shawn reached for his own gun, but before he could raise it the guard shot it out of his hand.

"That was a warning," the guard said. "Next one goes right through you. So do the hundred after that. Get the picture?"

"Got it," Shawn said. "What do you want me to do?"

"That depends," the guard said.

"On what?"

"On how much you piss me off," the guard said. "If you're nice, all I want you to do is die. But if you make me really mad, I'm afraid I'm going to have to insist you suffer the agonies of the damned."

"That sounds like fun," Shawn said, "but I'm kind of in a hurry. So I think I'll pass."

"Then die," the guard said, raising his gun.

There was no time for Shawn to grab one of his own weapons. He took a step backward, fumbling blindly behind him with one hand. At first there was nothing but concrete. And then he felt the cold, hard tube. Shawn closed his fist around the stick of dynamite and yanked it away from the face of the dam, then hurled it at the guard.

Just as the dynamite left his hand, Shawn heard O'Hara's voice screaming at him. "Shawn, no!"

*Let her be horrified,* Shawn thought. If she couldn't stand the thought of the guard spattering down on her like red rain, she should have stayed on her side of the dam. This was business, after all.

But if O'Hara was horrified she wasn't showing it. She whipped out her own gun and got off one shot. Thanks to the time-altering effect of the software, which slowed down the entire world from the moment a gun was fired until the bullet found its mark, Shawn was able to watch the projectile fly through the sky until he realized where it was heading—directly toward the dynamite.

Shawn dived to the ground just before the bullet struck the stick. Even so, he felt the blast wave slam him into the dirt. When he could finally get back on his feet he saw the security guard lying on his back and O'Hara standing over him with her pistol pointed at his head.

"Nice shooting," Shawn said. "What was the point?"

"The point was not letting you kill the guard," O'Hara said.

"That's a nice sentiment, but it kind of leaves us with a problem," Shawn said. "Because the instant you take your gun off that guy, he's going to pop up and kill us both. Believe me, I've played this game long enough to know exactly what kindness and gentleness get you."

That wasn't exactly a lie. Shawn *had* played the game long enough to have learned this lesson. He didn't actually know how goodness would be rewarded only because he'd never actually tried such a tactic.

"I'm not being nice," O'Hara said. "But if I let you kill this guard we'd never get out of this damn game."

"We can leave whenever we want, Jules," Shawn said patiently. "Even if we get caught and thrown in jail, we've just got to take off our helmets."

O'Hara sighed impatiently. "Look at the guard," she said. "What do you see?"

Shawn did as he was instructed. "It's a security guard," Shawn said. "Standard-issue in this game, right down to the beard stubble and the paunch."

"What about the uniform?"

Shawn looked a little more closely. "It's got the usual stains from coffee drips and doughnut crumbs, but it's a little less wrinkled than some other ones I've seen in the game," he said after some study.

"Yeah, there's that," O'Hara said. "Nice level of creativity with the cops eating doughnuts, by the way. Really raises my opinion of the programmers. But I was more interested in the buttons."

Shawn looked again. The buttons on the uniform shirt were standard plastic, with four holes for the thread to pass through. There was absolutely nothing special about them, no markings, no color, no insignia. He was about to say something to that effect when he realized what O'Hara was talking about.

"They're on the left side," Shawn said. "That's not a shirt—it's a blouse."

"And unless the security guards here are all cross-dressers . . ." O'Hara said.

She didn't have to finish. Shawn bent down over the security guard and grabbed him by the crew cut. "Hello, Fawn," he said.

Shawn gave the guard's scalp a tug and it tore off in his hand, leaving a jagged hole in his head. Inside, Shawn could see Fawn Liebowitz's long brown hair. He grabbed a piece of loose skin and tore down the guard's body. It ripped an opening all the way down, like the easy-open string on a twenty-pound bag of doggie kibble, and then the guard's body melted away, leaving the familiar form of Fawn Liebowitz behind.

"This is the one we've been looking for, right?" O'Hara said.

"Detective Juliet O'Hara, meet Fawn Liebowitz," Shawn said, giving the student a nudge with his foot. "Fawn, Jules has some questions for you. Although if you'd like to settle this with a hot-oil wrestling match, that would be okay with me."

"Hello, Fawn," O'Hara said. "You know what we want from you, don't you?"

The student stared up at her, impassive.

"That's how you talk to a student?" Shawn said. "Or is that the special language women use with each other?"

"I'm just getting started," O'Hara said.

"My name is Fawn Liebowitz," Fawn said. "I'm a student at Darksyde University. My major is library science."

"We know that, Fawn," O'Hara said. "I'm looking for information. Please."

Shawn looked down at Fawn and saw that she was reaching into her backpack. It couldn't be this easy. How could he not have thought of something so basic? There was only one possible answer—it was Gus' fault. All the years they'd been in the detective business, he'd let Gus handle all the intellectual issues like dealing with museum curators and college students because Gus liked talking to that kind of person. And Shawn had gotten out of practice. Thank God he was on his own again.

"Are you telling me it never occurred to you to ask her nicely for the information you needed?" O'Hara said.

"It was on my list of things to try," Shawn said.

"Uh-huh," O'Hara said. "And it never made it to the top because?"

Shawn glanced down at Fawn again. "Maybe because of that," he said.

O'Hara followed his gaze and saw that Fawn's hand was coming out of the backpack, holding a fist-sized green oval marked with striations. And it was ticking.

"Grenade!" O'Hara shouted.

Shawn took a step forward and kicked the grenade like he was trying for a game-winning field goal. It soared through the air and exploded in a fireball over the dam.

"Do you have any other brilliant ideas?" Shawn said.

"I'm thinking!" O'Hara said.

"That's a plan," Shawn said. "One strategy this game really rewards is standing around doing nothing. You get to learn all sorts of new and exciting ways to die that way."

"You worry about the threats, I'll deal with the girl," O'Hara said. "You're such an expert murderer by now, I'm sure there's nothing you can't handle."

"Absolutely nothing," Shawn said. "Except maybe for that."

He pointed up at the dam. Directly under the spot where the grenade had gone off, a spiderweb of cracks was crawling across the concrete surface.

"That's not fair," O'Hara said.

"Now you're learning," Shawn said. "So maybe you could speak to our friend before the Shawnstown flood begins."

O'Hara cast another glance up at the dam and saw how quickly the cracks were spreading, then turned back to Fawn Liebowitz. "Have you considered rushing Pi Phi? Because I'm sure they'd love to have you."

"You're kidding," Shawn said.

"Did you try asking her about sororities?" O'Hara said. "That can be an important part of a college girl's life."

"Well, unless Al-Qaeda's got a branch at Darksyde U, I don't think she's interested in social organizations," Shawn said.

While Shawn and O'Hara had been arguing, Fawn had reached into her backpack again and come out with a metal briefcase.

"Now what?" O'Hara said.

"My guess is it's a suitcase nuke," Shawn said.

"An atomic bomb?" O'Hara said, incredulous. "That's the dumbest thing I've ever heard."

Shawn grabbed the briefcase out of Fawn's hands and gave it a shake. It started to tick loudly.

"And the bar is raised," O'Hara said. "The suitcase nuke

is no longer the dumbest thing I've ever heard. A ticking suitcase nuke is even dumber. Nuclear bombs simply do not tick."

"Everything in this world ticks when it's about to blow up," Shawn said. "Ten ticks and you're done."

"Then get rid of it!"

Shawn hurled the briefcase down the hill. It bounced on its corners three times, then came to a stop.

"That's it?" O'Hara said.

"Two more ticks," Shawn said. "One—"

The briefcase exploded in a blinding flash, and then a miniature mushroom cloud.

"Now what?" O'Hara said when her ears stopped ringing. "Are we going to die of radiation poisoning?"

"I don't think that's going to be a problem," Shawn said.

"You sure about that?" O'Hara said. "The sick bastards who designed this thing seemed to think of every other possible torture."

"You're probably right about that," Shawn said. "It's just that we're not going to live that long. Look."

He pointed back at the dam. The nuclear explosion had accelerated the spread of the cracks and now they were wide enough that water was beginning to trickle through.

"This is so not fair," O'Hara said. "Why did I let you talk me into coming back into this damn, dumb game?" O'Hara said.

"Because you said you knew how to solve the puzzle," Shawn said.

"And I would if you'd let me think," O'Hara said.

"There's no time for that," Shawn said.

There was a thunk as a chunk of concrete from the dam landed at their feet, nearly taking off Fawn Liebowitz's head. Water blasted through the hole it had left behind, and more concrete was crumbling under the pressure.

"Come on, Jules. We've only got seconds left," Shawn said.

"I'm trying!"

"Try harder!" Shawn shouted over the roar of the water.

"Will you be quiet and let me think?" she said, but her words were lost as the concrete in the dam began to crack apart.

"What?" Shawn said.

"Quiet!" she yelled.

The water was rushing under their feet now. In another few seconds the dam would give way completely and they'd be swept away in the flood, drowned or pulverized or eaten by sharks. In other words, Shawn thought, another disaster.

He looked down, expecting to see Fawn Liebowitz grinning up at him as she always did right before he died. But Fawn wasn't smiling. She was twitching and shaking and blue smoke was coming out of her ears.

"You did it, Jules," Shawn shouted triumphantly. "Do it again!"

"Do what?" O'Hara said.

"I kept thinking of her as a college student and a woman," Shawn said. "I didn't realize that what's really important is what she's studying. She's a *librarian*."

Now O'Hara understood. She kneeled down by Fawn and yelled in her smoking ear. "Quiet!"

At the command, the student stopped shaking. The smoke stopped coming from her ears. She reached into her backpack again.

"Get back!" Shawn shouted, feeling disappointment flooding through him even more strongly than the water was coming out of the dam.

"Not this time!" O'Hara said. "You be ready in case she tries something."

The water was up to their knees now and it was getting hard to stand against it. Shawn braced himself as the librarian slowly pulled her hand out of the backpack.

"I see something!" O'Hara said.

It was long and straight. Shawn was so prepared to see a

weapon it took him a few seconds to realize that what was coming out of the backpack was actually a book.

"Grab it, Jules!"

O'Hara reached out and got one hand on the book and then the other. She gave it a yank and it came free.

"I've got it!"

There was no answer. O'Hara looked up, but Shawn was gone. So was the dam. The last thing she saw was the gigantic wall of water crashing down on her.

# Chapter Twenty

"I wish I could help you, Jules. I really do," Gus said. "I just don't have the time to get back to Santa Barbara."

"And I didn't have the time to fly up here," O'Hara said. "Or the money. And it's not like the department is paying for this trip."

As they walked through the wide hallways of the Benson Pharmaceuticals headquarters, O'Hara found she practically had to run to keep up with Gus. Of all the strange things that had been going on lately, this had to be the strangest. The Gus she knew was always the guy who was lagging behind shouting, "Hey, guys, wait up!" He wasn't the leader. But he strode through these offices as if he owned the place.

"I've given you every bit of information we have about Mandy Jansen, Jules," Gus said. "There just isn't any more."

O'Hara felt a tremor of guilt flit through her at the mention of the name. Since she'd gone to see Shawn two days ago she hadn't done a thing about that case. But the book in the game had pushed everything else out of her mind.

"You've been more than helpful on that case," she said. "But that's not why I'm here."

"Then what?"

"It's Shawn."

"What about him?" Gus said, his step slowing slightly.

"He needs your help on the Macklin Tanner thing," she said.

Gus stiffened and increased his pace. "If Shawn needs my help he knows where to find me."

"I'm not sure he does," O'Hara said.

"He's a detective," Gus said. "He tracked me to San Francisco when I was trying to keep my destination hidden from him. It'll be much easier now that he has my business card with my phone number on it."

"He doesn't want to bother you," O'Hara said. "He knows you're in an exciting new phase of your life, and the last thing he wants is for you to think he's trying to drag you back to Psych."

"So he sent you to do it instead."

Gus stopped outside a door. The nameplate read BURTON GUSTER, EXECUTIVE VICE PRESIDENT.

"Last time I was here, hadn't you just been promoted to senior vice president?" she said.

"It's one of the things that make this such an exciting company to work for," Gus said. "Lots of room for advancement. But it also means there's a huge amount of work for those who are ready to take it on. And I'm already backed up."

"All I need is a couple of minutes," O'Hara said.

Gus sighed and pushed open the door and led her into an office the size of the house she grew up in. Floor-to-ceiling windows looked out over the Ferry Building and the Bay Bridge to Treasure Island and the East Bay. She couldn't help but stare at the view—not only because it was so beautiful, but because she couldn't quite bring herself to reconcile it with its owner. People like Gus didn't get offices like this. And yet here he was.

Gus led her to a sitting area in one corner of the office, two armchairs and a couch all arranged for maximum appreciation of the view. He sat in one of the chairs and motioned for her to do the same.

"Tell me about Shawn," he said.

"There's not much else to tell," she said. "He's completely obsessed with this computer game."

"That's not much of a surprise," Gus said. "It's pretty addictive if you like that kind of thing—and Shawn likes that kind of thing."

"That's what I thought at first, too," she said. "Just Shawn being Shawn. But it's more than that. He's got to find Macklin Tanner or he'll tear himself apart. And he's convinced that the only clue is the one he'll find in the game."

"That's nothing new," Gus said.

"But this is," she said. "We found the clue."

"We?"

The look on his face told her he was reading much more into this pronoun than it could possibly carry. "I helped him out one time. It was the least I could do after all the cases you guys worked on for us."

"So you found the clue," he said. "That's great. Why do you need my help?"

"Because we can't understand what it means," she said.

"You're two great detectives," Gus said. "If you can't figure it out, why do you think I can?"

"Because it's a book," O'Hara said. "You like books. You understand books. I've always been something of a reader, but I never had the passion. And Shawn—well, you know."

He did. "I'll do what I can. But I'm not going to be able to get to Santa Barbara anytime soon, and I can't imagine there's a way to get into the game from here."

"You don't need to," O'Hara said. "I've drawn it for you."

She pulled a piece of paper out of her purse and unfolded it on his desk. She had drawn the book's front cover and spine.

"What about the back cover?" Gus said, studying the pictures.

"Nothing," she said. "Black leather."

"And inside?

"Blank page after blank page."

"It could be some kind of invisible ink," Gus said. "If so, you've got to do something to make it appear. If that's the case I can't help you."

"I don't think it is," O'Hara said. "We've already tried a couple of ideas, and the pages just get dirty. Whatever the clue is, it's here."

Gus picked up the paper and looked at it again. "It's by Edgar Allan Poe, which seems appropriate for the game," Gus said. "But what's this title?"

"The One That No One Has Actually Read," O'Hara said. "I have researched every word Poe ever wrote, and there's nothing with a title anything like this."

"Of course there isn't," Gus said, breaking into a broad smile. "Because this isn't a title. It's a description."

"We did think of that," she said. "But what good does it do us? I mean, sure, we can rule out the things we read in school—'The Raven,' 'The Tell-Tale Heart.' But he wrote dozens of stories and God knows how many poems and a lot of them are pretty obscure. Where would we start?"

"With 'actually,'" Gus said.

"I don't understand."

"The title isn't 'The One That No One Has Read,'" Gus said. "It's 'The One That No One Has Actually Read.' Which means that it's something people refer to as if they've read it, even though they haven't."

"And this means something to you," O'Hara said.

"It sure does," Gus said. "Would to you, too, if you'd ever worked as a private detective. Because people who think they're smart always like to suggest that the solution is much easier than you know it has to be. If you're searching for something, they want to suggest that the reason you're not finding it is because you're looking too hard, and not in the most obvious place. And when they do that, they always make reference to 'The Purloined Letter.'"

She looked at him blankly. "I'm thinking that's a Poe story."

"It is," Gus said. "Although I've never read it, either. Nobody has. But we all know the solution—that the reason the police were never able to find the stolen letter was because the thief knew they'd look in every elaborate hiding place, but they'd never notice it if it was left out in plain sight."

"That's ridiculous," O'Hara said. "The police always check the obvious places first."

"Maybe police work was different back then," Gus said. "Or maybe it's a lousy story. That would certainly explain why no one bothers to read it. But the solution is famous, and that's what this book title refers to."

"So it's saying that Macklin Tanner has been in plain sight all along?" she said. "But that doesn't make any sense at all. He's not like a letter you can stuff in an envelope. If he was at his home or at the office, someone would have noticed him a long time ago."

"Then maybe this isn't the clue you think it is," Gus said.

"It has to be," O'Hara said.

"What else can you tell me about the book?" Gus said.

"Just what's in the picture."

Gus squinted down at the drawing of the volume's spine. "What are these squiggles?"

"Those aren't squiggles," she said. "They're numbers."

"Not these numbers." Gus looked again. "They can't be."

"They are," she said. "Why can't they?"

"Don't you know anything about the Dewey decimal system?" he said, trying to mask his impatience at her ignorance.

"I know it's how books are classified in libraries," she said.

"Then I suppose you also know that the numbers aren't assigned randomly," Gus said. "That they have specific and precise meanings."

"Sure. I guess. I mean, they'd have to, or what's the point?"

"Exactly," Gus said. "What is this number you scrawled on the Poe book's spine?"

O'Hara started to answer, then stopped herself. She took the paper back, studied it closely, and then put it down again. "Six-eighty-two-point-seven MTN. Does that mean something?"

"I don't know yet, but I can tell you exactly what it doesn't refer to," Gus said. "The classification for literature, which is the only Dewey designation that makes sense for this book, is eight hundred. If I remember correctly, American Literature in English is classified in the eight-tens. Fiction, I believe, would put it in the eight-thirteens. So this book would be classified as eight-thirteen-point-something Po. But Poe might not be classified with the literature. It could be considered fiction, in which case it wouldn't have a number at all. The spine would just say FIC and then the first three letters of his last name—which in this case would be his entire last name."

O'Hara felt her heart starting to pound. This could be something. "So what do these numbers mean?"

"I might be tempted to say nothing," Gus said. "After all, we have no idea if the programmer responsible for this part of the game knew anything about the Dewey decimal system or if he just remembered there were supposed to be numbers on the spine of a library book. But those letters at the end suggest that's wrong."

O'Hara looked at them again. "MTN," she said. "Macklin Tanner."

"That's what I'm thinking," Gus said. "Which means that those numbers have to be a map to where he is."

"So what is six-eighty-two-point-seven?" she said.

Gus got out of his chair and walked across the office to the large desk that sprawled in the exact center of the window. He passed his hand through one of those light beams and the panel slid open to reveal the face of the computer. "Do you really think I'm such a nerd I'd know the entire Dewey decimal system?"

There didn't seem to be a way to answer that would actually move the conversation forward, so O'Hara didn't say anything. Gus started typing onto the computer screen.

"Okay," he said after the display loaded. "The six hundreds are all about technology."

"That doesn't do us any good," O'Hara said. "We already know that Tanner is a technological genius."

"But not this kind," Gus said. "Computer stuff all starts in the triple zeroes, because the entire system was developed a hundred years before Bill Gates was born, and there was no way to squeeze a new world of publications into existing categories."

"So what kind of technology are we talking about?" O'Hara said.

"The kind that existed in the nineteenth century," Gus said. "In terms of the six-eighties, we're looking at 'manufacture for specific use.'"

"How specific?"

"Well, six-eighty-five is leather, fur, and related items. Six-eighty-four is furnishing and home workshops."

"And six-eighty-two?"

He checked the display, then checked it again. "Small forge work," he said. "Blacksmithing."

# Chapter Twenty-one

As the door closed behind Detective O'Hara, Gus settled back into his desk chair and felt a familiar rush of satisfaction. He had grown tired of so much about the detective business, but he could never get sick of the thrill that came when the puzzle pieces finally began to fall together, when what had been a random set of facts and actions suddenly coalesced into a pattern.

It was true that they still had no idea exactly what the clue was telling them, what kind of connection might exist between Macklin Tanner's whereabouts and the art and industry of blacksmithing, but that would be a matter of grunt work, not inspiration. Now that they knew where to look, Shawn and Jules could start searching for any connection either Tanner or anyone who knew him had with metalwork.

That thought sent a little pang of jealousy through him. Shawn and Jules were going to have all the fun. They were going to track this clue down to its ultimate meaning, they were going to find Tanner and catch the bad guy—if there was a bad guy. And it would all be because Gus had spotted the misplaced number and understood the pattern.

Gus was so flushed with the excitement of the discov-

ery that he'd picked up the phone and dialed the first half
of Psych's number before he realized what he was doing.
Even then he wasn't sure why he'd stopped himself from
completing the call. He and Shawn had split on the best
of terms. There was no reason why he couldn't help his
old partner finish up a case they had started together. And
odds were O'Hara was still returning her rental car to the
airport lot—he and Shawn could jump on this new revelation and have it wrapped up before she even told Shawn
what he'd come up with.

But what had he come up with, exactly? He'd taken a
set of numbers and letters on O'Hara's sketch of a book
she'd seen in a computer game, made an assumption about
what they must have meant, and then jumped to an answer
based on that. And it all seemed perfectly logical, as long as
his basic assumption was right.

But what if it wasn't?

Gus had no idea who had put those numbers on the spine
of the digital image of a book. He had no way of knowing
if that person knew anything about the Dewey decimal
system. Maybe he'd just remembered that there were supposed to be numbers on a library book and slapped some
on at random. Or maybe there was a message encoded
there, but not the one that Gus had puzzled out.

Gus knew he hadn't necessarily deduced the truth of
these numbers. He'd simply made a decision. When he saw
that the spine bore the wrong Dewey decimal classification,
he leaped to the idea that the numbers were to be inter-
preted via the system. That gave him an answer—but was
it *the* answer?

The truth was those numbers could have meant anything. A date, for instance: Maybe 682.7 should have been
read as June 7, 1982. It would be odd to write it out that way,
but if they were looking for a rogue programmer, would it
really be so hard to believe he'd write it out as a *Star Trek*–
style star date? If that was right, then Shawn would have

to search through Tanner's life to figure out what had happened on that day—and since the game designer had only been three at the time he'd also have to look at whatever else might have been going on at the same time. June 7, 1982 was, for example, the day that Priscilla Presley first opened Graceland to the public, although she kept the bathroom where Elvis died off-limits. Could that conceivably have anything to do with Tanner's disappearance? It seemed unlikely, but was it that much less plausible than the notion that Festus from *Gunsmoke* had snatched the guy?

Or maybe it wasn't just the numbers. He'd stated as a fact that MTN had to stand for Macklin Tanner, but there was no way of knowing that for sure. For all he knew the correct way to read the spine was as a seven-digit telephone number: 682-7686, once he'd swapped out the three letters for their corresponding numerals. Granted, that was not a common format for writing out telephone numbers, but there were no standardized rules for leaving clues in computer games.

And those were just the first two possible alternative interpretations that popped into his mind. Who was to say the kidnapper—if there was a kidnapper—hadn't actually given out the address of Tanner's hiding place: 6287 Mountain? Maybe he was bragging that he'd shot Tanner with a Remington Model 700 Mountain LSS Bolt Action Rifle 6287. MTN could have referred to the Military Training Network of the Uniformed Services University and the number to a course or a research study.

Those letters and numbers could have meant anything. Gus had chosen his own interpretation and O'Hara had run out to act on it. But if he was right and his hunch led them to find Tanner, it would really only be luck. And if he was wrong—and he was so much more likely to have been wrong—then he might have just condemned the man to a terrible death.

Gus realized the phone was shaking in his hand. He lowered it gently to its cradle and waited until the tremors passed, then dug a Kleenex out of his drawer and wiped the sweat off his palms.

This, Gus knew, was why he couldn't call Shawn and spitball ideas about what kind of mad blacksmith had taken Tanner hostage.

It was the fear.

It was why he'd left Psych in the first place.

Gus had tried to convince himself that he had grown tired of being a detective, that now he had become a man and it was time to put aside childish things. That the thought of being an executive was simply more exciting than working with Psych.

But now he had to face the truth. He'd left Psych because he had been scared.

He'd tried to deny it to himself, and when that didn't work, he'd simply ignored the sensation. Because every time he even thought about working on a case, he had been filled with fear.

It didn't used to be like this. When Gus teamed up with Shawn he'd managed to share his best friend's blithe assumption that as long as they were having fun that was all that mattered. And for years, the world seemed to follow that dictate. Gus and Shawn would take the most outrageous risks, play the most ludicrous scams, and accuse the least likely suspect of the vilest crimes. And every time they turned out to be right.

It was like they were charmed. Shawn could do something as ridiculous as announce that a sea lion had been murdered, and not only would no one ever point out that the definition of the crime extends no further than the willing extermination of a human being, but they'd also end up catching a band of international diamond smugglers.

It was wonderful. And then the charm wore off.

It happened last year. When his old art history professor

Langston Kitteredge became the prime suspect in a vicious murder, Gus insisted that he and Shawn were the only ones who could clear his name.

The story Kitteredge told them was as fascinating as it was frightening—the professor was the victim of a centuries-old, global cabal that only he knew about. To clear his name of the murder charge, they'd have to unmask the conspiracy.

It sounded impossible. But Gus and Shawn had tackled so many cases that sounded crazy at first blush; one of their clients had seemed to be possessed by the devil, for heaven's sake. This one wouldn't be any different.

Except that it was.

Everything Gus thought about the crime had turned out to be wrong. He had allowed himself to be blinded—not only by his fondness for the professor, but by his belief in his own skills as a detective. It simply never occurred to him that he could have been mistaken.

Until it was too late. Too tragically, horribly late. He watched as a man was murdered in front of him, all because Gus had been so convinced he had it all right.

Since that case had ended Gus had simply had no appetite to take on another one. Every time a potential client came through the door, Gus would envision that dead man lying on the floor and he'd want to flee the room.

He'd tried talking to Shawn about this. When Brenda Varda came in to ask them to find Tanner, Gus had pleaded with him not to take the case. But when Shawn asked why, Gus couldn't find the words. He rambled on and on about the Kitteredge case and how badly he'd screwed up, but Shawn just chucked him on the shoulder and said something about getting back on the horse.

The trouble was, there was no horse anymore. His instincts, which had been so infallible for so long, had completely failed him with Kitteredge. And since neither he nor Shawn had any formal detective training, if such a thing even existed, Gus' instincts were all he had to go on. If he couldn't trust them, he couldn't trust himself on a case. Because if he was wrong, people could die.

So he wouldn't call Shawn and help him figure out what a blacksmith had to do with the disappearance of a computer-game mogul. He wouldn't share his theories about the other possible meanings of the clue, and he definitely wouldn't do to Shawn what he had just done to himself. He wouldn't sow doubt and fear when the only thing that could help the situation was confidence.

Gus had made his choice. He used to be a detective; now he was an executive vice president of a rising pharmaceuticals company. He'd loved being part of Psych, but that time was over. There was no going back.

# Chapter Twenty-two

It was only a few hundred feet from one side of the ridge to the other, but it felt like they'd traveled a thousand miles. The climate they'd left behind was temperate and practically tropical, cooled by the gentle breezes blowing off the ocean. Now they'd stepped into a desert of dead grasses and blasting heat.

Detective Carlton Lassiter had always loved crossing the hills that separated Santa Barbara from the rest of the world. Sure, the city he lived in was widely considered a paradise, and the backcountry was barely livable for rattlesnakes. But there was a truth to the arid heat that was hidden by the green and pleasant climate of the city below: Life was cruel and death was always waiting around the corner for you. The hills told you that. Bums lived out on the streets of Santa Barbara for years—there was one old guy he was sure had been camping outside a shopping mall since Carter was president. But you couldn't survive a summer in the hills without running water and air-conditioning and shelter. In August you'd be lucky to make it through a day.

As much as he enjoyed the physical experience, though, Lassiter had little interest in being here now. He had work to do, cases to close, criminals to catch. He couldn't afford to waste most of a day trying yet again to solve the murder of a woman who hadn't been murdered.

This was his partner's doing. She had insisted they follow some mysterious lead in the Mandy Jansen case and slog up this way. At least she said she'd had a lead; she refused to tell him where it had come from. For all he knew it had been revealed by a gypsy woman reading her palm.

Normally he wouldn't have cared where she'd gotten the tip. Juliet O'Hara was as good a detective as he'd ever met and the best partner he could imagine.

But lately she had begun to change. As far as he could tell it had started when they'd been called to the scene of that hanging cheerleader. For some reason the sight had affected her more deeply than she would acknowledge. Lassiter had offered her the advice that had always helped him through the tough times on the job. But when he'd pulled her aside and said "walk it off, Detective," she had only given him that vacant smile she reserved for civilians who came into the station to report that space aliens were eating Jell-O on their lawn.

Lassiter was still willing to trust her instincts—he was here with her, wasn't he? But he found himself questioning her judgment far more than he ever had before.

And now, as their unmarked sedan bounced down a dirt road leading into a deep canyon, he had to wonder if she'd lost her senses completely. There was no crime to investigate at all, just a poor, unfortunate girl who had taken her own life. And yet O'Hara was insisting they search for some kind of phantom evidence in Southern California's answer to Appalachia.

"Are you sure you've got the right address, Detective?" Lassiter said.

"No, Carlton," O'Hara said, not taking her eyes off the rutted road. "The other fifteen times you asked me that, I lied. But now that you've hit the magic sixteenth, I'm compelled to tell the truth. I've actually got the wrong address, and I'm just going to keep driving through the middle of nowhere because I'm too embarrassed to admit it."

"At least that would be behavior I could understand," Lassiter said. "I can't imagine what else would possibly drag you up here."

The car rounded a tree and suddenly Lassiter could imagine. There was a small blue car sitting under the branches, the one bit of shade for miles around. Shawn Spencer was stretched out on the hood.

"This was your tip?" Lassiter said.

"It wasn't a tip. It was a lead," O'Hara said. "We found it together."

She pulled the sedan up behind the blue Echo and got out. After a long moment Lassiter followed, but only because she'd turned off the ignition and the cabin was already starting to heat up.

"Sorry we're late, Shawn," O'Hara said, as he ambled over to meet them.

"No problem," Shawn said. "It's hard to move fast when you're stapled to a lead weight."

Lassiter glared at Shawn. "What does this loser know about Mandy Jansen?" Lassiter said. "I doubt she would have given him the time of day."

"I don't think he knows anything about her," O'Hara said. "We're here searching for Macklin Tanner."

Now Lassiter turned his glare on her. "The Mandy Jansen case would be bad enough," he said. "At least that's technically an SBPD case, even if it's only still open because you've got some strange fixation with it. But Macklin Tanner isn't a case at all. Our detectives looked at it, determined there was no foul play, and dismissed it. So if you are using the time of two Santa Barbara Police Department detectives to help a private detective out on his own case, that is theft, and despite my great respect and admiration for you, I will have no choice but to report you to the proper authorities."

"And then Santy Claus won't bring her any presents," Shawn said. "I bet you'll feel guilty come December twenty-sixth, Lassie."

"I'm at a dead end with Mandy Jansen's case," O'Hara said. "I asked Shawn to consult, but since the department wasn't prepared to pay I told him I'd give him a hand on his case."

"Unfortunately she didn't mention she'd be bringing some other body part, as well," Shawn said.

"I refuse to have anything to do with this," Lassiter said.

"Too late, Carlton," O'Hara said. "The mileage is already on the vehicle. If you report me, what are you going to say—that I kidnapped you?"

"Don't think I won't report myself, as well," Lassiter said. "You know I will."

"Poor Lassie," Shawn said. "Doesn't have any friends, so he's got to do everything on his own."

"I don't see your little sidekick anywhere, Spencer," Lassiter said. "Oh, that's right. He dumped you to take a real job."

"He didn't dump me," Shawn said, rolling off the car's hood and landing on his feet. "If you ever had a friend you'd know that sometimes you've got to go off in separate directions for a while."

"I'd say three hundred miles and eighteen tax brackets north is about as far as Gus could get away from you," Lassiter said. "So, what, you kept his car as a souvenir?"

"He doesn't need it in San Francisco," Shawn said. "So I offered to look after it when he's out of town."

"Thoughtful of you," Lassiter said. "If I ran the plate, I bet I'd find this piece of junk is owned by Gus' old company. And since Gus doesn't work for them anymore, and in fact has started working for their competitor, I wouldn't be surprised at all to find that they requested its return weeks ago. By now it might even have been reported stolen."

"Carlton, stop," O'Hara said.

"It's not stolen," Shawn said. "Gus asked me to turn it in. And I'm going to. But I have to make sure to clean all of our stuff out of the glove compartment first, and I haven't had a chance to do that, what with all the official police business you can't seem to wrap up without help from me."

"The Santa Barbara Police Department is perfectly capable of closing its cases without you, Spencer," Lassiter said.

"Really?" Shawn said. "You should try it someday."

The two men stood toe-to-toe, and if the tension radiating off them got any hotter the dried grass under their feet would soon be bursting into flame. O'Hara took Lassiter's arm and pulled him back a step.

"He's helped us plenty," O'Hara said. "And if Tanner is in trouble, then it doesn't really matter whose case it is, does it?"

Lassiter thought that over. "And if this turns out to be as big a waste of time as I think?" he said finally. "What do we do if Macklin Tanner hasn't been kidnapped?"

"We'll have to deal with that issue if it comes about," O'Hara said. "Maybe if we just keep negative thoughts in our heads, everything will work out for the worst and we'll be okay."

Lassiter muttered something under his breath, but he gave her a shallow nod. "What is this brilliant tip we're chasing?"

"We're going to see a man about a horse," Shawn said. "No, wait. That's not right. We're going to see a man about a horseshoe. Or are we going to see a horseshoe about a man?"

"I'm so glad we took the afternoon off to have this experience," Lassiter said. "How I've missed this sparkling repartee."

"There's reason to believe that there's a connection between Macklin's disappearance and a blacksmith's shop in the Santa Barbara area," O'Hara said.

"What reason?" Lassiter said.

"If I told you we learned it from an exploding librarian, would that convince you?" Shawn said.

Lassiter couldn't bring himself to waste the energy to make his tongue form the word "no." He let his eyebrows do the work instead.

"Then I won't tell you that," Shawn said. "I won't even mention that an entire neighborhood perished so that we could get this information. Let's just say it's an anonymous tip and leave it at that."

"Happy to," Lassiter said. "Detective O'Hara, you can come back with me now or get a ride in a stolen car from this felon. At this point it's all the same to me."

He snagged his car keys out of his partner's hand and headed back to the sedan.

"There are at least a dozen blacksmiths in the Santa Barbara area," O'Hara said. "Not to mention all the various other businesses that work with wrought iron."

"I'm glad you clarified that," Lassiter said. "Now, let me see if I have this straight: There's absolutely no reason to think that any blacksmith shop has anything to do with Tanner's disappearance, aside from some idiotic fantasy of young Kreskin here. But even if I were to accept his word on the subject and go chasing off on this fool's errand, this is just one of potentially hundreds of locations where I might want to look. Does that about cover it?"

"You left one detail out, Carlton," O'Hara said. "Of all those hundreds of potential locations, there's only one that belongs to a subsidiary of VirtuActive Software, and that's Winter Brothers Ironworks, which is right up ahead."

"So the company's hedging their bets in case kids finally wise up, get sick of computer games, and go back to wholesome outdoor entertainment like horseback riding," Lassiter said.

"The ownership is hidden in a series of nested holding companies," O'Hara said. "Someone went to a lot of trouble to keep anyone from finding out about this place."

"But you got the last laugh on them," Shawn said. "They put all that time and energy into hiding the fact that they owned this place, and what did they get? A police detective who couldn't be bothered to walk five hundred yards to find them, let alone dig through layers of corporate shells. Bet they'd feel pretty silly if they knew. Which of course they never will, since you're too lazy to walk the five hundred yards to let them know."

Lassiter thought he detected something strange in Shawn's voice, a note verging on hysteria. Of course it was possible he was just choking on the dust that filled the air, but it sounded like Shawn was, for the first time since they'd met, losing that patina of hip detachment he undoubtedly thought of as his cool or his mojo. That was the first interesting thing that had happened since Lassiter let O'Hara talk him into this field trip, and he was about to follow it up with a piercing jab to Shawn's protective shell, when O'Hara stepped between them again.

"The blacksmith's shop is just around the next curve," O'Hara said. "We're going to knock on the door and ask a couple of questions. Then we can all head back."

Lassiter stopped with his hand on the door handle. "And if there's no sign of Tanner?"

He waited for either O'Hara or Spencer to say something. For a long moment, there was silence.

"Then I'll never ask for SBPD help on this case again," Shawn said finally.

"And?" Lassiter drew the syllable out longer than he ever had before, hoping that his partner might pick up on the subtle signal.

Apparently she did, further proof of what a good detective she could be when she wasn't obsessed with trivia. "I will sign off on Mandy Jansen's death as a suicide," O'Hara said.

Lassiter pulled open the sedan door, then peeled his fingers from the handle where his flesh had begun to sizzle on the blazing metal.

"Let's go, then," Lassiter said. "Looks like this trip is going to turn out to be worth my time after all."

# Chapter Twenty-three

The Hittites of Anatolia developed a process for smelting iron ore fifteen hundred years before the birth of Christ. Shortly after the invention, a couple of the more enterprising members of that long-forgotten nation took their skills with metal and set up a blacksmith business in the hills outside Santa Barbara.

At least that seemed to be the case if you judged by the exterior of the decaying barn that stood in the middle of a weed-choked lot at the end of the road. The yellow paint had faded to the same dusty brown as the dying vegetation all around it and was peeling off the siding. The once-shining tin roof was encased in dust, and birds flew out through holes in the metal. Where once the word "blacksmith" had been painted in gigantic black letters, now there was only the faint outline of barely recognizable shapes.

As Shawn led the two detectives down toward the barn, he studied the ground for signs that anyone had been there recently. It was impossible to tell. The dirt road had been sunbaked until it was harder than concrete. The grass and weeds had been dead so long that the trampled stalks could have been crushed ten minutes ago or last year.

And yet Shawn was positive that Macklin Tanner had

been in this barn. Or that his kidnappers had used it as their hideout. Or that it was at least in some tangential way related to the kidnapping.

That was what he was telling himself, anyway. That he was positive.

The trouble was, he wasn't. Not about this. Not about anything.

This was not the way it was supposed to be. Shawn was always positive. His subconscious would toss out an idea and the rest of his mind would grab it and chew it into shreds like a dog with a plush toy. He didn't always know why he knew something, but he never had any doubt that he did.

But that was not the way it had been working lately. The ideas his subconscious threw to him were barely more than half-formed notions, and his brain could hardly get in a nibble before its teeth started to hurt and he had to stop.

This had started when Gus left Psych to take the executive position with Benson Pharmaceuticals. But that couldn't be the reason. Shawn didn't need Gus. He never had. He liked having his old friend with him on cases, of course. He liked the camaraderie, the company. And there was nothing better than having a buddy around when you were stuck on an all-night stakeout, if only to stay in the car when you ran out to look for a bathroom.

But in terms of solving the cases, Shawn had never needed Gus. Shawn was the one with the eye and the mind and the skill. Gus was along for the ride. It was true that he had come in handy from time to time, but his greatest use was as Shawn's sounding board. Shawn hardly needed a full-fledged partner for that. And, in fact, shortly after Gus left Shawn had replaced him with an actual board. He peeled off a piece of plywood that had been covering one of the office's rear windows since it had been broken in a game of extreme handball, drew a rough approximation of Gus' face on it, and propped it up on a shelf. Then he started to run his theories by the board.

Unfortunately that didn't work nearly as well as he'd hoped, and after an hour Plywood Gus was back covering the broken pane. Apparently Shawn needed his sounding board to ask obvious questions before he could come up with his brilliant answers. If only he'd thought to record the real Gus over his last few days in the office. Since his questions were always the same variations on "What the hell are you talking about?" Shawn could simply have pushed play after every inquiry.

Since he hadn't taken that precaution Shawn decided to move away from inanimate objects and try to replace Gus with a real human being.

He'd thought briefly about bringing a professional detective into the agency. But Shawn had a unique way of working that tended to annoy people with actual law enforcement experience, and while that was one of his favorite parts of the job, he didn't feel like bringing that kind of conflict into the agency. Besides, private detectives generally wanted to be paid in money for their labors, and for the position he was looking to fill Shawn was planning on a salary measured in Yoo-hoo and Skittles.

There was only one man who could fit all of Shawn's needs. Hank Stenberg. Hank didn't know a lot about law enforcement, but Shawn was pretty sure that he'd seen enough TV cop shows to know when Shawn was deviating from standard fictional police operating procedure and would object loudly. And his voice was even higher than Gus', so there would be an extra layer of outrage in the complaint.

But Hank turned out to be no more useful than Plywood Gus had been. Sure, he asked plenty of questions in that high, piercing voice, but they were mostly along the lines of "Where's the Butterfinger you promised me?" and

"Why haven't you fixed that window?" Not exactly the kind of intellectual challenge that would inspire Shawn to the deductive leaps he needed to make.

He might have tried to work things out with Hank, until Shawn's father, Henry, came to ask him for help. It seemed that one of his neighbors was growing frantic because her son hadn't come home from middle school that day and it was nearly dark. Henry was planning to search the area between the school and the boy's home, and wanted to draft Shawn to join the posse.

At least he had before he saw the object of his search sitting behind Shawn's desk, watching old Hong Kong kung fu movies on the agency computer. Without a word Henry scooped Hank up in one arm and marched him to his truck, and Shawn was once more without a partner.

Which was, he decided, the way it should be. Shawn wasn't the type who needed people. He was a lone wolf. A rebel, a rogue, a one-man army who didn't play by anyone's rules. He was every tagline from every action movie made in the 1980s, except the one about how in space no one could hear him scream, because he wasn't planning any interplanetary excursions, and "Part man, part machine, all cop," because that would require attending the police academy.

But try as he might, he couldn't make himself feel like a one-man army. His eyes worked the same way they always had and the neurons of his mind still flowed along the same old pathways, but whatever had made Shawn into the great natural detective he had been only weeks before seemed to have disappeared. He could still spot tiny details and his mind could still weave them together into patterns, but he had lost the crucial piece of himself that told him which pattern was the right one. He had lost his confidence, and with that had gone his ability.

That was what he told himself, anyway. Because that was better than the other thought that was constantly nibbling away at the back of his mind—that he had it backward. That he had only lost his self-confidence because he knew his ability was gone for good.

The Poe book that had led them here was a perfect example. It was true that the clue in the Dewey decimal number was the kind of thing that Gus would usually have been helpful with, because he was the kind of person who cared about boring things like library classification systems. But Shawn should have spotted the discrepancy. It wasn't that hard. He must have stared at the spine a thousand times and it never even crossed his mind to check its classification number.

If it hadn't been for Jules, they might still be back in the game, trying to figure it out. And Shawn was beginning to think that would not have been a completely positive thing. Although it contradicted everything he'd ever believed, he was coming to the conclusion that you could, indeed, spend too much time with a computer game. It wasn't just that he was dreaming about Darksyde City—his dreams had always been surrealistic landscapes incorporating whichever pop culture tropes he'd been ingesting that day. It was the way his instincts were beginning to change. When he'd gone out for lunch yesterday some clown in a battered Mustang had cut into the drive-through line in front of him and Shawn had had to stop his right foot from slamming down on the accelerator to take out the jerk in a massive fireball. He accepted the possibility that this was simply a measure of the frustration he'd been feeling about being unable to crack the Tanner case, but he thought he'd better cut down on his *Criminal Genius* sessions before he found himself attempting to blow up the Paseo Nuevo Shopping Center in an attempt to solve it.

Once Jules had given him the reference to blacksmithing it was an easy Google search to find out just how many metalworkers there were in the Santa Barbara area. The next part of the investigation took a little longer, but there was no inspiration involved, just a few long hours slogging through incorporation records and other public files to find the link between Macklin Tanner's company and Winter Brothers Ironworks.

When he'd made the discovery, he waited for the old feelings of triumph to flow through him. He sat in front of his computer for a full five minutes, expecting to find himself leaping out of his chair and high-fiving the light fixture.

But that sense of satisfaction never came, and neither did the old, familiar certainty. What he'd found seemed to be a plausible connection and a probable lead, but he didn't *know* it the way he always had before.

At least he still remembered what it was supposed to sound like, so when he called O'Hara he was able to use the proper mixture of elation and self-worship. He hadn't thought she'd heard anything off in his voice, and she did agree to meet him up here this afternoon.

But now that they were all standing outside the barn that once housed Winter Brothers, Shawn was feeling doubt creeping through him. What if he had been wrong? What if Macklin Tanner had never been here?

"Great lead you found, Spencer," Lassiter said as he came up to Shawn. "Doubt you found your missing person, but at least we'll all get skin cancer from standing around in the sun like this."

O'Hara stepped up to Shawn, a look of concern on her face. "It doesn't look like anyone has been here in years," she said.

It didn't. Shawn knew it. He'd gotten this one wrong. The right thing to do would be to turn around and go home, lie on the couch, and watch all five *Planet of the Apes* movies back-to-back. Not that he deserved that kind of reward. It would be much more fitting to make himself sit through the Tim Burton remake five times over, although if he wanted to punish himself that severely he might as well just hang himself in Mandy Jansen's basement.

But just because Shawn felt defeated, he didn't need to show it. He gave Jules his best cocky grin. "Looks can be deceiving," Shawn said. "I mean, Lassie here looks like Mr. Bean. But that doesn't mean he's a bumbling, incompetent boob with a turkey on his head."

"Gee, thanks," Lassiter said.

"Unless I'm wrong about this barn, of course," Shawn continued, "in which case looks really aren't deceiving and no one has been here in years. Then the whole turkey-on-the-head thing is up for grabs."

"That's good, Shawn," Lassiter said. "If you're wrong and you dragged us out here for absolutely no reason, then I'm the idiot."

"Hey, you listened to me," Shawn said.

"Not anymore," Lassiter said, drawing the gun from the holster under his polyester-blend jacket.

"Don't you think you're overreacting a bit?" Shawn said.

"I'm doing my job, which is to check out a tip, no matter how little credibility its source might have," Lassiter said. Gun held pointing down at the ground, he started toward the barn. "O'Hara, you take the back."

"What about me?" Shawn said. "If you've got the front and she's got the back?"

"Personally I think you should go ahead and walk into the barn," Lassiter said. "That way if there are gunshots you're almost certain to get caught in the cross fire. But as a law enforcement officer, I'm telling you to stay here until I give the all clear."

"The what?" Shawn said.

"All clear," Lassiter said.

"That's what I was waiting for." Shawn sprinted past the detective and made it to the barn door before Lassiter could grab him.

"Shawn, stop!" O'Hara whispered urgently.

But Shawn couldn't stop. Right or wrong, this was his

call and he wouldn't let Lassiter take that away from him. The way he was feeling, he might never have another one.

Shawn pushed against the barn's sliding door, but it wouldn't budge. Glancing back he saw that Lassiter was closing in on him. In a second he'd grab Shawn and pull him aside and then whatever was in the barn would be all his. Shawn gave the door another shove and this time it slid open. He stepped through.

After the bright sun outside, the barn seemed to be pitch-black aside from the shafts of light that poured through the holes in the roof. Shawn stood in the doorway, waiting for his eyes to adjust. "Hello," he called. "Kidnappers? Victims? Insane computer-game designers? Anyone?"

There was no answer other than some faint scrabbling of rodents in the walls. And as Shawn's eyes got used to the darkness, he could see why.

There was no one here. The floor was rotting bare boards, except for a stone square in the center where an ancient forge sat. Blacksmith tools, bent and blackened by use and age, were scattered around it.

"You've really cracked this case wide-open, Spencer," Lassiter said in his ear.

Shawn felt that same sinking feeling that had assailed him outside the barn. But he was even more determined now not to let it show. "I'm glad you see it, too," he said.

"See what." It wasn't a question, more like an expression of all the contempt Lassiter had ever felt for Shawn squeezed into two syllables.

"The clues," Shawn said. "The evidence. You know, the kind of things that crime solvers use to crack their cases."

"The only thing that's going to be cracked is your skull if you try to keep me here one minute longer," Lassiter said, heading back to the door.

Shawn looked around the interior of the barn again, desperately hoping to find some tiny sign that Macklin Tanner had been there. But unless the game designer had been in the habit of excreting tiny black pellets, he didn't see anything.

That was it, then. His one lead and it was a false one. He might as well give up the detective business altogether. Not right away, of course. He could coast on his past glories for a few more cases before people started to notice he'd lost his gift, the way *Friends* had still attracted vast audiences for three years after the last time it had actually been funny. But once the police beat him to the solution on a couple of cases, word would begin to get out that Psych was a fraud and he'd be out of business. Maybe if he jacked up his rates before then he could build himself a financial cushion that would last until he chose his next career.

He was so lost in his thoughts that it took him a couple of seconds to register the shouts that were coming from the back of the barn. "Carlton! Shawn!"

Shawn ran across the barn's floor and when he reached the back wall he gave it a hard kick. Two of the planks flew off and landed on the dirt, and Shawn stepped through the hole just as Lassie was coming around the corner.

"What is it, Detective?" Lassiter said.

O'Hara didn't say anything. She just pointed to a high stack of old lumber.

"That's very good," Lassiter said, slamming his pistol back in its holster. "You've found the woodpile. If we start to get chilly, it's nice to know we'll be able to build a fire. Of course we'll probably burn down half of Santa Barbara when the first spark drifts out, but still, a good thought."

Shawn didn't listen to Lassie. He was staring at the woodpile, trying to understand what Jules was pointing at. He shifted slightly on his feet and he saw something—a glint of red sparkling in the sun.

Then he knew what it was. He pushed past Lassiter and ran to the woodpile, tearing logs off and hurling them aside. Dodging the flying wood, O'Hara came up and worked beside him until they opened a large hole in the stack.

Gleaming red metal sparkled up at them. Stacks of it, cut into shards and scraps, hacked into chunks.

"What's that?" Lassiter said as he peered down at the heap of metal.

"Right now, scrap metal," Shawn said. "But before someone took a set of blacksmith's tools to it, I'd say it was a cherry red 1964 Impala."

# Chapter Twenty-four

He was back, baby.

All that doubt, all that fear—all pointless. Shawn had followed his own instincts where they led him and he'd found the first evidence that Macklin Tanner had been kidnapped. The police quickly confirmed that the metal scraps had been the car Tanner disappeared with, and now there was a full investigation into his abduction.

Of course this hardly meant Shawn's role in the case was over. He'd discovered where Tanner had disappeared to, but who took him and why and where he might be now were still completely unknown.

Or almost completely, anyway. Thanks to Shawn's sleuthing methods, the police were fairly certain that at least one of the kidnappers worked for VirtuActive. After all, it was a clue planted in the game that had led to the barn and the discovery of the dismembered automobile. The cops were running background checks on every member of the programming team and had already started questioning everyone who'd ever worked for the company.

Shawn was content to let them take over this part of the case. That was the kind of thing the SBPD was good at—the hard, boring grunt work. His job was the brilliant flashes of insight that broke cases wide-open.

This time, though, he couldn't take all the credit for himself. It was true he had figured out that the librarian in the game was the key to figuring out Tanner's location, and that he had persisted in trying ways to worm it out of her no matter how many fictional people had to die along the way.

But once he'd gotten the book he hadn't known how to interpret the clue. He had no doubt that if he'd had a little more time it would have come to him. After all, the Dismal Dewdrop system number, or whatever it was called, was a pretty obvious sign, and once he had exhausted all the less likely possibilities he would have had to investigate the obvious ones. Still, he'd had help on this part and it had shortened the investigation substantially.

That help hadn't come free, of course, and that was why he was standing next to Juliet O'Hara in the basement apartment of a fabulous Spanish house in one of the nicest parts of town. She'd agreed to help him with the Macklin Tanner case if he'd take a look at her cheerleader suicide, and now he was paying off his debt.

He was trying to, anyway. Even with his mojo back he was having trouble trying to understand what it was about the case that was troubling her. And she was having just as much trouble explaining it.

"So, in terms of evidence you've got what exactly?" Shawn said as he looked around the immaculately clean room. There was a bed in one corner and a small kitchenette directly opposite it. Just in front of the window overlooking the garden sat two armchairs and a small coffee table. The floor was covered in a cheerful blue carpet. If it hadn't been for the exposed water pipes running along the ceiling there would have been nothing to say that this was a basement conversion.

"Nothing that indicates anything other than suicide," O'Hara said morosely.

"That's a good start," Shawn said.

"It is?" O'Hara looked at him with a little glimmer of hope.

"Sure," Shawn said. "You know you're dealing with a master criminal if he didn't leave any evidence behind."

"Or I'm not dealing with a criminal at all," O'Hara said. "That's the standard interpretation of complete lack of evidence."

"The standard interpretation!" Shawn scoffed. "The standard interpretation of the sun setting into the ocean every night was that it was moving around the earth. The standard interpretation of a yellow light is that you're supposed to prepare to stop. There's always a standard interpretation and it's always wrong. Except for why people actually watch *Two and a Half Men*. No one's been able to explain that. But the rule stands."

O'Hara let out a heavy sigh. "It would be nice to think that's true," she said. "But the standard interpretation is almost always the right one, because it's a product of many minds working from the same set of facts and coming up with identical answers. And in this case we're not going to be able to change any of those minds if all we have to go on is the complete lack of evidence."

"Well, in that case, the solution is simple," Shawn said. "We have to find some evidence."

If he'd actually unplugged a valve in her neck and let out all the air filling her body, O'Hara couldn't have looked more deflated. "That's kind of why I asked you to meet me here."

"And you were right to do it," Shawn said. "Evidence of murder, coming up."

Shawn looked around the room and he *saw* . . . nothing. No wayward pill, dropped out of the handful that had been ground up and poured into Mandy's evening cocoa. No carpet fibers torn up as Mandy's high-heeled feet were dragged across the floor so that her unconscious body could be strung up from the beam. No button that would at first seem to be from Mandy's blouse but on closer examination would reveal itself to be made out of a unique type of plastic that was only used by one designer of men's shirts, which were sold to only one store in California and which would turn out to have had only one customer in the last ten years.

Shawn felt a new stab of panic. Before, when he'd thought he was losing his mojo, he knew it was mostly about confidence. But this was completely different and entirely worse. Before the confidence could come into action he needed the *eye*. It was great to be able to take tiny details that no one had noticed and then spin them into a web of meaning, and then invent some psychic vision to explain what he'd figured out. But that ability wouldn't do him much good if he'd lost the ability to spot those details in the first place.

He took a deep breath. He was getting way ahead of himself. It was quite possible that the only reason he wasn't seeing any details out of place was that there were none. Everyone else who'd looked at this case had concluded that Mandy Jansen had killed herself. Maybe that was what happened, in which case there would have been no reason for anyone to drop pills or buttons or carpet fibers.

But Jules was sure Mandy had been murdered, sure in a way that transcended evidence and came straight from her instincts as a detective. Shawn had known her long enough to know that she was good at what she did, and if she was feeling this strongly she was probably right.

Which meant that Mandy had been murdered. And unless the killer was the most brilliant criminal in history he had left evidence behind. Evidence that Shawn wasn't able to see.

Shawn looked again, harder this time, straining the muscles in his eyes as if he thought they'd pop out of their sockets and roll across the carpet, looking for clues. But he still saw nothing.

"What is it?" O'Hara said. "What do you see?"

For one brief moment Shawn contemplated telling her the truth. Or at least his own version of the truth, something about how the spirits had been chased away by the aura of sadness lingering in the apartment. That might actually work, he realized. He could say that the spirits wouldn't return until the place got a lot more cheerful, so they should tune the flat panel to the *Full House* marathon on TV Land, and then come back in a day when they'd been drawn in by the warm family humor.

But everyone had been blowing O'Hara off on this investigation. She'd been told by her fellow cops, by Mandy's friends, and probably by complete strangers that this was an obvious suicide and she should just close the case and move on. If he gave her some nonsense about spirits not wanting to cooperate, she'd assume that he was doing the same thing. He didn't want to let her down that way, especially after the help she'd given him with Macklin Tanner.

He was going to have to admit the truth. This was all Gus' fault. Shawn had never had any problems like this when he was still around. Even though Shawn couldn't remember anything he'd ever actually done, apparently his presence worked on Shawn's subconscious like a security blanket.

But Shawn wasn't five years old anymore. He didn't need a security blanket. He didn't need any kind of blanket. Well, there was that nice wool one he liked to snuggle in when the weather turned cold, but he was willing to throw that on the dustbin of history if it would help bring his mojo back for good.

"There's nothing, right?" O'Hara said softly. "You're not getting any emanations or seeing any spirit trails or doing whatever it is you do instead of what I do."

She was giving him a chance to get out of this easy, he realized. Maybe she was looking for a way to extricate herself from the case, too. All he had to do was say there was nothing here and it would be over. She'd close the file on Mandy Jansen and everyone could get along with their lives, with the obvious exception of Mandy herself.

But if he did that here, what would happen on his next case? It was exceptionally rare that a client hired a detective only to tell him that it was okay if he wasn't able to solve the case. He had to fight his way through this.

And if there was one thing he'd learned from watching TV, it was that he could do it. Had there ever been a single private detective who didn't get blinded at some point in his career? And whether it was Spenser or Dan Tana or Mannix or Magnum or even Monk, none of them ever gave up. Instead when the acid was thrown in their face or the gunshot creased their brows or they had been exposed to superbright light intended to kill the brain-parasite–Jell-O thing stuck to their backs, they wrapped a bandage around their eyes and set out to solve the crime they'd been investigating.

So maybe Shawn was blind now. He'd find a way to carry on. If Robert Urich could do it, so could he.

"Maybe this was a bad idea," O'Hara said. "Mandy's death was probably a suicide, just like everyone thinks, and I'm wasting your time dragging you here."

"I owe you," Shawn said. "If it hadn't been for you, I'd still be in Darksyde City."

"You don't owe me anything," O'Hara said. "You owe Gus."

Shawn pulled his eyes away from their search of the floor and gave her a sharp stare. "Because he's done so much to help solve this case?" he said.

"Not this one," O'Hara said. "Macklin Tanner."

"Believe me, he was even less use on that case than here," Shawn said. "Every time I brought him into Darksyde City he spent the whole time whining about how he didn't want to kill anymore. It was like having the Dalai Lama as a sidekick, except that Gus can't shoot laser beams out of his eyes."

"He was the one who came up with the explanation of the Dewey decimal classification," O'Hara said. "When neither of us could figure out what the book clue was, I flew up to San Francisco to talk to him about it. He told me about the blacksmiths."

"Mighty helpful of him," Shawn said. "Although I guess it felt pretty good to do some real work instead of pushing papers across a desk."

"He seemed pretty excited about what he was doing at Benson," O'Hara said. "Said he felt he was really going to be able to help a lot of people there."

"Oh," Shawn said. "Well, it was nice of him to put off saving the world for a few minutes. I hope you gave him a big thanks."

"I wanted at least to take him to lunch, but he didn't have time," O'Hara said. "He said he was absolutely swamped and couldn't leave his desk."

"I guess that's what it's like when you're the bottom guy on the old totem pole," Shawn said.

"He's not," O'Hara said. "He's been promoted twice since he got there."

"Twice?" Shawn said. That couldn't be right. Gus was a great guy and all, but he wasn't promotion material. He was a sidekick, not a star.

"He started off as a junior vice president, then moved up to senior VP within a couple of weeks," she said. "Now he's an executive vice president, whatever that is. Part of it is all the coincidences, sure, but they must really like him to move him up so quickly."

Shawn felt a little tickle from his subconscious. He took a quick glance around the room to see if he had spotted a piece of evidence without being aware of it. But the little apartment was just as clue-free as it had been before. The dark part of his brain must have been responding to what she had said.

"Coincidences?" Shawn said as casually as he could.

"A bunch of them," O'Hara said. "It's really kind of weird. If you read it in a book you'd have trouble believing it."

"And if it wasn't in a book, but in real life?" Shawn said, trying to keep the edge out of his voice.

"Well, it actually all starts in this room," O'Hara said.

"You asked Gus for help on this case, too?"

"Yes, but not in the way you think," O'Hara said. "It turned out that Mandy Jansen used to work in sales for Benson Pharmaceuticals. She resigned a few weeks before she died. Lassiter and I drove up to San Francisco to talk to her employers, and it was Gus who took the meeting. That's how I found out he'd left Psych, by the way."

If there was reproach in that sentence, Shawn chose to ignore it. He was too interested in the rest of her story.

"So Gus knew Mandy?"

"They missed each other by a few weeks," O'Hara said. "In fact, if Mandy hadn't died, Gus might never have been offered his job. The company had wanted her for the position."

There was another jab from Shawn's subconscious. Something was definitely weird here.

"Okay, that's one coincidence," Shawn said. "Or is it just happenstance at this point?"

"Either way," O'Hara said.

"I'm still not sure why you ended up talking to Gus about Mandy Jansen," Shawn said. "If he was hired after she quit and they'd never actually met, what did he have to tell you about her?"

"Not much," O'Hara said. "Although he did give us her complete personnel file. We were sent to him because Mandy reported to the senior vice president of marketing, and that was the job Gus had just been promoted into."

"What happened to the former senior vice president of marketing?" Shawn said. "They erased his memory when they gave him a different job?"

"We were told that if we wanted to pick his brain, we'd have to scrape it off the tree first," she said. "He'd gone skiing the weekend before we got there and died in a freak accident."

Shawn's subconscious was screaming at him, and now there was no doubt what it was trying to say. "That's not the last coincidence, is it?"

"Once Gus got the promotion to senior VP, he was reporting to a guy named Jim Macoby, who was second in command of marketing for the entire world," she said.

"Don't tell me," Shawn said. "His plane crashed."

"You think that's funny, but you're closer than you know. There was a problem with the electrical system in the office where they work. He went to get a cup of coffee from the machine and was electrocuted."

Shawn felt a chill run through his body. "Is that the last of them?" he said carefully. "The last of your coincidences?"

"As far as I know," O'Hara said. "Isn't that enough?"

"It's more than enough," Shawn said. "More than enough to tell me none of these deaths was coincidence."

"Then what?" O'Hara said.

"They were murders."

# Chapter Twenty-five

"We are doing well, but we can do even better by doing good."

That sounded right. Gus had been practicing his closing line for half an hour now, and he thought he had finally perfected the intonation. As long as he made sure to add that note of surprise to the last phrase, as if he had just stumbled across the formulation in the middle of speaking it, all taint of self-righteousness disappeared.

Gus was ready. He'd been preparing for this staff meeting for a week, although in a way his entire tenure at Benson Pharmaceuticals had been a warm-up for what he was about to do. "We are doing well, but we can do even better by doing good," he said again, this time with a perfect little fillip of surprise when he hit that last phrase.

Gus glanced at his watch. Fifteen minutes until the meeting started. Just enough time to practice his presentation one last time. He straightened his tie, shrugged his shoulders like a fighter entering the ring, and stood to address his imaginary audience. And he froze.

He knew his closing; there was no doubt about that. But that was all he knew. The beginning and the middle were completely gone.

Gus snatched the index cards off his desk and riffled through them quickly. He recognized his handwriting, but he couldn't read any of it. What were these words scribbled down? What was it he was supposed to say? His mind was blank.

There was a gentle knocking, and the door cracked open. Jerry Fellows' beaming head appeared in the doorway. "All ready?"

Gus dropped the index cards and let them scatter all over his desk. "Ready for my career to end."

Jerry pushed the door open and wheeled his steel mail cart into the office. "Now you're just being silly, if you don't mind my saying so. You're going to be great."

"I've been here for weeks," Gus said. "Before that I was a half-time salesman, and not a very good one at that."

"I find that hard to believe," Jerry said. "I can see the fire in your eyes. I bet you had that in your last job."

"One of them," Gus said. "But I don't think it was for the sales route."

"Then maybe you were simply waiting for this opportunity to come along," Jerry said.

"Yeah, the opportunity to humiliate myself completely," Gus said. "Look at the new guy. He's barely got his business cards, and he's already telling us how to restructure the entire company. Who do I think I am?"

Jerry left his cart behind and walked up to Gus. "I can't answer that, but I can tell you who I think you are," he said. "I think you're the kind of man who sees an opportunity to make the world a better place and won't rest until he seizes it. I think you're the kind of man who knows he could hide behind his desk and make a lot of money for doing not much of anything but chooses to risk his job for the chance of helping the company and its customers. I think you're the kind of man this company needs and that Bobby cherishes."

Gus felt some of his panic start to ease away. "Really?"

Jerry gave him one of his leprechaun grins. "But what do I know about anything?" he said. "I've been pushing a mail cart for thirty years, so pretty obviously I don't have a clue about how business works."

Gus looked at his watch again. He still had a few minutes before the meeting. He scooped his index cards into a pile and flipped through them to make sure they were in order. "And why is that, Jerry?" he said. "I've seen how D-Bob promotes people around here, and I'm getting an idea of the kind of person he likes. Seems to me if you'd wanted to be an executive you could be running the place by now."

"That would be one of those questions that answer themselves," Jerry said.

"You mean the part about if you wanted to, right?" Gus said.

"When I go home at the end of the day I leave my mail cart right here," Jerry said. "It never wakes me up with a phone call in the middle of the night, it never demands I come in on a weekend, and it doesn't add ten years to my age because of stress. I went through my world-changing phase when I was young, and I managed to get over it. Now I've got a nice little apartment, and thanks to Bobby's generosity I won't have to spend my golden years standing outside BART stations with a Styrofoam cup, asking for spare change. So why would I want any other job in the world?"

"That's a good question," Gus said. "Maybe I should get a mail cart."

"Only one per company," Jerry said. "Besides, I know people, and I can see you wouldn't be happy in any job where you weren't making a serious impact on the world. I don't think I've seen anyone with your drive since Carlton Eastlake had this job."

"I don't think I've met him," Gus said. "Is he running one of our foreign branches now?"

"Not unless we've got one in heaven," Jerry said, doffing his cap and touching it to his chest.

"He died?" Gus said.

"Almost a year ago now," Jerry said, replacing his cap over his mop of red hair.

"What happened to him?"

"It wasn't that he ate too many oysters, just that one of those he ate turned out to be the wrong one," Jerry said.

"Food poisoning?" Gus said.

"One of the few things this company doesn't make a pill for," Jerry says. "It's always felt like some kind of tragic irony there. But his loss to the company wasn't ironic at all, especially since he was the only one pushing on the very same issue as you."

"He was interested in orphan drugs?" Gus said.

"It was a passion for him, just as it has been for you," Jerry said. "I really thought he would be the one to convince Bobby that was the direction the company should be moving in. And he might have, if it hadn't been for that mollusk. And so does history move on."

"I didn't realize that other executives had tried to broach this subject," Gus said.

"It doesn't come up a lot," Jerry said. "It's easy to explain how you're going to alleviate suffering by developing drugs for diseases, even if they only affect a tiny percentage of the world's population. It's a lot harder to figure out how to make money doing it. But I really think you've come up with a novel and exciting approach."

"I appreciate that," Gus says. "I hope the executive committee agrees with you."

"There's only one person on that committee who really counts," Jerry says. "If you can convince Bobby, the rest of those sycophants and parasites will fall in line."

"That's what I'm hoping for," Gus said, picking up his note cards and sliding them into the breast pocket of his suit coat. "Wish me luck."

"One second, if you don't mind," Jerry said. He reached across the desk and straightened Gus' tie, then stepped back. "Now you're perfect. I think you've got a better shot at making this work than Jim Macoby ever did."

Gus was halfway across the office before the last of Jerry's words struck him. "Jim Macoby?" he said. "Jim Macoby was planning a presentation on orphan drugs?"

"That he was," Jerry said. "Until that sad accident with the coffeemaker."

Gus took a long look at Jerry to see if the mailman was sending him any kind of coded message. He'd just told Gus that the last two executives who attempted to do what Gus was about to try died in freak accidents. Was there some kind of warning there?

"You're going to be great in there," Jerry said without a trace of subtext or hint of caution. "I look forward to hearing all about it."

Gus took one last look at Jerry, then headed out of his office.

# Chapter Twenty-six

"Turn off the television and do your homework." That was what Gus' father used to say to him whenever he came home from school, went to his room, and flipped on the little black-and-white TV that sat on his desk. "Turn off the television and go outside and play," he'd say on the weekends when Gus chose to indulge in his favorite activity. "Homework makes you smart. Sports make you strong. TV just rots your brain."

Even at the tender age of ten Gus knew that was wrong. TV didn't rot his brain; it filled him with knowledge. What was he going to learn from school? How to add stacks of numbers, how to spell the names of state capitals. What could he learn from watching television? Everything.

Especially if he was lucky enough to come across one of those "very special episodes" that existed to instruct and educate its viewers. Did his father know how the grand jury system could be used to intimidate, harass, and ruin an average citizen who came up against the district attorney's office? Gus did, because he'd seen it happen to Jim Rockford. Did his father know that sexual assault against innocent young girls was wrong? Gus did, because he'd shared Natalie's terror on *The Facts of Life*. Did his father understand how much harm alcoholism could do to a family? Elyse Keaton's adorable younger brother taught Gus all about that, too.

Gus had tried to explain this to his father, but it never did any good, and every time he tried he ended up losing TV privileges for a couple of days. Finally he gave up.

Now Gus was standing in front of the executive committee of Benson Pharmaceuticals, proposing a plan to restructure a large piece of the multinational company to refocus its mission on the manufacture and distribution of drugs to aid people suffering from orphan diseases. And it was all because he'd watched TV as a kid.

Specifically it was because he had happened to flip on the set one afternoon when he was avoiding a mountain of math homework, only to find that his usual afternoon lineup of *The Brady Bunch*, *The Partridge Family*, and *What's Happening!!* reruns had been replaced by a baseball game. Desperate to find something to keep him away from the rigors of mathematics, he had flipped over to the UHF band and started twirling the dial slowly, hoping to find anything that looked remotely entertaining.

When he saw Oscar Madison testifying before a jury, he stopped. He'd only seen a handful of *The Odd Couple* episodes, but they had all made him laugh. So he settled in for a few premath chuckles. It took a couple of minutes for him to realize there was something strange about this particular episode. For one thing, it wasn't funny. Okay, that could happen to the best of sitcoms, but in this case even the studio audience wasn't amused. There wasn't a single chuckle on the laugh track. Second, people kept calling Oscar "Quincy." And he seemed to have a surprisingly large number of lab coats in his wardrobe for a sportswriter.

By the time he finally realized he must be watching whatever show Jack Klugman had starred in after *The Odd Couple*, Gus was hooked. Because while this Quincy guy might not be as lovable as Oscar, what he had to say was as compelling as anything he'd ever seen on TV.

In the show Quincy started off by investigating the tragic death of a teenage boy. But the mystery quickly petered out as the crusading M.E. found the real culprit: a rare disease. Rare but not incurable. There was a drug that could have saved him. Unfortunately there were not enough people suffering from the disease to make it profitable to manufacture the cure for it.

Even as a young boy Gus had been shocked by this revelation. He knew it was wrong and he wanted to do something to change it. And while there wasn't a whole lot he could do in his preteens, that desire never left him, and had helped move him toward his first job in the pharmaceutical industry.

Now Gus felt the spirit of Jack Klugman flowing through him as he delivered his presentation to the executive committee of Benson Pharmaceuticals. He tried to capture Quincy's mixture of compassion and outrage, his passionate devotion to the cause with the self-deprecating awareness that he was just one little guy taking on the system. While he was preparing he'd even flirted with the idea of using Quincy's signature attitude and informing the committee that if they didn't do exactly what he said thousands of people would die and it would be their fault, but at the last minute he decided that kind of confrontation wouldn't go over well with D-Bob.

Now that his presentation was almost finished, Gus glanced around the room to see how it was going over. D-Bob was smiling happily and nodding at all of Gus' key points, but Gus had been at the company long enough to know how little that meant. D-Bob liked ideas, and he liked people who were passionate about them. If Josef Mengele's grandson had appeared in the boardroom and laid out a case for kidnapping children off the street and conducting medical experiments on them, D-Bob would have smiled and nodded exactly the same way through the presentation. Then, when Mengele Junior was finished, he'd lay into the guy, tear apart every one of his points, and throw him out of the building. He'd probably end up calling the police. But during the presentation he'd be the soul of courtesy.

Gus would find out later what D-Bob thought of his idea. But he wasn't going to have to wait to learn where his colleagues would come down. They hated his plan. At least that was how they all looked. Gus knew he could be misinterpreting their hostile stares, though. It was just as likely that they hated him, too.

"We are doing well," Gus said, "but we can do even better by doing good."

Gus stopped and dropped his hands to show he was finished and ready to field questions. But the three executive vice presidents sitting across the table from him looked like they were more interested in throwing knives than queries.

Of all the angry faces staring at him, none was angrier than that of Stephen Ecclesine, who was in charge of worldwide manufacturing. His shaved scalp had turned bright red, nearly matching the hibiscus flowers in his tie, and even the diamond stud in his nose seemed to glow more brightly than usual. Gus had generally managed to avoid Ecclesine during his tenure at Benson, mostly because until he'd joined the executive committee he was never sure if the bald hipster usually dressed in a black T-shirt and jeans was a member of the team or a local musician hoping to make a few bucks volunteering for clinical trials. But now that Gus had spent a few hours sitting in meetings with Ecclesine, he had seen that the club-crawler outfit was a disguise to hide the classic company man. Ecclesine was interested in only two things in life: the success of his division and the amount of money that success would bring him.

Ecclesine had hated Gus from the first time they met. Not out of any particular animus, but a basic theory that the existence of any other human being could present an obstacle between him and the sack of gold he was searching for. Now that Gus had finished presenting a plan that would cost manufacturing millions in retooling and re-equipping the company's factories, Ecclesine was just about ready to declare war.

The woman next to Ecclesine presented a much more welcoming face. Like most of the women she hired to work in her sales force, Lena Hollis had spent her teen years on cheer squads, and along with the perpetual tan and the toned muscles she'd never lost that perfectly gleaming cheerleader's smile. But Gus knew that smile too well, having been on the receiving end of it every time he tried to ask one of his high school's cheerleaders out on a date, or even offered help with homework. It looked friendly, but the message it sent was *You are so far beneath me that it's not worth my effort to be rude.* The fact that she was flashing it at him now was telling him that she considered his plan so pathetic it wasn't even worth arguing over.

That wasn't the case with Ed Vollman, but then it never was. Vollman, who was in charge of the company's worldwide finances and operations, had never found any plan, or any subject for that matter, that was not worth an argument. The oldest person on the executive committee by at least two decades, Vollman tried to show he was as vital as any of his youthful counterparts by staying perpetually angry.

Vollman was capable of flying into a rage over a badly stapled report or a coffee with a micron too little soy milk in it. But Gus had never seen him quite as furious as he was now. The only thing holding him back from exploding into a tantrum was his awareness that D-Bob hadn't weighed in on Gus' plan yet.

That was clearly what was keeping the other two at bay, as well. They were all desperate to tear into Gus' proposal, but they didn't dare make their opinions known until they knew which way the boss would come down on it. It was true that D-Bob always insisted that there was no penalty for bad ideas at Benson Pharmaceuticals, but it was equally true that it was never a good idea to get too far out of synch with the guy who ran the company.

And so they waited. Gus turned to the end of the table to see if D-Bob was ready to offer an opinion. The broad smile on his face suggested he was.

"That is a profound and moving idea, Gus," D-Bob said, his ponytail jiggling in agreement. "Everyone in this business is aware of the problems with orphan diseases, of course, and I've heard elements of your plan in other presentations. Specifically the notion of encouraging foreign governments to establish crown corporations that we would then run on management contracts is something we have explored in the past and still find potentially interesting. But you've managed to put together a lot of diverse ideas in a way that they become complementary pieces of a grander whole, and that is new. Of course what is really fresh and different about your proposal is the idea that we could afford to do all this if we were willing to greatly reduce the profits we make as a company. I'm sure that Ed will have some strong opinions on that score."

Vollman forced his deep scowl into some semblance of a smile. "I'd like to take a longer look at the numbers before I commit myself," he said, although Gus was pretty sure that what he really wanted to do was rip out Gus' throat with his teeth.

"Of course, of course," D-Bob said with a laugh. "There's plenty in here to absorb, and we should all take a few days and give it the attention it deserves."

"Yes," Ecclesine muttered. "Every bit of attention it deserves."

"In most companies this wouldn't be an option," D-Bob said. "But we are blessed with the freedom of not having shareholders to whom we have to answer. We can do whatever we feel is right for the company, even if it does hurt our short-term profitability. Or even our long-term survival. So as you study Gus' proposal before our next executive committee meeting, I want you to clear your minds of preconceptions and prejudices. Let's approach this with open minds and open hearts."

Gus had a pretty good idea whose heart the other three vice presidents would like to open, but he didn't care if they hated him. D-Bob was giving his idea serious consideration, and that was all that mattered.

"In that spirit, we'll table Gus' proposal until our next meeting and move on to our next bit of business," D-Bob said. "As we are all aware, our company has suffered a series of tragic losses in the past few weeks. Treasured members of our family have perished, leaving holes in all our hearts."

Gus doubted there was enough heart in the three people sitting across from him to house even one hole, but they all did a good job of looking suitably grief-stricken.

"What I finally realized was that we are far too lax about safety and security," D-Bob said. "I think we can all agree that something needs to be done."

Gus was pretty sure that the only thing the other three executives could agree on was the notion that it was a bad idea to publicly oppose the boss' new initiative, no matter how stupid it sounded to them. They all nodded with feigned enthusiasm.

"But doing just anything without knowing what or why is even worse than doing nothing," D-Bob said once it was clear no one would be arguing with his previous point.

"Absolutely, D-Bob," Lena Hollis said. "You've hit on something that's real and important. I think you've also come up with a solution. We need a committee to study the issue from all sides, bring the heads of all the departments together and really get to the root of the issue. I don't think it should be a quick process, but an in-depth exploration of all the aspects of security, possibly starting with an investigation into the very nature of safety itself."

She delivered the suggestion with the conviction her former self would have used to urge a crowd to cheer their team on to victory. Somehow, Gus had a feeling she might not be completely sincere about the subject, and that suspicion was confirmed when Vollman seized on the idea, as well.

"That is a brilliant idea," Vollman said. "One that is worthy of this company and the ideals we stand for. This committee could change the way every corporation in the country addresses issues of safety and security. It's hard to imagine how we could be prouder of the company we work for, but this could actually do that."

"I agree entirely," Ecclesine said. "And I think that this committee needs to be led by a true visionary, someone who has the ability to think outside the boxes we've all built for ourselves. Fortunately we now have one such creative soul among our number. I nominate Burton Guster to lead the new safety and security committee."

Before Gus could open his mouth to object, Hollis and Vollman had seconded. Now that it was too late, he understood what Lena Hollis had been doing. The only thing D-Bob liked better than an idea was a newer idea, and this overhaul of the company's safety and security agenda would completely push the orphan drugs out of his mind. And even if it didn't, Gus would be expected to gather every department head in every office across the world for daily teleconferences until he could say he'd gotten input from all of them. Then he'd have to synthesize everything he learned into a report at the same time he needed to overhaul his orphan drugs project. The three executives knew that the first negative word they said about Gus' original plan would have been enough to put D-Bob firmly on its side; now they had found a way to kill it with kindness, love, and encouragement.

The smile splitting D-Bob's face certainly suggested they had succeeded. "That's the spirit!" he said. "You know, in other companies there would have been a struggle between the top executives over who could seize this opportunity to increase their own portfolio. But you guys are so great, you all chose the man you believed was best suited for the job without a thought for yourselves. Let's all take a moment to pat ourselves on the back."

In any other company this might have been meant figuratively. Not at Benson, as Gus had learned over the previous weeks. Each of the executives reached over their shoulders to pat their own backs. Another one of D-Bob's morale boosters.

"Gus, I want to thank you for jumping on this with both feet," D-Bob said. "I know it's going to mean some extra work, but I have no doubt you'll find it worth your time. And, of course, I'm here to help you at any time of the day or night."

Gus knew that was true. D-Bob was famous for the e-mailed memos that went out around the clock. He also knew that if he took his boss up on the offer, Gus, too, would never sleep again.

"Thanks, D-Bob," Gus said. "I need a little time to wrap my head around the totality of the issue. Then we'll talk."

"I've got two things that will make that first step a little easier," D-Bob said. "The first is a guideline: Keep in mind at all times that the word 'security' comes from the Latin roots *se*, which means 'without,' and *cura*, meaning 'care.' That's how we want our employees to be able to live. Without care."

"Good thinking," Gus said automatically. "That makes my job a lot clearer."

"And this should help even more," D-Bob said. "This is such a massive undertaking, it wouldn't be fair to ask you to do it all by yourself."

Gus noticed worried glances on the faces across from

them, as the other executives began to feel like they had hoisted themselves on their own petards. In another situation this might have made Gus feel better about his new position, but the only thing he wanted less than to rethink security for a multinational corporation was to do it alongside any of these three.

"I wouldn't be alone, D-Bob," Gus said. "I'll have the whole company behind me."

"Yes, you will," D-Bob. "But sometimes even that isn't enough. Which is why I've hired an outside consultant to help define our security future. And not just an ordinary security expert, but one whose talents and skills spring from a higher place."

"He's a Fed?" Hollis said.

"He's a psychic," D-Bob said, walking over to the conference room door.

Gus felt his stomach churn. He'd spent too many years working with a fake psychic to have patience for any fraud who called himself clairvoyant. *This new job can't get any worse,* he thought.

Which, of course, meant that it could.

D-Bob threw open the door and invited in his consultant. "I'd like you all to meet Shawn Spencer."

# Chapter Twenty-seven

Gus waited until his office door was closed before he let a single word out of his mouth. That was unfortunate, because during the long walk down the hallway they had all gotten jumbled together, and when he finally started to allow them egress, they refused to reassemble themselves into anything resembling orderly sentences.

"What are you how did what do you can't you even ruin own business leave what are alone," he sputtered, trying unsuccessfully to arrange the individual words into some kind of meaningful pattern.

Shawn plopped down on the sofa and gazed out at the view. "I couldn't have said it any better," he said. "Nice view, by the way."

The smugness in Shawn's voice did what Gus' brain could not—set the words in Gus' mouth marching out in the proper order. "What are you doing here?"

"Same thing you are," Shawn said.

"You're not fooling anyone but yourself," Gus said. "You're here to destroy my new career."

"Like I said, I'm doing the same thing you are," Shawn said. "You really think it's a good career move to drive your company into bankruptcy before you've been on the job for a full year? Most corporate executives wait at least until they've got the key to the executive washroom before they start tanking the business. Although maybe that kind of thinking is out-of-date these days."

"There is no executive washroom here," Gus said. "D-Bob believes that all our employees are equal, and he doesn't give the execs any better perks than the most junior secretaries."

"That's good to hear," Shawn said. "Say, do you think the girl who makes the coffee can see Berkeley from her corner office window, too?"

"If she gets promoted to executive vice president, she will," Gus said.

"Then you might as well find out what color curtains she wants, because she'll be taking possession in about three weeks," Shawn said.

"Right," Gus said. "After you destroy my career here."

Shawn jumped off the couch and tiptoed to the door, then flung it open. The doorway was empty. He let it close again and came back over to Gus.

"Okay, no one's listening," Shawn said. "We can talk freely now."

"I was talking freely," Gus said. "And you were talking gibberish, which sounded pretty free to me."

"I see what you mean," Shawn said. He put his finger to his lips, then went to the desk. He picked up the phone and turned it upside down, then put it in a drawer and closed it. He picked up the coffee cup Gus used for pen storage and upended it, sending writing instruments flying in every direction.

"What are you doing?" Gus said, picking up the pen that rolled to his feet.

"I don't see any bugs here," Shawn whispered. "But maybe we should step out on the balcony to talk."

"There is no balcony," Gus said. "Just a sixteen-story

drop to a fast and messy death. So please feel free to step outside."

Shawn moved close to Gus and spoke softly. "We'll have to chance it, then."

"Chance what?"

"That your office is bugged," Shawn said.

Gus moved away from Shawn and spoke loudly and freely. "First of all, there is no chance that my office is bugged. And if it was, I wouldn't care, because I'm not planning on saying anything in it that I wouldn't want anyone else to hear."

"That's good," Shawn whispered. "If anyone's listening, I'm sure you fooled them. Or made them deaf, anyway. Now let's get to business."

"We don't have any business, Shawn," Gus said. "When I took this job I left Psych behind. And I guess it's kind of flattering that you've gone to all this trouble to get me to come back, but it's not going to happen. I'm happy doing what I'm doing now."

"That's even better," Shawn whispered. "Now tell me to get out of your office."

"Why would I tell you to get out of my office?" Gus said. "You haven't answered a single one of my questions."

"Good point," Shawn whispered again. "You should call security and have me thrown out. That'll convince them!"

"Convince who of what?" Gus said.

"Exactly!" Shawn said, then grabbed the phone from the drawer and hit the button for the operator. "Get me security."

Gus reached to take the receiver away from him, but Shawn snatched it away. "It's ringing," Shawn said.

Shawn's pocket started playing the theme from *Magnum, P.I.*

"That's your cell," Gus said.

Shawn handed the office phone to Gus. "When they finally answer, you should give them hell. What if this was an emergency? What kind of security team do you have here?"

Gus considered slamming the phone back down in its cradle, but he had to admit, he found it a little strange that it was taking so long for security to pick up. He held the receiver to his ear and heard it ring on the other end.

Shawn yanked his cell out of his jeans pocket and pressed the answer button. "Talk to me," he said.

Shawn's voice hit Gus' ear just a second before its echo spoke through the phone. "Shawn?"

"We shouldn't talk on this line," Shawn whispered into the phone. "It might be bugged."

Shawn hung up his cell as Gus slammed the office phone down into its cradle. "I guess I forgot," Shawn said. "I'm security now."

"Shawn, this is a serious business," Gus said. "You can't just march in here with some ridiculous story and take over the entire security department."

"Apparently I can," Shawn said. "And I think the key was to make the story even more ridiculous than usual. I told Dirt Bag—"

"D-Bob," Gus said.

"Right," Shawn continued without missing a beat. "I told him that the company had suffered what seemed to be a tragic series of accidents."

"That's not ridiculous at all," Gus said. "That's a fact."

"Yes, but I didn't stop there," Shawn said. "I went on to explain that these weren't accidents at all. That they were murders."

"He didn't believe it," Gus said, although his sinking heart insisted that this was not the case.

"He had to," Shawn said. "I made a very convincing case."

"How could you?" Gus said. "It's absurd."

"Look at the pattern," Shawn said. "One guy skis into a

tree. Another one crashes his car. A third guy goes for a cup of coffee and he's turned into barbecue."

"Exactly," Gus said. "There is no pattern."

"That's what Dive Bomb said."

At least the entire world wasn't going insane. D-Bob didn't jump at Shawn's insane theory. Except that he had hired Shawn.

"So, how did you convince him that you were right?"

"I didn't," Shawn said. "You did."

"I did?" This had to be a dream. Soon there would be a knock on the door and Nana the dog would come in and tell him it was time for tea, or the entire building would turn into a rocket ship heading for Mars. "How?"

"I told him the truth," Shawn said. "That you had figured it all out weeks ago and taken the job here so you could work undercover. And now that you were getting closer to the killer you needed me to come in to help."

# Chapter Twenty-eight

There were something like a bazillion restaurants in San Francisco, but Gus and Shawn ended up back at the same diner where they'd shared their last meal. It seemed appropriate. After all, this is where Gus' career with Benson Pharmaceuticals had really started; it might as well mark the end as well.

"I'm going to try to explain this one last time," Gus said after the waitress had taken their order and disappeared with the menus. "This is not an undercover operation."

"Not anymore," Shawn said. "Not now that the boss knows what you're doing."

"I'm not doing anything." Gus had to fight to keep his voice from rising an octave and several decibels.

"It's okay," Shawn said. "I understand why you had to do it this way. I'll admit I was getting a little obsessed with the whole *Criminal Genius* thing, and all those times you tried to tell me about the serial killer at Benson Pharmaceuticals, I didn't exactly give your fascinating theory the attention it deserved."

"All *what* times?" It was getting harder to keep his voice from turning into a shriek.

"I don't know," Shawn said. "Didn't I say I wasn't listening?"

"You're not listening now," Gus said.

"Yes, but only because now I already know," Shawn said. "So it's a waste of our time if I spend it listening to you rehashing the past instead of moving on into the future."

Gus felt a sharp pain in his right hand. He looked down and discovered he was clenching his fork so tightly it was about to draw blood. He forced his hand to relax until the fork clanked back down onto the table.

"I am trying to tell you that I took this job—"

"Because you couldn't find any other way to get me on the case, I know," Shawn said. "It was one giant cry for help, and I was so distracted I couldn't hear it. Looking back on the past few months, I'm so embarrassed. To think I actually believed you were trying to ditch me when you flew up for your final interview, when it's so obvious that you were leaving bread crumbs the size of Buicks for me to follow."

"Umm, sure," Gus said.

"And when you said you were leaving detective work for a job pushing pills, you probably expected me to fall down laughing," Shawn said. "You must have been so shocked when I said okay."

"I was a little surprised," Gus said. It was true, although not for the reasons Shawn now believed. "But I was always serious about this job."

"You would have had to be," Shawn agreed. "Just like when Steve Sloan went rogue and Mark Sloan had him committed to that asylum for loony cops on *Diagnosis Murder*."

Now Gus was sure this was a dream. "You watched *Diagnosis Murder*?"

"I was dating a girl who worked in a nursing home," Shawn said. "She had to keep up on the episodes so she'd have something to talk to her patients about. Anyway, the point is if Mark and Steve hadn't been completely convincing the guy from *Jake and the Fat Man* would never have broken down and led them to where he'd walled up his family."

It occurred to Gus that if he had taken the simple precaution of walling up Shawn somewhere before he'd taken the job at Benson, he might still have a future there. But it was too late for that now. Still it was possible he might be able to salvage his new career, if only he could figure out what Shawn was talking about. Or better yet, if he didn't even try, and simply made his own point as plainly and forcefully as he could.

"Shawn, if you've never listened to me before, you've got to listen now," Gus said.

"I'm sure I've listened some," Shawn said. "Like that time I was about to try parasailing, and you said that it was just like jumping off a cliff with a kite strapped to my back."

"You went anyway and you broke your ankle," Gus said, despite having just taken a vow not to be dragged off the subject at hand.

"Yes, but not because I didn't listen," Shawn said. "I thought you meant it as a recommendation."

"Fine," Gus said. "In that case I'm going to ask you to listen first and if there's anything you think you might not understand, ask questions afterward. Can you do that?"

"I can do even better," Shawn said. "I can ask questions before I listen. Or even during, although that doesn't save quite as much time."

Gus sighed heavily enough that Shawn took the hint and stopped talking.

"Shawn, when I left Psych to take this job, I left Psych to take this job," Gus said. "I wasn't going undercover, and I wasn't trying to convince you that you had missed out on a string of murders. I was offered a position as a vice president in a multinational pharmaceuticals company and I accepted it. I never wanted you to leave Santa Barbara and join me up here to investigate some case that never existed in the first place. So if that's the reason you've invented this job as head of security for yourself, you don't need to stick with it any longer. You can go back home."

Shawn waited patiently for several moments after Gus had stopped talking. "That's really interesting," he said finally.

"What's that?" Gus said.

"This whole listening thing," Shawn said. "You'd think you might learn a little more by doing it, since presumably people scatter information throughout the entirety of a speech like that. But no matter how long I kept quiet, I didn't hear anything I didn't already know from your first sentence. Look, food's here."

It was. The waitress was hovering over their table with trays that could easily tip over the Flintstones' car. She dropped them in the center of the table, leaving it for Shawn and Gus to figure out which plate belonged to whom, and disappeared again.

Shawn grabbed one of the plates, picked up the head-sized burger and crammed two eyes' and a nose's worth into his mouth. Gus took advantage of what would be at least a few seconds of enforced silence to make his point again.

"What I'm trying to say is that while I appreciate the faith you put in me, it's wrong," Gus said. "I didn't come here because I believed there was a case. In fact, I still don't believe there's a killer out there stalking pharmaceuticals executives. It's just a series of coincidences."

Gus spat out the last syllables as quickly as he could, since he could see the giant mass of food moving down Shawn's throat like a rabbit in a python.

"There is no case here, Shawn, but there is one back in Santa Barbara," Gus said before Shawn could usher the last traces of food all the way into his stomach. "I appreciate your faith in me, but you've got to tell D-Bob that whatever you told him about the serial killer was wrong and that you're resigning as head of security."

Shawn studied Gus closely. "You're sure about this?"

"About everything except telling D-Bob," Gus said. "I have no idea how you can stuff that bit of toothpaste back into the tube."

"Nothing to worry about there," Shawn said. "I wouldn't squeeze that tube if your life depended on it."

It took Gus a moment to realize what Shawn was saying. "You didn't tell him about the killer?"

"He was my favorite suspect," Shawn said. "I wasn't going to share my suspicions with him."

"Then how did you get the job?"

"The same way you got yours," Shawn said, taking another huge bite out of the burger.

"You landed this job by spending years working in pharmaceuticals sales and having a unique point of view on the issues that confront our industry in these troubling times?" Gus said.

Shawn managed to get the wad of beef and bun down his throat. "Wouldn't it surprise you if I said yes?"

"If by 'surprise' you mean drive me into a such a rage I'd gouge out your eyes with this spoon, then hurl myself off the Golden Gate Bridge, then definitely it would," Gus said.

"You make it tempting to say yes," Shawn said. "But I have to tell the truth. I did it the old-fashioned way. I earned it."

"Earned it how?"

"By lying," Shawn said. "He knew we were old friends from the last time I met the guy. So I told him that your presence in the company had established a psychic link for me to see its aura. And that emanation was pulsing red for danger."

"He bought that?" Gus said, dismayed.

"Your boss is kind of a moron," Shawn said. "Unless he's actually the killer. Think we have time for dessert before we go back to the office?"

Gus slid out of the booth, fished in his pocket, and dropped a couple of bills on the table. "You do," he said. "In fact, you should have dessert for both of us. You don't need to stop by the office before you head back to the airport. I'll tell D-Bob you're on a vision quest or something. He'll like that."

Shawn took one last suck on his milk shake and scrambled out of the booth to follow him. "I can't go back to Santa Barbara now," he said. "I've got a job to do."

"Making my life miserable?" Gus said as he pushed open the door and stepped out onto the busy sidewalk.

"That's part of it," Shawn said.

That was so astonishing Gus stopped dead in the middle of the sidewalk. At least until a kid texting on his phone while he rode his skateboard slammed into him, propelling him into the street. Just before he flew into traffic Gus grabbed the pole of a NO SKATEBOARDS sign and swung himself back into the mass of pedestrians, nearly knocking over a trio of secretaries.

Shawn waited patiently until his acrobatic display was done, then fell into step alongside him.

"You're admitting it?" Gus gasped once he had his heart rate back down to sustainable levels. "You only took this job to make my life miserable?"

"Not only," Shawn said. "Also to make your life happy. And exciting. And boring. And easy. And difficult."

"Are you planning on doing this in sequence?" Gus said. "Because you could start by making my life a little more lonely."

"I'll put that on the list," Shawn said. "Along with all the other sorts of things your life can only be if it's a going concern."

"You're saying you took this job to save my life," Gus said.

"I took this job because I thought we were going undercover to expose a murderer who had found a way to kill without ever being noticed," Shawn said. "That is, by going after people no one would ever mourn—pharmaceuticals executives."

"I'm a pharmaceuticals executive," Gus said.

"That's what I'm saying," Shawn said. "I took this job because I thought we were going undercover together. But I'm keeping it because I'm not going to let you be the next victim."

"I can't be the next victim, because there haven't been any previous victims," Gus said. "There's just been a series of unfortunate accidents, which is not that surprising when you consider how many thousands of people Benson Pharmaceuticals employs worldwide."

"And one suicide," Shawn said.

"And one suicide," Gus agreed. "If it makes you feel better I'll promise not to put on a cheerleader's outfit and hang myself in my mother's basement."

"That's good, because you really don't have the legs for it," Shawn said.

Gus stopped as they reached the corner of Market Street. He pointed at the long escalator that descended to the subway stop under their feet. "Here's the BART station," he said. "You can take that right back to the airport."

"Only if you come with me," Shawn said.

"I'm not coming back," Gus said. "I've got a life here."

"Sure, but for how long?" Shawn said.

"Shawn, there is no danger at Benson Pharmaceuticals," Gus said. "How can I convince you?"

"You can start by explaining that."

Shawn gestured down Market to the glass-and-steel tower that housed Gus' office. A thick crowd of people had formed outside the lobby doors. As Gus watched, a steady stream of onlookers squeezed forward to get a better view, then pushed their way out of the crowd, looking sick. One woman threw up on the curb.

Gus was running before he knew he'd meant to. His

flat shoes slapped on the bricks of the sidewalk and sent a sharp sting of pain through his feet with every step, but he barely noticed. He reached the edge of the crowd and let his momentum carry him through the close-packed bodies. He could feel the onlookers push back against him, but he kept going, using knees and elbows to clear any obstruction his combined mass and velocity couldn't move. After what felt like an eternity he broke through into a clearing, a wide, empty space on the sidewalk, ringed by spectators.

But that space wasn't completely empty. The first things Gus noticed were the clear pebbles that littered the sidewalk. He realized he'd been walking on them since before he'd entered the crowd; some of them were still stuck in the soles of his shoes. They looked like the bits of windshield that were left on the highway once a serious crash had been cleaned up.

Gus could easily have spent the next few minutes thinking about the marvels of safety glass, wondering what kind of technology was required to make it shatter into beads instead of jagged shards. It was thicker than normal glass, true, but was that enough? Or did it have to go through some kind of chemical process? Gus had heard it referred to as tempered glass, but he had no idea how you would go about tempering something. And could a sheet of glass lose its temper the way a person could? That would make a kind of sense, since a person who lost his temper would fly into a rage, and a pane of glass that lost its temper would fly into jagged shards. Maybe this was just an etymological accident. Or perhaps Gus had stumbled onto some great truth about glass or emotions or flying into things.

Gus wanted to explore all these ideas in detail. All he had to do was turn around and push his way back through the crowd. Then he could walk around the corner to the Drumm Street entrance, take the elevator up to the sixteenth floor, lock himself in his office, and spend the rest of the day in rapt concentration. He might have to ignore the cold wind blowing through the corridors, but he was willing to do that, because the alternative was so much less appealing.

That alternative was to focus on what lay in front of him, spread out on the sidewalk. And that was the last thing he wanted to do. The last thing, but the only thing.

Gus forced his eyes to look down at the ground. He tried to avoid taking in the whole picture and instead to focus on the tiny details. Like the cracks in the bricks where the shock wave from the body's landing had rippled out across the sidewalk. Or the brown loafer that had come off either in flight or on landing and now lay by its owner's head. Or the tie. That hideous floral tie he had spent so much of the morning staring at across the conference table. The one Steve Ecclesine put on whenever he planned to engage in an act of corporate brutality, as if the cheery flowers could hide the cruelty of his actions.

There were short bloops of police siren from the street behind him, and Gus felt the crowd jostling as a pair of uniformed cops muscled their way through to the body lying on the ground.

"Okay, let's move on, people," a gruff voice said from behind him. "There's nothing to see here."

*How wrong that voice is,* Gus thought. There were things to see in every direction. If you looked down, there was the body. If you looked up, you could see the hole in the building where the window had popped out of its sixteenth-story frame. And if you looked to your left, you could see Shawn looking right back at you.

"So," Shawn said. "We still working on that string-of-unconnected-accidents theory?"

# Chapter Twenty-nine

"I quit," Gus said.

"A bold statement," Shawn said. "Forcefully spoken. Brief and yet eloquent. If I could give you the tiniest smidge of advice, I'd just say that it would be more convincing if you weren't on your knees while you said it."

Gus looked back over his shoulder at Shawn, who was spread out over one of the sofas in his office. Then he turned back to the carpet in front of him and pulled another stretch of silver duct tape off the roll. He laid the top half of the tape along the bottom edge of the closed curtain, then pressed the bottom of it against the floor.

"As long as I'm within ten feet of this window, I'm keeping low to the ground," Gus said. "The lower my center of gravity, the less chance I'll plunge to my death if the glass falls out."

"First of all, if the glass does fall out a strip of duct tape and a curtain won't stop you," Shawn said. "If Goldfinger could get sucked out through that tiny airplane window, there's no way you're not going out a hole the size of a billboard."

"That would be true if we were two miles in the air,"

Gus said. "As it is, explosive decompression is just about the only thing I don't have to worry about."

"You also don't have to worry about whether you're such a man that one romp in the hay is enough to make a criminally oriented lesbian aviatrix turn straight in both ways," Shawn said. "And also you don't have to worry that the glass will come out," Shawn said.

"Says the company's chief safety officer," Gus said.

"Exactly," Shawn said. "I commissioned an inspection of every window in these offices, and they are all firmly glued. Or however they're stuck in there."

That was at least partially true. There had been an inspection and it had cleared all the windows, although it had been performed by engineers working for the building's owners and their insurance company. The fact that they still had no explanation for the sudden failure of Steve Ecclesine's window did tend to undercut Gus' confidence in the security of his own, however.

Gus pulled another strip of tape off the roll and overlapped it on the piece holding the curtain to the carpet. "That doesn't exactly fill me with confidence."

"Then this should," Shawn said. "The killer hasn't repeated himself yet. Skiing accident, electrocution, suicide. I don't think he's going to feel that the window gag was so good he needs an encore."

"That's great," Gus said. "As long as there really is a killer. I'm still not convinced this isn't one more in a tragic series of accidents."

"Yes, you are," Shawn said. "You just don't want to be."

Gus got up on his knees, then hurled the roll of tape directly at Shawn's head. Shawn ducked and the tape bounced off the wall behind him.

"All right, I am," Gus said. "I'm convinced."

"Don't forget, I'm also right that you don't want to be," Shawn said.

"I haven't forgotten." Gus slid across the carpet on his

knees until he reached an armchair opposite Shawn's sofa and pulled himself into it. "Believe me, I'm never going to forget that. Because I want this job. I want to stay here."

"No, you don't," Shawn said.

Gus might have jumped out of his chair and grabbed Shawn's shirt to shake some sense into him if that hadn't required standing up within a football field's distance of the window. "You don't know what I want," he said. "You only know what you want."

"That's right," Shawn said. "But we always want the same thing, so what difference does it make?"

"It's not that we want the same thing," Gus said. "You always manage to get what you want, and I find a way to convince myself that that's what I'd wanted all along."

"So everyone's happy," Shawn said.

"One of us is happy and one of us is pretending to be," Gus said.

"That works, too," Shawn said.

That was enough to propel Gus out of his chair. Let the window blow out if it wanted to. He couldn't sit here and listen to this.

"Not anymore," Gus said. "I've got to have my own life. You can stay ten years old forever if that's what you want, but I've got to grow up."

"I'm sure your voice will change one of these days," Shawn said calmly.

Gus stalked over to the door. It would be so easy to fling it open and walk out, never to see Shawn's face again. Of course it would have been easier if they hadn't been sitting in Gus' office, to which he would have to return sooner or later. All Shawn would have to do to foil Gus' plan was to continue to sit on the comfortable guest couch.

And it wasn't what Gus wanted, anyway. At least it wasn't what his calm, rational side wanted, and he'd never been able to shut up that part of him, even in the heat of rage.

Yes, Gus realized, he wanted to leave childhood behind and step with both feet into the adult world. But he didn't want to leave Shawn back there in his preadolescent days. He wanted to bring his best friend along with him. Would that even be possible? He had no idea. But he owed it to their friendship to give it at least one good try.

Gus turned back from the door. "It is a string of coincidences," he said. "Tragic accidents and a suicide, all completely unconnected except by happenstance."

"You know that's not true," Shawn said.

"I know part of me wants it not to be true," Gus said. "That's the part of me that wants the world to conform to my idea of fun. Where there are Russian spies working behind the counters of dry cleaners, pirates plotting to take over oil rigs, and serial killers hiding inside every corporate office."

"Why would a Russian spy go undercover in a dry cleaner's?" Shawn said. "It would make much more sense to operate out of a shoe store."

"See?" Gus said. "If I gave that one second of thought, I could probably find a way it made sense."

"People are at their most vulnerable when they've got their shoes off," Shawn said. "Combine that with—"

Gus slapped his hands over his ears. "Stop!"

Shawn shrugged. "Okay, but don't blame me if you find yourself blabbing state secrets next time you go in for a pair of Keds."

"I don't wear Keds anymore, Shawn," Gus said. "And that's kind of the point. We're not in *The Goonies*. There isn't a pirate ship wrecked in a cave under every abandoned restaurant."

"You never know if you don't look," Shawn said.

"I don't want to look for what's underneath anymore," Gus said. "If a sea lion washes up on shore, I don't want to check to see if it was murdered, because it wasn't."

"Except for Shabby."

"A couple of years ago all the sea lions disappeared from Fisherman's Wharf here," Gus said. "No one knew why."

"They were all murdered?" Shawn said.

"The next year they all came back. Because that's what sea lions do in the real world," Gus said. "Just like people ski into trees or get electrocuted by bad wiring or even hang themselves when life gets to be too much for them."

"Of course they do," Shawn said. "That's why all those things make such good cover for murder."

"One out of a million times maybe it's murder," Gus said. "I want to live in the world of the nine hundred ninety-nine thousand nine hundred ninety-nine, not the crazy world where the one just might possibly be right."

"What fun is that?"

Gus took a deep breath. This was the hardest thing he'd ever tried to explain, and if he didn't get it right he'd have lost the chance to bring Shawn along. "It's not fun," Gus said. "It's not supposed to be fun. It's real."

"Real." Shawn rolled the word around in his mouth as if he'd never heard it before.

"I need to accept the real instead of jumping after the fun," Gus said. "Because while I've been chasing that one in a million, I've been missing what everyone else has. I don't want to spend my time wondering if an accidental death is actually a murder. I don't want to meet a perfectly nice new person and immediately jump to the conclusion that—"

There was a knock at the door. Then it cracked open. Jerry Fellows stuck his smiling face into the office. "Is this a bad time, Mr. G?" he said.

"I guess not, Jerry," Gus said. "Come on in."

Jerry wheeled his mail cart to Gus' desk and deposited a stack of letters. "Ah, I'm sorry. I didn't realize you were meeting with our new safety officer," he said. "Are we still on for later, Mr. Spencer?"

"That we are, Jerry," Shawn said.

"Anything I can do to help end this string of terrible accidents," Jerry said. "Although if you don't mind my saying so, Mr. G, poor Mr. Ecclesine's passing may end up doing the world a world of good, bless his soul."

"What do you mean?" Gus said.

"Of all the senior executives around here, he was the one most opposed to your orphan drugs campaign. Did the same back when Jim Macoby was pushing his own plan. So maybe now that he's gone you've got a chance."

"Hate to have it come at such a price," Gus said.

"Too true, too true," Jerry said. "But on the other hand, if you've got to suffer through such a terrible tragedy, it's a blessing that some good can come out of it."

"Thanks, Jerry," Gus said.

"For what?"

"For reminding us that there's more to life than the occasional bit of violence and misery," Gus said.

"That's what I'm here for," Jerry said as he pushed his cart toward the door. "Just want to leave the world slightly better than it was when I got here."

Gus held the door open for Jerry's cart, then let it close behind the mailman before turning back to Shawn. "See?" he said. "That's what I'm talking about. Here's a man who can bring joy to everyone around him because he's not busy running around trying to prove that something statistically absurd has actually happened."

"I won't argue with you about Jerry," Shawn said. "He's a great guy."

"And I want to live in a world where a great guy is just a great guy," Gus said. "Where I don't have to think someone like him could ever be—"

Gus broke off as a dark thought started forming in his head. He pushed it away. He couldn't go down that path. He wouldn't.

"No way he'd ever be what?" Shawn said.

"He isn't," Gus said. But the harder he tried to push the

thought out of his mind, the stronger it came back. He gave it one last shove and managed to free himself. He breathed a sigh of relief, and the thought rushed back at him like a wave crashing onto a sand castle, obliterating everything in its path.

It wasn't just a thought anymore. Gus knew the truth. The horrible, awful, inescapable truth.

# Chapter Thirty

"**A**re you all right?" Shawn asked. "Because you look like you just swallowed a Volvo."

Gus was not all right. His head was pounding from the effort of denying what was so obviously right in front of him.

"This is exactly what I mean," Gus said. "I'm tired of living like this."

"If you mean like someone out of *Mad Men* but without any of the good parts, I certainly understand," Shawn said. "If you've got to wear a suit to work every day, at least you should take up smoking and drinking and sleeping around on your wife, so it's all worth it. Of course you'd probably need to pick yourself up a wife, too. And a childhood where you were thrashed daily for not slopping the hogs, and a secret identity no one knows about. I've got to tell you, I don't see how anyone sticks with this corporate life for long. I'm exhausted just thinking about it."

"What I'm tired of," Gus said tensely, "is seeing murders wherever I go."

"I thought you'd taken care of that by closing your eyes and refusing to look at what's obvious," Shawn said.

"I'm tired of looking at the nicest man the world has

ever seen and leaping to the conclusion that he must be a murderer because he's the least likely suspect," Gus said.

It took Shawn a moment to realize what Gus was saying. "Really? Jerry? A killer?"

"Don't tell me you hadn't already gone there," Gus said.

Gus thought Shawn seemed completely astonished, although a lifetime spent trying to look innocent whenever he was caught red-handed could have explained that. "Why would I?"

"Why would you?" Gus sputtered. "Because he's the last person anyone would ever suspect of anything."

"Exactly," Shawn said. "So why would we start now?"

"Because that's how it works," Gus said. "You always say the least likely suspect is the one who did it."

"Doesn't sound like me," Shawn said. "Oh, wait a minute. 'The least likely suspect is the one who did it.' Yeah, it's a little closer when the voice isn't all squeaky and shrill. But still—Jerry? How could you even think such a thing?"

"I don't want to," Gus said. "That's what I've been saying. I want to be part of the real world where the guy the police catch standing over the corpse with a smoking gun is the guy who pulled the trigger."

"Now you're just talking nonsense," Shawn said. "Why would you shoot a guy and stand around with a smoking gun, waiting for the police to show up? And how do you get a gun to smoke, anyway? Because today's modern firearms are pretty much emissions-free, if you don't count the bullet, so you've got to be lighting cigarettes and sticking them in the barrel, and anyone who would do that probably doesn't have the intellectual wherewithal to figure out how to pull the trigger."

"That's exactly what I mean," Gus said. "That's the kind of gibberish that leads us to accuse the Jerry Fellowses of the world."

"Yes, but gibberish isn't enough," Shawn said. "This is not as easy as you make it sound. For instance, why would

Jerry want to kill all these pharmaceutical executives?
I mean, aside from the same reasons everyone else who
didn't do it has."

Gus felt the pounding in his temples ease a little. Shawn
was right. Maybe he was nuts. There had to be a motive.
And then the same dark thought came rushing back again,
only this time it was far more detailed.

"Orphan drugs," Gus said. "That's his motive."

"Orphan drugs?" Shawn said. "They've got pills for that
now? What do they do—you take one and you grow a new
set of parents?"

Gus sank down in the armchair, lost in dread. "They're
not drugs for orphans," he said mechanically, his mind
spinning through the ramifications of what he'd realized.
"They're drugs for diseases that are too rare to make mass
production possible, which means that they're too expensive to produce at all. Millions of people all over the world
die of illnesses that could be cured, except that the financial
rewards aren't there and—"

"Okay, this is getting boring," Shawn said. "You're not
going to start making speeches like that Quincy guy, are
you? Because that show should be an object lesson for all
of us: When he was solving crimes and sleeping with day
players it was a lot of fun. But once he got all serious and
started tackling social issues it got to be just about unbear-
able. Something to think about."

Gus considered explaining to Shawn that certain social
issues were far more important than whatever entertainment value they might contain for an audience, but he knew
that would lead directly to an argument about the value of
the very special episode of a sitcom compared to one that
was actually funny, and then half the day would disappear.
He needed to stick to the subject he started with.

"The issue of orphan drugs was something I was interested in from my first day here," Gus said. "I really thought
I could make a difference."

Shawn's thumb started twitching. Gus slapped his hand away.

"Stop that," he said. "You can't change the channel just because I'm talking about something serious for one minute."

"Another reason real life can't compare to television," Shawn said.

"Just listen," Gus said. "One day I was talking to Jerry Fellows and I mentioned my interest in the subject. He was thrilled. He said that in all the decades he'd been with the company he'd thought we should have a real program to address the issue. From then on he always asked about my progress. He encouraged me when I was feeling hopeless, cheered me on when I was doing well, and did everything he could to subtly keep me focused on the problem."

"You sold me," Shawn said. "He's got to be the killer."

Gus wondered briefly if Shawn felt now the way Gus always had when Shawn announced some ridiculous theory of the crime at hand, and if he'd feel as foolish when Gus proved to be right.

"Just before my big presentation to the executive committee, he let something slip," Gus said. "Jim Macoby had been working on a plan to address the orphan drugs issue before he died."

"Jim Macoby?" Shawn asked, and then remembered. "Oh, Mr. Coffee."

"Steve Ecclesine was my primary opponent on the committee," Gus said. "I'm pretty sure he was planning to do whatever he could to stop me."

"I'm beginning to see an issue here, but let's keep going with this for the moment," Shawn said.

Gus didn't need Shawn's permission. He was already at his desk and typing furiously onto his computer monitor. "I knew it!" he said.

"You can't put a red six on a red seven?" Shawn said. "Because Hank Stenberg made a patch for the Psych computer so that you can put any card on any other card. It's made the long workday a lot more fun, I've got to tell you."

"Sam Masterson," Gus said. "I've got access to all his files, and here's one marked 'orphan drugs.'" He tapped twice on the image of the file and it spread open. His face fell. "It's empty."

"This certainly is a slam-dunk case you're putting together against Jerry," Shawn said. "You've got one dead guy who was all in favor of giving drugs to Little Orphan Annie, one who was opposed to it, and one who was so passionately involved on one side or the other that he couldn't be bothered to invest any more time in the subject than it took to label a new file. I'm definitely seeing a pattern here."

Shawn might not have seen the pattern, but Gus did. At least he was feeling the general shape of it. The details were still hazy, but he could tell there was something. "Did it ever occur to you that this file might be empty because somebody erased everything in it?" he said.

"Sure," Shawn said. "And when I buy a frying pan and get it home to find there are no pancakes in it I know it's because some kid ate them all before I could."

"Jerry Fellows is passionate about the issue of orphan drugs. Can we agree on that?" Gus said.

"We can agree to take your word on it," Shawn said. "Then if you turn out to be wrong we can agree to make fun of you for the rest of the week."

"He's been supporting me and doing whatever he could to help me prepare my presentation to D-Bob," Gus said. "So I'm going to make a leap and say that he would have done the same for Jim Macoby."

"Leap on."

"D-Bob was impressed with my presentation—there's no question about it," Gus said. "But Ecclesine managed to derail it at the end. It was obvious he was going to be the biggest obstacle in my way. So he had to go."

"I'm still with you," Shawn said. "Or I would be if I hadn't already gotten to this point about the time you started down this path. Now I'm up ahead waiting to see if you notice that it plunges off a cliff."

Gus shot him a scowl. "The big question is Jim Macoby," Gus said. "If he was pushing the issue why would Fellows have wanted him dead?"

"You're not at the plunge yet, but at least you've skipped through the minefield," Shawn said.

Gus thought hard until he finally had a glimmer of an idea. He typed furiously and a different file cabinet opened on his screen. He opened the cabinet. "Nothing here labeled 'orphan drugs,'" he said. "But we've already established that it could have been deleted."

"In the same way we've established what happened to my pancakes," Shawn said. "Which reminds me, where's the kitchen in this place? All this talk about breakfast is making me hungry."

Gus opened another file. "This is it," he said. "I've got it. Macoby's calendar."

"If he's got dinner reservations for tonight, let's see if they're for someplace good," Shawn said. "Because if we show up instead of him I don't think he's going to object."

Gus flipped through screens. "He had reservations, but not for dinner," he said. "It looks like he kept scheduling meetings with D-Bob to talk about orphan drugs, but then they all got canceled."

"I know I'm not exactly the expert on how business works, but doesn't that happen all the time?" Shawn said.

"Yes, but from the notations, Macoby canceled the meetings himself," Gus said. "He talked a big game about tackling the issue, but he chickened out every time."

"And you think Jerry doesn't like chicken?"

"It makes sense," Gus said. "If Jerry has a real sense of urgency about the issue, then he'd take this as a betrayal.

Who knows how much time and energy he put into helping Macoby get his proposal together?"

"For that matter, who knows if any of this has the slightest connection to the truth?" Shawn said. "Oh, right, nobody."

Gus wasn't listening. His fingers were flying over the virtual keyboard, and after a few seconds another file opened up. "What about Mandy Jansen?"

"Well, if she did know, it's not going to do us any good," Shawn said. "Not unless you know someone who can talk to the dead."

"Like Shawn Spencer, psychic detective?"

"Exactly," Shawn said. "Just like him, only with actual psychic powers. Give me a call when you find the guy and I'll buy him lunch."

"We don't need to talk to Mandy Jansen," Gus said. "All we need to know is right here in her file. She said she quit Benson Pharmaceuticals to take care of her mother, and in fact here's a digital copy of the letter she mailed just before I was hired. She said her mother had been diagnosed with mesenchymal chondrosarcoma and that she needed constant care."

Shawn just looked at him. "You know, I feel like I'm supposed to come up with a witty riposte here, but you've left me completely blank."

"Mesenchymal chondrosarcoma is a cancer of the cartilage, one of the rarest cancers there is," Gus said. "There haven't even been a hundred cases diagnosed in all the world. So obviously there's no treatment for it."

"Still waiting for my opening," Shawn said.

"Don't you see?" Gus wanted to hit Shawn in the face with the facts. Unfortunately they were nothing more than pixels on a screen, so he was reduced to waving his arms in the air to emphasize his point. "Mandy's mother was suffering from an orphan disease. Mandy, who was supposed to take the job that eventually went to me, was the perfect person to lead the charge for the cause in the company. She would have had the passion, the firsthand knowledge, and the moral gravity to force Benson Pharmaceuticals down this path."

"Instead she decided to stay home and take care of Mom," Shawn said. "How selfish can you get? No wonder she killed herself."

"That's what I'm trying to tell you," Gus said, arms flapping so hard that if the glass had fallen out of the window right now he could have flown down to a safe landing. "She didn't kill herself. She committed the same sin that Jim Macoby did: walking away from the cause. And for that sin she was murdered."

"By Jerry Fellows."

"By Jerry Fellows," Gus agreed. "Don't you see? It all makes sense."

And for one brief, shining moment of clarity, it did. He had found the pattern. But that was only the first step. After he found it he needed to prove it, which meant using the pattern as a guide to find another instance that would fit. And he had done that, too. Gus had solved a series of terrible crimes when no one else had even suspected that the crimes had been committed, except for Shawn, and that didn't count.

So why didn't he feel that sense of triumph that always used to come with the solving of the puzzle? Where was that satisfaction as the last piece snapped into place and proved him right?

It wasn't there. And, Gus realized, it wouldn't be there. Because he hadn't actually solved anything, except theoretically. Yes, everything he said held together, and he could connect every one of his dots to make a sound, logical case.

But there was nothing real about it. Nothing tying these bold rhetorical declarations down to reality. It was all fine as a word puzzle, but if he took it any further it would actually impact people's lives. Living people, breathing people,

people with hopes and dreams, all of which might be shat-
tered by his little game. It might be fun to calculate where
the train leaving New York at eighty miles an hour would
meet the one heading out of Los Angeles at twice that
speed, but once you realized that both of them were running on the same track and their meeting would entail the
deaths of hundreds of innocent passengers, it seemed irre-
sponsible to keep calculating instead of doing something to
stop the catastrophe.

And Gus had caused enough catastrophes in exactly
this way. When Professor Langston Kitteredge had come
to him for help in battling the global conspiracy that only
he knew about, Gus had leaped to his aid and worked out
an entire theory about who had murdered the museum's
curator and why. It was logical, it was plausible, and all the
pieces fit together.

The only trouble was that it was all based on a faulty
assumption, and because of that everything he'd come up
with afterward had been completely wrong. Logical, defen-
sible, and wrong. And a man had died because of it.

Now he was doing exactly the same thing. He had taken
a set of incidents and strung them together into a pretty
pattern. But that didn't mean the pattern represented what
had really happened. It just meant that he was really good
at coming up with arguments he could use to persuade
himself.

When he stepped back and looked at what he was really
talking about, he could see how stupid and dangerous the
exercise was. And not just because he was already falling
into the least obvious suspect trap. The theory about Jerry
Fellows killing Benson executives rested on one necessary
assumption—that a string of accidents and one suicide
were actually murders that no one had noticed. Which was,
of course, the most ludicrous part of the whole argument.
There was no evidence to suggest that all these deaths

were anything other than what they appeared. Shawn had skipped over that by simply assuming its opposite, and Gus had started piling details on top of that declaration.

Gus could feel the fear overtaking him again. His palms were sweating; his heart pounded against his ribs.

He wouldn't do this again. Not to himself, and certainly not to Jerry Fellows. There was a reason Gus had given up working as a detective, and this was it. What was fun in the abstract could destroy people's lives once he started to pretend he knew what he was doing.

That was why he was here at Benson Pharmaceuticals. That was why he had put on a suit and a tie, why he had decided to live as a grown-up in the grown-up world.

And it was why he would refuse to play the detective game anymore. If it turned out he was wrong and there was a mysterious murderer killing people, then let someone who knew what he was doing figure it out. He would do the job he was being paid to do.

Gus forced his mouth into a grin. "Got you with that one, didn't I?" he said. "You have to admit, it sounded pretty good for a while."

Shawn didn't smile back. "Not all of it," he said. "But it sounds like you got some of it right."

Gus tried to keep the grin on his face, but he could feel it sagging away. "No," he said. "I was making it all up. It was all a joke. None of it was real."

Shawn gave him a long, hard look. "You don't believe that."

"I do," Gus said. "More than I've ever believed anything."

"You know there's a killer at this company," Shawn said.

"I know there isn't," Gus said.

"Think about what you're saying," Shawn said. "Because if we don't stop this guy before he kills again, the next victim could be you."

Gus had known that. He'd accepted it at the same time he decided that the killer was a phantom of his own logic. "I'll be really careful if I go skiing," he said.

Shawn studied his friend closely, as if looking for the smallest chink in his armor of denial. Then he let out a sigh, got up from the couch, and headed for the door. "If that's the way you want it . . ."

"It's the way it is," Gus said. "Thanks for all your help."

"Don't thank me now," Shawn said as he opened the door. "I haven't caught this guy yet."

"What do you mean 'yet'?" Gus said. "There is no killer. I forbid you to look for a murderer in this company!"

But Gus was yelling at a closed door. Shawn was gone.

# Chapter Thirty-one

There was an obstacle in level six of *Criminal Genius* that had taken Shawn a few lives to figure out. It didn't look complicated. At the beginning of the level you were approached by a beautiful young woman who begged you to save her from her abusive husband, and in return she would introduce you to Morton, the game's evil kingpin. This could be a shortcut to winning the entire game, since the ultimate goal was to kill Morton and take over his crime syndicate; you spent much of your game play trying to inflict enough damage on Darksyde City that he'd invite you to join his organization.

Every time Shawn'd played this level, however, he could never get past the brutal husband. No matter what kind of ambush he'd planned, the husband always spotted it and killed him. Shawn tried attacking him directly, but was over-powered and killed yet again no matter what weapons he used. One time he'd managed to infiltrate the abandoned warehouse the husband used as a headquarters—the game designers alternated between abandoned warehouses and deserted amusement parks for their criminal lairs, apparently having learned everything they knew about the underworld from watching the same '80s cop movies Shawn had grown up on—he was immediately captured, hung by his feet from a chain that dangled from the ceiling, and dissolved in a hailstorm of machine-gun bullets.

This was still before Shawn had discovered the mysterious librarian, and he had thought the clue to Macklin Tanner's disappearance would lie with Morton, so he believed he couldn't move forward with his own investigation until he'd beaten this level. Still, no matter what he tried he couldn't get past the woman's brutal husband.

It was after he'd died for the eighth time on this level that he finally came up with a plan. This time he asked the victimized wife to come along with him to the abandoned warehouse. He'd expected they'd be captured or killed along the way, but she seemed to work like a magic charm, and they were able to walk right in.

The husband was waiting for them inside, surrounded by at least a dozen armed goons. "What do you want?" he growled, with no memory that he'd asked that question eight times before, often emphasized with jolts from a stun gun or blasts from a flamethrower.

"Your wife has been complaining," Shawn said. "She says you've been hurting her."

The husband didn't kill him right away, which Shawn took as a positive sin. "What business is that of yours?"

"Absolutely none," Shawn said. "Except that I don't like people who complain."

Before any of the thugs could move, Shawn yanked down on the chain that dangled from the ceiling. There was a rumbling Shawn could feel in his feet, then a trapdoor opened in front of him. Shawn gave the woman a shove and watched her fall in.

There was one moment where nobody moved. Then the husband jumped forward, threw his arms around Shawn's avatar, and gave him a hug. "I should have done that years ago," he said. "Because I don't like complaining, either.

And, say, you know who else doesn't like complaining? My boss Morton. He's going to like you, my boy."

That was it. End of level six, move on to seven and the next test to prove if he was indeed brutal, vicious, and sick enough to merit a meeting with the great man of Darksyde City. And all it took was the will to betray the one person in the world who trusted you.

Even though it had moved him up a level Shawn hadn't felt good about that particular play for a couple of days. It had left him feeling soiled in a way that all the game's massacres and murders never could.

But no matter how dirty he'd felt afterward Shawn couldn't argue that the simple act of betrayal hadn't propelled him further and led him closer to the clue he was searching for. In the end wasn't that really what was important?

He wasn't searching for a hidden message in a computer game anymore. He was trying to solve a string of murders. More important than that—much more than that—he was trying to save Gus' life. If Gus refused to acknowledge that a killer was stalking his company he would never see the ax before it fell.

Which meant that Shawn couldn't afford to worry about his own feelings. If the only way to protect Gus was to commit an act of personal betrayal, he'd do it and he'd take the consequences.

The question, Shawn thought as he walked down the corridor away from Gus' office, was what kind of betrayal would work for him now? Obviously he'd need to keep his position in the company for a little while and continue to investigate while he was here, but that might not be fast enough. That would make Gus mad enough, since he'd explicitly asked Shawn to go back to Santa Barbara and leave him alone. But Shawn knew he'd need to do a lot more than simply hang around. The killer had been too careful up until now to allow himself to believe it would be easy to spot him setting up his next murder.

No, Shawn had to do something active. Or even proactive, if that word had any meaning at all, something he'd doubted for a long time.

Shawn was so deep in thought he barely noticed he'd started down the steep stairs to the lobby until he was passing the receptionist's desk.

"Are you coming to the memorial service for Mr. Ecclesine tonight?" she asked. "I need to put together a list for the caterer."

"Of course I'll be there," Shawn said. "Wherever there's a caterer serving hungry people, you'll find me. It's kind of like my motto."

Chanterelle gave him a warm smile, then stood to grab a flyer announcing the reception from the far side of the desk. Shawn wondered briefly if there was a store that specialized in mourning clothes for the adult-film community, or if the receptionist simply shopped in the short girls' section to save money on her wardrobe and never noticed how little of her body she managed to cover. Before he could make a decision she handed him the flyer, which gave driving, biking, and public transportation directions to the San Francisco Bay Yacht Club, where the ceremony was going to be held.

"I'm glad," she said with a smile that made Shawn think the San Francisco fog had been replaced by Santa Barbara sunshine. "People come and go so quickly here these days. Sometimes it feels like I never really get to know anyone."

"Everyone certainly knows you," Shawn said, only half thinking of the way that the men in the company would find any excuse to learn more about the receptionist by following her up those steep stairs. "Although I'm a little surprised that you haven't gone off to run some other company."

A faint blush colored her cheeks and her smile turned

shy. "I'm not very ambitious," she said. "Everybody around here seems to be trying to fix the world or at the very least use their jobs here to climb to some better position. I'm more like my da. We're lifers here and we're happy about it."

"Some of the people who've left recently were also lifers," Shawn said. "They just didn't know it."

She gave him a blank smile as if to acknowledge that she realized he'd said something funny even if she didn't have the slightest idea what it could have been.

"You father is Jerry Fellows, right?" Shawn said.

"Since the day I was born," she said. "Or even longer, if you believe the biology books."

"He must like the company, since he was willing to bring you in to work here," Shawn said, an idea beginning to percolate in his mind. "But all those years delivering mail must get kind of dull after a while."

"Nothing's dull when your mind works the way his does," Chanterelle said.

"And which way would that be?" Shawn said. The phrase would be equally appropriate for the kind of mind that could understand string theory or one that couldn't figure out how to untie a knotted string.

"He delivers mail now, but that's just a temporary gig," Chanterelle said. "He can do almost anything he puts his mind to. As a little girl, I used to spend hours watching him as he taught himself whatever caught his interest, from electrical work to construction to hypnotism. He's going to do great things for this world. As soon as the time is right."

"Glad to hear he's not rushing anything," Shawn said.

"I used to urge him to take a better job. But he loves what he does. It's like he used to tell me: You don't have to be the king to help the country," she said.

"That's what I say all the time," Shawn said.

"Really?"

"No," Shawn said, but when that lovely smile turned to a

frown he was quick to amend his statement. "But it's a nice saying and I'm sure I would have said it if I'd ever thought of it."

He was heading toward the elevator when the thought hit him. Hit him so hard and fast he almost gasped for breath. This was the moment he lived for, when everything became clear and bright. Out of habit he turned to Gus, meaning to give him some cryptic comment that would let him have a hint that he had figured everything out without actually giving him any information, only to remember just before the words left his mouth that Gus wasn't next to him anymore.

That was going to change soon, though. It would have to. Gus was going to be a detective again or he was going to be dead. Shawn was going to make sure of that.

# Chapter Thirty-two

This was her punishment, self-imposed and self-administered. Detective Juliet O'Hara had spent every night for the last weeks canvassing the homeless population of Santa Barbara's main business street, trying to get even one of them to say he'd seen a pedestrian knocked down by a speeding car.

This was a nothing case, she knew. Walon O'Malley, the victim, hadn't been anyone important, just an older retiree who had stepped out of his adult living community late one night to grab a pack of smokes. His wife had died years ago, they'd never had any children, and if he'd had any friends in or outside of the home where he lived, none had materialized. He was apparently an unhappy old grouch, passing his final days waiting for the Reaper to swing his scythe.

The department would never let her waste this much time on the case; there was no question of that. So she didn't ask them and she didn't use their time. She put in a full day at work, clocked out, and then hit the streets. No one had to know until she got results, and even then she wouldn't put in for the overtime. This was her own personal mission. Her penance.

Even as she walked down State Street she knew she was

wasting her time. She had talked to every homeless person on the street who was ever going to talk to her. At first she tried to tell herself the reason she kept going back was so that the street people would get used to her presence there and finally begin to trust her. She even started bringing them the occasional cup of coffee or box of cookies.

Now most of them knew her by sight, and she was greeted as a friend almost every night. *Which isn't all bad,* she thought to herself as she set off for one more point-less patrol. Maybe one of them would see evidence in some other crime someday. At the very least she'd always have a place to go if she lost her job, her apartment, her savings, and her ability to function in society.

But as the hit-and-run receded further into the past, she knew it was increasingly unlikely she'd find anyone here who had seen it or who would remember if they had. *A couple more nights,* she thought, *and I can give this up for good.*

Of course she could have given up on it anytime in the past weeks. The case was technically still open, but no one in the department expected it to be solved, and realistically no one cared. There were bigger cases with more important victims. There were missing children and murdered wives and stolen life savings; there were people hurting whose pain could only be salved once the ones who had injured them were behind bars. There was no one pushing the chief to solve Walon O'Malley's killing; there were no anguished calls to members of the city council, no angry letters in the *Santa Barbara Times*. Even the homeless coalition people had moved on to more pressing issues. There was simply no reason for her to keep pursuing it.

And so she hadn't. Not when it might have mattered; not back when it was still fresh. It was almost certainly true that it wouldn't have made any difference then, either, but that wasn't the point.

She hadn't been focused on Walon O'Malley's case.

She'd put in the hours, but her heart and mind were still with Mandy Jansen. She'd been convinced that the former cheerleader had been murdered and could not let that go. So she put in her obligatory hours on the hit-and-run, but she was always aware she was only going through the motions.

Not that her focus on Mandy Jansen had done any good for that case. It was still sitting open on her desk, but she had given up any hopes of finding more evidence unless Mandy herself clawed her way out of the grave and explained exactly what had happened to her. The only reason O'Hara had left the case open was that there was no more pressure on her to do anything else with it. Mandy's mother had taken a serious turn for the worse in the last few weeks, and now she was in the hospital, slipping in and out of consciousness. O'Hara had been to visit Mrs. Jansen once, and the poor woman had thought she was Mandy and kept talking about how beautiful she looked in her cheerleader's outfit, as if she were still in high school.

At least she'd been spared the Macklin Tanner case. That was the department's big black eye and everyone who'd touched it walked away badly burned. The detectives originally assigned to the case, Bookins and Danner, had been sure Tanner was a walk-away, and closed the case early on despite Brenda Varda's entreaties for them to keep looking. After the clue O'Hara and Shawn had found in the game led them to the abandoned barn and the chopped-up remains of Tanner's car, the case had been reopened. Chief Vick had threatened to put O'Hara and Lassiter on it, but Mickey Bookins begged her to give him and his partner a chance to redeem themselves, and she consented.

Since then the detectives had come up with precisely nothing. They'd traced the ownership of the blacksmith workshop to some division of VirtuActive Software, as she and Shawn had done before, but the financial trails were so complicated and the holding companies so gnarled that even the forensic accountant the department hired from outside couldn't say with any certainty who had been responsible for the purchase, or even who might have known about it.

Bookins and Danner had spent a week investigating Brenda Varda, who was not only Tanner's colleague and ex-wife, but also his primary beneficiary. They had a theory that she killed him but did too good a job of hiding the body and then couldn't collect her inheritance. That was why she'd been nagging the police to find him; if he was believed to be alive the company would never be hers.

O'Hara never believed that for a second. She'd met Brenda Varda and seen that she was honestly worried about her ex-husband. And just to prove she hadn't lost all her instincts, she checked Varda's financials and confirmed that even with Tanner alive she had enough money to buy most of Central California. Bookins and Danner should have been able to figure that out, too, but they were blinded by the hope that the woman who'd made their professional lives hell would turn out to be a bad guy.

Now the case was toxic. Bookins and Danner had been assigned to desk duty pending review and the FBI was investigating what everyone finally had to admit was a kidnapping. O'Hara had originally hoped that the department would bring Shawn in as a consultant on this one, since it was his clue that had provided the only break in the case. But Shawn had disappeared shortly after they'd found the remains of the Impala. He hadn't shown up at the station, hinting around for the gig, and he hadn't even responded to any of her voice mails.

As she got closer to the doorway she could see that her regular was there as usual. Frank was what he called himself, and over the weeks he'd let a few bits of information about his previous life slip out. None of it was unique or surprising: the standard story of youthful promise disappointed, middle-aged disappointment drowned in drink or drugs, drink or drugs destroying careers and relationships, and finally a home on the streets. But he still managed a twinkle in his eye and he seemed to enjoy the semblance of a life he'd made for himself on the streets. And, as Frank liked to say, if you had to be homeless Santa Barbara was where you wanted to be.

Frank sat up in his sleeping bag as she got close. "Got a nip for old Frank, Detective?" he said with a gap-toothed smile.

"If by nip you mean a doughnut, help yourself," she said, holding out a box.

"Wasn't exactly what I had in mind," Frank said, helping himself to a glazed old-fashioned, "but it'll do. How's the patrolling going?"

Since the first time they met Frank had thought of O'Hara as an officer walking her beat. The first time he'd made this mistake she pointed out that Santa Barbara didn't have beat cops, and even if they did, she wasn't wearing a blue uniform. But apparently in his mind she was, down to the nightstick on the Sam Browne she hadn't worn since her earliest days as a rookie in Florida. Since he seemed to like the idea that the local force was out looking after people like him, she stopped arguing early on.

"Pretty quiet tonight," she said truthfully. "So I've got some time to look into that hit-and-run that happened here a few weeks back."

"Seem to recall somebody talking about that just yesterday," Frank said, screwing up his eyes as he struggled to squeeze the memory out of his brain.

O'Hara offered him the doughnut box again, and this time he plucked out a glazed jelly. "Do you remember who it was? Or what they said?" She tried to keep the excitement out of her voice.

He thought this over as he bit into the doughnut. He

didn't seem to notice the jelly squirting out over his gray-ing beard. "It was a woman," he said finally. "Yeah, a pretty blonde."

"Can you remember anything else about her?" O'Hara asked impatiently. This was the first lead she'd had in all the nights she'd spent down here.

"She was maybe around thirty," he said. "Like I said, real pretty. I couldn't figure out why such a nice girl would be asking so many questions about such a dismal subject."

"What kind of questions?" O'Hara said. Who was this woman and what could she have been looking for? Was somebody else trying to find the driver—or to see if anyone had spotted her leaving the scene?

"She kept asking if I'd seen anything or if I'd talked to anyone else who might have seen something," Frank said. "And then she gave me a cookie."

O'Hara felt any trace of excitement vanish. "That was me, Frank," she said.

He squinted up at her, unsure. "It was?"

"Oatmeal raisin, with a hint of cinnamon, right?" she said.

He broke into a broad smile at the memory. "Could have done without the walnut pieces, personally, but on the whole a damn fine cookie," he said. "That was you, wasn't it?"

She nodded wearily and held out the doughnut box again. At this rate she'd run out before she made it down one block, but she was having a hard time caring about that. She'd been down this street too many times, asked the same people the same questions and gotten the same non-answers over and over again. Maybe this was finally the sign she should stop.

"I don't suppose you've remembered anything else since last night," she said without any real hope.

"Not me," Frank said.

"I didn't think so," she said. "Thanks for trying, anyway."

"The other guy might have, though," Frank said.

"The other guy?" This time she wouldn't let herself get her hopes up. "Do I know him?"

"Don't think so." Frank chuckled to himself. "Takes off like a startled rat every time you come around here. I always tell him he should stick around, at least on brownie night. But he just takes off like a startled rat scurrying for the sewers."

"You've never mentioned this man before, have you?" she said.

"Haven't I?" Frank said. "I don't know."

"And you think he saw the hit-and-run?" she said, fighting against the excitement that was building inside her.

"Can't say for sure he did or didn't," Frank said. "All I know, when I mentioned there was a police officer asking questions about some car thing and paying for answers with treats, he ran away. And then whenever you started coming down this way he just took off like—"

"A startled rat, right," she said. "Can you describe him for me?"

"He's got beady little eyes, white whiskers sticking out this way from his face," Frank said, making sure she was writing all this down. "And don't forget about that long tail."

She slapped her notebook shut, disappointed. "Frank, that's a description of the startled rat, isn't it?"

He just chuckled in response.

"There is no other man, is there?"

"Oh, but there is," he said. "I was just having some fun with you. This guy's about six feet tall, maybe thirty years old. His hair's about your color, and he's got a month or two's worth of beard. Don't think he's been on the streets long."

"Why's that?" she said. This was sounding promising, the first possible break they'd had in the case yet.

"His face doesn't have these wrinkles you get from living out under the sun all day," Frank said, pointing to his own. "And his hands are too soft."

"Do you know where he is now?" O'Hara asked, scanning the street for any sight of the new man. This could be the break she'd been searching for. At the very least he was a witness. But the way he was so terrified of being asked about the accident suggested he might be much more.

"Hiding where any startled rat's going to hide," Frank said. "Someplace you're not going to be able to find him."

*That's what he thinks,* O'Hara said to herself. *There is nothing that's going to stop me from finding this guy if I have to talk the chief into putting every officer in the force on State Street every night for a week.*

"Do me a favor, Frank," she said. She wrote her name and cell phone number on the pink cardboard of the doughnut box and handed it to him. "When he comes back, give him these for me. Tell him to call me, day or night. There's a lot more than doughnuts waiting for him if he does."

# Chapter Thirty-three

Gus had been to the Santa Barbara Yacht Club only once in his life, on a sales call to a plastic surgeon who was concerned the Feds were spying on his office and didn't want to take a chance on asking for a kickback where they might be listening. He hadn't made a sale that day, since the only bribes he was authorized to offer came in the form of T-shirts and tote bags with pharmaceutical logos on them and the doctor was hoping for someone who would at least pick up his moorage fees at the club. But that unpleasantness aside, he'd had a wonderful time sitting out in the sun, watching the waves lap against the dock as the rich and beautiful sailed their multimillion-dollar boats out for the day.

When he saw on the invitation that Steve Ecclesine's memorial service was going to be held at the San Francisco Bay Yacht Club, he'd felt guilty for looking forward to it so much. He was remembering the Santa Barbara club and anticipating another lovely afternoon, sitting out on the water, knowing that he could safely zone out because nothing important was going to transpire. Which was the wrong way to approach what was, for all intents and purposes, a funeral. He should spend the ceremony contemplating the tragedy of a life cut short. Even if it was true that he hadn't particularly cared for Ecclesine, he should use the occasion to meditate on the nature and purpose of human existence. That was what you did at these things.

But as he walked down Market toward the waterfront, he couldn't focus on the meaning of life or any other deep issues. He felt the warm sun and the cool bay breeze against his skin, and no matter how many times he reminded himself this was a solemn occasion, he couldn't stop feeling like school had just let out early on the first day of summer.

Gus was feeling so good that he barely noticed where he was going until he had crossed the wide Embarcadero and found himself heading away from the new baseball stadium. The GPS on his phone told him he wanted to keep going past AT&T Park and continue for half a mile. But as he scanned the waterfront walk ahead of him all he saw were industrial piers and warehouses. The Santa Barbara Yacht Club had a rolling lawn in front of it; if the Bay Club had ever had any such thing it had already rolled into the water. More perplexing, given that his phone was telling him that he was within five hundred yards of the correct address, was the complete absence of anything that could be described as a yacht. There were a couple of vessels bobbing on the gray water, but even someone with as little nautical knowledge as Gus would have had a hard time describing these decaying houseboats as yachts.

By the time the GPS had beeped to announce his arrival at his destination, Gus was ready to toss the phone into the bay. Clearly it had sent him to the wrong place. He was standing outside a small, shabby, whitewashed wood building. It looked like the kind of bar that did most of its business selling vodka to people who couldn't afford to be seen drinking during office hours.

He was about to turn back in disgust when a burst of laughter from inside made him look up, and now he noticed the small sign over the door: SAN FRANCISCO BAY YACHT CLUB.

Of course, Gus realized too late, this was San Francisco. There probably were real yacht clubs for the superrich, but for every one of them there would be a dozen of these ironically named establishments. *Yacht clubs for the rest of us,* they'd call them.

Once again, Gus considered turning back to the office. His vision of a day spent playing hooky in the sun had vanished, and now he was facing the reality of spending who knew how many hours sitting in this dump, listening to people who'd never liked Ecclesine when he was alive talking about how much they were going to miss him.

But Gus knew that wasn't an option. He was an executive at Benson Pharmaceuticals. He was part of the company's public face. And if that meant putting on a mask every now and again to pretend he was something he wasn't—in this case, a grieving colleague—then that was part of being an adult. The days of skipping out on obligations simply because he felt like it were over.

He pushed open the door. The space inside was divided into two rooms, but the divider had been pushed aside to make one large space. A long bar ran across the back wall; just beside it was a table heaped with salads and cold meats and breads. In between the bar and Gus was a solid mass of people packed in like the New Year's Eve crowd in Times Square.

*Great,* Gus thought, *I'm the last one here*. And it did seem as if everybody else who worked in the San Francisco office of Benson Pharmaceuticals was already there. Gus spotted Ed Vollman standing by the bar, finishing up a martini as the bartender slipped him the next one in the sequence. Lena Hollis was leaning into a younger man, clearly her intended target for the evening. But he seemed to be interested only in a spot over her shoulder, and when

Gus followed his gaze he understood why. Chanterelle had apparently decided that her usual minidress wasn't formal enough for such an occasion and had managed to find one that was even shorter. She was leaning into her father, who was whispering something in her ear. Gus was wondering if he was suggesting she might want to put on a slightly longer dress. Probably not, since she smiled and nodded when he finished.

Gus scanned the crowd quickly, checking out the faces familiar and new. There was one face he was eager not to see, and his heart lightened greatly once he realized that Shawn wasn't there. It wasn't that Shawn couldn't be trusted to behave at funerals—although his picture was posted in the guard shacks at several of Santa Barbara's better cemeteries—so much as what his absence here would mean. Maybe Shawn had actually listened to him and decided to go back home, to go back to his own life and let Gus have his new one.

He'd miss Shawn. He already did. But seeing him at work was too hard. Whenever he was with his old friend, all he wanted was to fall back into old patterns, old rhythms. He wanted to run and play and joke and bicker, and these were not behaviors that were appreciated in the adult world he'd moved into. As soon as he had some vacation time saved up, or maybe even at the next three-day weekend, he'd head back south and he and Shawn could spend all the time they wanted just hanging out. But for now balancing his old self and his new made him dizzy, and he knew everything would be immeasurably easier if he didn't have to run into Shawn whenever he popped into the kitchen for a cup of coffee.

Gus took a step into the room and let the door swing shut behind him. It hit its frame with a bang, and every head swiveled to look at him. He gave them a little wave and moved away from the door.

The entire crowd turned to follow him.

This was weird. If this had been Gus' memorial service, it would have made perfect sense for the attendees to treat his appearance as worthy of note. But Gus was just one of hundreds of employees in the office. True, he was an executive, and one on the fast track at that, but all these people saw him at work every day and never found him quite so fascinating as this. He glanced over his shoulder to see if someone more interesting had slipped in behind him, but unless everyone in the company was desperate to buy the used sofa, bed, and dining table that were advertised on a flyer above the light switch, there was nothing that could garner such rapt attention.

Gus looked back at the crowd. They were still staring at him. He glanced at Chanterelle and her gaze was exactly what it was when she entered his late-afternoon daydreams, asking if there was any way he might be willing to come to her apartment that evening. That would have been gratifying, if he wasn't getting exactly the same look from everyone else in the company. It looked a lot less appealing on the unshaven face of Fat Walter from accounting.

What was going on here? Sure, he'd been a few minutes late, but he couldn't imagine that all his coworkers had decided he was some kind of superhero simply because he'd dared come last to a memorial service. He played with the idea that D-Bob had circulated a memo describing Gus' plan for tackling the issue of orphan drugs. Certainly some of them would have thought highly of him for doing that. But he noticed at least six people in the crowd who had fairly major profit sharing in their deals, and his plan was almost certain to depress the company's income for at least a couple of years. Even if they approved emotionally of what he was trying to do, there was no way they would be this thoroughly enamored of him.

Most likely this was some kind of prank, a practical joke played on whoever was last to show up. But that would have been in dubious taste if this had been a staff meeting.

They were at a memorial service. Who would hijack a funeral and turn it into an episode of *Punk'd*? Aside from the people who actually made the show, of course, and Gus was pretty sure they were all too busy counting their money to waste their time on him.

Before Gus could figure out what to do there was a stirring at the back of the room, and for the first time since he'd come into the building people turned away from him to watch D-Bob climbing up on the bar and clinking two beer mugs together for attention.

One by one the assembled employees of Benson Pharmaceuticals pulled their gazes away from Gus and toward their leader. He waited until he was sure he had everyone's attention before he started speaking.

"Steve Ecclesine," he said thoughtfully. "What can I say about him? That he was a dear friend? A great humanitarian? A warm and loving man who cared about this company less because of the money it could bring in than for all the good it could do in the world?"

Gus managed to catch his deep sigh before it escaped his throat. This was beginning to look like it was going to be a very long afternoon. He wished he'd brought some of his work with him.

"It's true. I could say all those things about Steve," D-Bob said. "And you know why that is? Because I own this company, so I can say whatever I want. But the flip side of that is that I don't have to say anything I don't want to. And I'm pretty sure that none of you want me to take up your time lying about a man many of you despised and most of the rest loathed."

Gus had been so busy going over a to-do list for the rest of the week that it took a moment for the words to sink in. Once they did, all thoughts of planning his agenda flew from his mind.

"This is not to say that there is no one here who thought of Steve as a friend and who will miss him," D-Bob said.

"That's one of the great truths of the human race—as my grandmother used to say, for every old sock, there is an old shoe. To those of you who are feeling the loss of a companion and a compatriot, I salute you."

D-Bob bent down to the bar and picked up one of the beer mugs, which had now been filled with brown, foamy ale. He hoisted it in the air, held it there for a moment of tribute, then lowered it to his mouth and drained half of it in one gulp.

"But for the rest of you, the ones who are here because you felt it was required, or because it was a day away from the office, who knew Steve as a bully and a brownnoser, or a sanctimonious hypocrite who talked about making the world a better place but really only cared about making a better place for himself, let me just say that I understand your feelings, and maybe even share them a little," he said.

A ripple of assent ran through the crowded room. Gus expected some angry protests, maybe even a walkout or two, but no one spoke or moved. Maybe D-Bob had been overly kind when he suggested there was anyone in the company who actually cared that Ecclesine was dead.

"Even for those of us who do not mourn the specific loss, the fact of Steve's death must come as a shock to us," D-Bob continued. "Because it can only remind us of our own mortality. It was the window in Ecclesine's office that happened to fall out, but who is to say that it couldn't have happened to any one of us lucky enough to have an office with a view? Or to any of our female employees that Steve might have called in for one of his standard sessions that never quite crossed over to the level of harassment?"

This time the murmur in the crowd sounded a little angrier, as several women seemed to realize for the first time that their experience was not unique.

"We are all going to die," D-Bob said. "And it is times like this that we must stop and face that fact. That is what this memorial service is for. We come not to bury Steve

Ecclesine, not to mourn him, but to let his death serve this great purpose for all of us. We are going to die, ladies and gentlemen, and in acknowledgment of that sad fact, let us seize this moment to vow that until that blackness descends we will live our lives to the fullest. Let us seize every day, embrace every moment, and cherish all that has been given to us. My employees, my friends, this memorial service is for you!"

He raised the beer glass again and saluted the crowd, who cheered loudly and raised their own glasses back to him.

"We love you, D-Bob!" Gus craned his neck to see who had yelled out, but it could have been almost anyone. The assembled employees were all gazing up at him with such affection he might have been their guru or their sainted father.

"I can tell you this death has affected me greatly," D-Bob said once the shouts and cheers had died down enough for him to be heard. "Following the other tragic losses at our company, it has forced me to deal with the fact that I won't be around forever to lead you."

There were shouts of "No!" and "We love you" from the audience. He smiled and shook them off.

"Don't worry. I've got no plans to go anywhere for a while," D-Bob said. "But even when I do it's not going to be a bad thing. A company needs new blood. And even though I like to think my ideas are every bit as fresh as they always have been, one man's mind can only work in certain ways. We need other voices to stay young. And that's why I've chosen this moment to announce a major change I'm going to be implementing at Benson Pharmaceuticals."

The mass intake of breath from the crowd nearly sucked the light fixtures from the ceiling. Even Gus found that he was holding a lungful of air and he had to force himself to exhale.

"For years our executive structure has been simple and

direct," D-Bob said. "There's me and then there's everyone else. Sure, some of you have bigger offices or fancier titles. You've probably noticed we've got a lot of vice presidents in our company. But in terms of decision making, it's been you wonderful people coming up with ideas, and me choosing whether or not to implement them. And it didn't matter if that idea came from a senior vice president or the parking attendant in the garage. A good idea is a good idea and a bad idea can spark a good one."

The crowd cheered at the sound of D-Bob's favorite saying, but Gus was still stuck on the earlier part of the paragraph. There was no difference in the company between a vice president and a secretary? Had all his progress been meaningless? Was he simply fooling himself when he believed that he'd really found a place where he was valued?

"Our love of ideas isn't going to change," D-Bob said. "No matter what else happens, I can assure you of that. But I've realized it's wrong for me to be the sole decision maker in this company. It's time for me to start sharing some of those responsibilities, so that if something does happen to me, the company can still go on the way we all envision it. And that's why I'm announcing that I am stepping aside as president of Benson Pharmaceuticals."

For a moment, the audience was completely still. Then it erupted into murmurs, and then shouts of "No!" and "We love you!" D-Bob let the noise build, and then held up his hands for quiet.

"Don't worry. I'm not leaving you," he said. "I will be keeping my position of CEO and chairman of the board. But I'm tired of talking only to myself. So at our company-wide annual retreat next week in Santa Barbara, I will be announcing that I am appointing one person to be president of Benson Pharmaceuticals."

The murmur now was mostly confusion and some concern. No one knew what this was going to do to their own jobs, or if they should even care.

Gus cared. He had fought his way to the level of executive vice president, which was the highest office in the company below D-Bob himself. Now he was going to be shoved down in the ranks, forced to answer to some corporate lackey. He'd had unbelievable freedom in his job, almost as much as he had with Psych. But he knew a little about corporate politics from his position in his old pharmaceuticals company and there was no way the new executive was not going to clamp down on everyone beneath him. Sure, he'd play the game, pretending to hold to D-Bob's ideals, but at the same time he'd be spending every waking hour consolidating his own power base. This had been a dream job for Gus, but there was no way that was going to last once the new guy took over.

Gus was so lost in thought he missed D-Bob's next few words.

"... a man who has shown not only wisdom but compassion," D-Bob was saying. "Who understands what our business needs, but also what the world needs from our business. I have come to admire and even love this man, and as you see what he brings us I know that you will love him as much as I do."

*Sure,* Gus thought. *Kiss up and kick down. That's what they'd be getting.* The new corporate hack would make sure to echo D-Bob whenever the boss was around, but as soon as his back was turned, out would come the knives. First order of business would be to start eliminating any potential competition. One by one he would find reasons why the vice presidents had to be demoted or transferred to Kabul or forced out of the company. There would be a crisis overseas that only this longtime executive could handle, an incipient scandal that could only be prevented by the immediate firing of a vice president who could be made to take the fall. Gus wondered which excuse the new president would use to get rid of him, but deep down he knew it didn't really matter.

"I'm sure that many of you already do love this man, as you've had the opportunity to get to know him over the past few weeks," D-Bob was saying. "For the rest of you, you've got something great to look forward to. As I said, the official announcement will be made at our company retreat, but I wanted you all to have a chance to get to know our new president before he takes on that title. Friends, employees, partners, I'd like to introduce you to the president of Benson Pharmaceuticals: Burton Guster!"

# Chapter Thirty-four

Gus must have walked back to the Benson building, but he had no memory of the trip. The past two hours had gone by in a blur. From the moment D-Bob had called his name Gus had barely been able to think or even to breathe. He'd been mobbed at the meeting and every one of Benson's employees had shown him the love that D-Bob had urged. They pressed food and drinks on him, they hit him with ideas for moving the company forward, or they just came up and hugged him.

But none of it meant as much to him as when Jerry Fellows came up and took his hand. "I'm so happy for you," he said. "Chanterelle and I both are."

And indeed Chanterelle did seem impressed. She was gazing at him with an intensity he'd never noticed before, at least not when her eyes were pointed in his direction.

"Thanks," Gus said, pulling his own gaze away from hers.

"No, I'm the one who should be thanking you," Jerry said. "Because you're in a position now where they'll have to listen to you. I've seen so many people take a stab at the orphan drugs issue, and they've all fallen short. But I know you won't. You'll make us all proud. Won't he, Chanterelle?"

She nodded, still staring at Gus with eyes that seemed to see straight through to his musculoskeletal system. "It's my da's passion, you know," she said. "And now you're in a position where you can do something about it."

Gus felt an odd tingling at the base of his skull and turned back to Fellows. But the elfin gentleman was still smiling happily at him. He was nothing but pleased. How could Gus ever have been so crazy as to think of him as a killer?

Finally the party had broken up around three. D-Bob had told everyone to take the rest of the day off, and the employees filtered out to enjoy the perfect afternoon. Gus had tried to find D-Bob to talk to him about this promotion, but when he was finally able to extricate himself from the mass of well-wishers the boss was nowhere to be seen.

Gus hadn't planned to go back to the office. Actually he hadn't planned anything at all. He felt incapable of thinking. He just wanted to experience this day, to feel the uncomplicated joy that this expression of confidence in him brought. Later, he knew, there would be nothing but complications. There would be the terror of facing the new job, the difficulties of dealing with the other executives who had been passed over in favor of him, the responsibilities that came with the presidency. But for now he wouldn't worry about any of it.

When Gus stepped back into his own office he was feeling so good he didn't even notice that the duct tape had been peeled from the carpet and the curtains were now open. If the window had fallen out, Gus felt he could have floated down to the ground and landed like a feather.

He also didn't notice that he had a visitor.

"I think they bought it," Shawn said, popping up from the couch he'd been lying on.

Until this moment Gus hadn't realized what was missing about this day. He'd had no one to share it with.

"You will not believe what happened today," Gus said,

delighted that the afternoon's deficiency had been addressed. And then he felt that delight dissolve into confusion as he realized what Shawn had said. "Bought what?"

"But you realize this was only the first step," Shawn said.

"The first step toward what?" Gus said. "What are you talking about?"

"I think you know," Shawn said.

"If I knew I wouldn't be asking," Gus said.

"I think you would," Shawn said.

"I've had enough of this," Gus said.

"I think you haven't," Shawn said.

"Stop that!" Gus shouted.

"I think you—" Shawn said, then broke off. "You're seriously interfering with my rhythm here, you know."

"And you're seriously interfering with my life," Gus said. "Here I was all excited to tell you my big news, and you start talking like Darth Vader."

"Vader, really?" Shawn said. "At least you mean the Darth Vader from the first films, right? Because if you're comparing my silk-smooth delivery to that whining little punk from the sequels, we are going to have serious issues."

"We can deal with your issues later," Gus said. "I want to know what was bought and who bought it and what you're doing here when you're supposed to be in Santa Barbara."

"Can I take the second part of that question first?" Shawn said.

"Whatever," Gus said.

"Okay," Shawn said. "What was the second part again?"

Gus tried to reconstruct his thought: Although he'd only uttered it seconds before, the sequence was completely jumbled in his mind. "Just tell me what you're talking about."

"They did," Shawn said.

"Who did what?"

"I remembered the second part of your question,"

Shawn said. "It was 'Who bought what?' and the answer is, 'They did.'"

"That's not an answer," Gus said. "It's not even a hint. It's completely meaningless. 'They' only has any value if there's a precedent in the sentence."

"There is a precedent," Shawn said. "That's you."

"What?"

"Precedent Gus," Shawn said. "Didn't Damp Blouse make the announcement?"

"That's *president*," Gus said, then broke off. "Wait a minute. How did you know about that?"

"What do you mean how did I know about that?"

"If you study my question I think you'll find that there's absolutely no ambiguity about what it means," Gus said tightly. "It is simple, straightforward, and without any possibility of misunderstanding. So the fact that you are stalling and refusing to answer it is telling me that you are up to something."

"We're up to something," Shawn corrected.

The thought occurred to Gus that what they were up to was 160 feet above the sidewalk, and if there were a way to get the window open he could count how long it took Shawn to hit the ground. But that brought images of the late Steve Ecclesine to mind. He took a step away from the window.

"How can *we* be up to anything?" Gus said. "*We* don't work together anymore. You're a private detective and I'm the incoming president of a multinational pharmaceuticals company."

"It's great, isn't it?" Shawn said. "No one's ever going to suspect a thing."

"Because there's nothing to suspect," Gus said.

"That's exactly the right tone of outrage," Shawn said. "Keep that up."

Keeping the level of outrage high enough was not going

to be Gus' problem. He took a deep breath and then another before he spoke again. "I need to know what's going on," he said. And then before Shawn could answer he started over. "I take that back. I know what's going on. What I need to know is what you think is going on."

"Nothing big," Shawn said. "Just your undercover assignment."

"My what?" Gus said. "We've already had this conversation. I'm not undercover."

"I realize that the phrase doesn't really do your mission justice," Shawn said. "The way you've burrowed into this company is really inspiring. All I can say is wow."

"Why?"

"Why what?" Shawn said. "Why wow?"

"Yes, fine," Gus said. "What are you talking about?"

"The way you were willing to walk away from your old life so completely," Shawn said. "Giving up your apartment, quitting your job, pretending that the Echo had been stolen so the company wouldn't insist on taking it back."

"What about the Echo?" Gus said.

"Just part of your master plan," Shawn said. "And what a plan it was. I've got to say, if I hadn't known better, there were times when you would have fooled even me."

"I wasn't trying to fool you," Gus said.

"Why would you?" Shawn said. "We've been in this together all along, haven't we?"

"We have not." Gus felt a familiar throbbing at his temples, the special kind of headache that only a particular type of conversation with Shawn could bring on. Although in the privacy of his own skull, he had to admit that now that he was feeling the pain he had missed it a little bit.

Shawn gave a chuckle of wry amusement, or what he imagined wry amusement would sound like if you were able to experience such a sensation without wearing a smoking jacket. "There is such a thing as going too far undercover," he said.

"There's also such a thing as getting to the point," Gus said.

"See, that's what I mean," Shawn said. "You sound exactly like a busy corporate executive when you say things like that. You don't have to keep up the cover when we're alone together. Although if we're together we can't really be alone. Which is either kind of a deep thought or something I read on a Hallmark card."

"Shawn!"

"Don't use my name," Shawn said. "They might be listening."

"Who might be listening?" Gus said, now hopelessly lost. "And why does it matter if I use your name?"

"Good point," Shawn said. "Since you're the one who's undercover here."

"You have to listen, Shawn," he said with as much patience as he could muster. "I am not now and have never been undercover here. I'm not on a secret mission. I didn't just pretend to leave Psych and take up a new life as an executive here. This is all true. This is all me."

Even as he was speaking the words the true meaning of them hit him with a force he hadn't anticipated. It wasn't the restatement of his current reality; he'd more than come to peace with the fact that he'd joined the grown-up world and left childish things behind. But why was he saying them? If Shawn was playing games, trying to get him to come back to Psych, that was okay. But Shawn seemed really convinced that he and Gus were still working together and that all the changes Gus had made in his life had been nothing more than a gambit to solve a case. And if that were true, then something was seriously wrong with Shawn.

Because Shawn had always been one of those miraculous people who had the ability to shape reality to his own desire. It was a matter of will over the world. Gus saw how things were and he adjusted. But Shawn simply refused to. If things weren't going the way he wanted them to, he acted as if they were. And more often than not, reality got tired of trying to force itself on him and twisted itself into whatever shape he had wanted.

But this wasn't one of those occasions. No matter how much Shawn wanted to be working on an investigation at Benson Pharmaceuticals with Gus, that simply wasn't the case. And if Shawn was unable to accept that he was leaving behind the territory of will and moving into psychosis.

Shawn, who had been pacing the carpet while Gus talked, now stopped. He peered closely at Gus. Took a step forward so their noses were nearly touching, then squinted. He stepped back. "I don't mean any disrespect," Shawn said, "but you're not this good an actor."

"I'm not acting," Gus said.

Shawn squinted at him again. "You've either gotten a lot better at this kind of thing, or you're really telling the truth," Shawn said.

"The only thing I've gotten better at in the last few months is being a corporate executive," Gus said. "Which is why D-Bob named me to be the president."

"You're really serious," Shawn said.

"Of course I am," Gus said. "I have been all along."

Shawn took a step back, then collapsed onto the couch. "Then I've made a terrible mistake."

Gus could see the reality crashing down all around his friend. He knew how this must feel. It had been the same for him in seventh grade when he finally realized that Tanja Traber hadn't been joking when she'd told him she was only going to hold hands with him after school until he finished writing her term paper on Ecuador, and that they really didn't have a future together unless at some point in the far future she decided to become a Latin American scholar and didn't feel like doing the work.

Gus sat next to Shawn on the couch. "It's okay, Shawn," he said. "This transition has been tough on everybody."

"No, I mean I made a terrible mistake," Shawn said again.

"You followed your heart," Gus said. "That's never a mistake." Except, of course, if that heart led you to Tanja Traber's birthday party, even though you hadn't been invited and she had specifically told you to stay away.

"You're really not listening very well," Shawn said. "When I said I made a terrible mistake, I didn't mean I misunderstood your motives. If you're not able to express yourself clearly, that's really your problem, not mine."

"How much clearer could I have been?" Gus said. "I did everything but ask the San Francisco Police Department to have you arrested if you crossed into the city."

"That would have been a start," Shawn said. "But we're not talking about you now. I'm the one who made the big mistake. And I don't know how to fix it."

"You could start by telling me what it was," Gus said.

"I made you president," Shawn said.

Gus jumped up off the couch, outrage propelling him like a jet pack. "You did no such thing," he said. "I earned this. Me. On my own. You had nothing to do with it."

"I wish that were true," Shawn said. "Then whatever happened next would be your fault instead of mine."

"You are just trying to steal my moment," Gus said. "You can't stand that I've been so successful here, so you're going to do whatever you can to make it seem less important."

"That's pretty good," Shawn said. "And I appreciate your effort to make me feel less guilty. But I did it, and I've got to take the blame."

"Okay, then," Gus said. "How did you do it?"

"I told Dem Bones that it was the only way to turn the auras from red to blue," Shawn said. "Or blue to red. Either way, it's amazing how easy it is to talk that man into anything," Shawn said. "Can you believe some clown proposed a new business plan for the company that would drive the

whole place into bankruptcy in about six weeks, and because it was delivered with passion, Dil Bert was ready to
sign off on it? You can thank me for talking him out of that
particular bit of madness."

This couldn't be happening. First Shawn had taken
credit for Gus' promotion; now he was proudly announcing
he'd just destroyed Gus' key policy initiative. Shawn had
to leave, to leave and never come back. It didn't matter if
Gus was going to be lonely without him. There was simply
no way that President Gus and Shawn could coexist in the
same universe, let alone the same company.

"First of all, I don't believe that," Gus said. "I realize
that in the world you've created in your mind, you have
complete control over everything and everyone, but this is
reality. This is business. And it's a lot bigger than whatever
scheme you've cooked up. Billions of dollars are at stake
and the man who owns this company isn't going to risk
them just because you tell him to."

"You think so?" Shawn said.

"It doesn't matter what I think. It's a fact," Gus said.

Shawn didn't respond directly. Instead he pulled out
his cell phone and hit two keys. Even from where he was
standing, Gus could hear the ringing on the other end of
the line, then a voice answering. "Are you at the Krab
Shack, D-Bob?" Shawn said, then waited for the answer to
come over the line. "I just wanted to warn you, I'm getting
a very negative vibe from one of the oysters there. I can't
tell you which one it is, so I'm going to warn you off eating
anything in a shell."

Shawn held the phone out to Gus in time for him to hear
D-Bob thanking Shawn profusely, then ordering a waiter
to remove something from his plate. Shawn disconnected
the call and put the phone back in his pocket.

"Okay, so you've convinced him you're some kind of
psychic dining guru," Gus said. "That doesn't mean he's

going to take your orders when it comes to running his company."

"No, but he does," Shawn said. "And you know it as well as I do."

Gus did. This was San Francisco, after all, where the question of what to have for dinner was considered far more crucial than little issues like life and death.

"Okay, fine," Gus said. "For the sake of argument, let's say it was your idea that D-Bob make me president. It's done. So thank you. What's the big deal?"

"The big deal is that the president thing was part of the plan when I thought we were working together undercover."

"Again, I say, what's the big deal?" Gus said.

Shawn looked at him gravely. "The big deal," he said, "is that the president is going to be killed next week."

# Chapter Thirty-five

Gus took a deep breath and held it in his lungs. He'd only been gone for a few months but he'd forgotten how sweet the Santa Barbara air tasted. Funny how you could spend an entire lifetime in one place and never notice how special it was until you went away.

It wasn't just the soft breeze from the ocean or the light scent of jasmine that made this air smell so good to Gus. There was another scent. The aroma of triumph.

Gus had left Santa Barbara as a failed detective, a part-time salesman, and an all-around loser. He'd spent close to thirty years on the earth and what had he accomplished in all that time? He'd lived in a crummy one-bedroom apartment, driven a company car that was barely one step above a skateboard, and spent all his free time hanging out with the one close friend he'd ever made, arguing about nonsense and doing nothing.

*Now look at me,* he thought as he walked along the edge of the cliff that marked the western edge of the fabulous Zahara Resort and Spa. In a few minutes he would be striding to the stage of the resort's conference center to be named president of the world's largest privately owned pharmaceuticals company. He had a penthouse apartment in San Francisco, thousands of devoted employees, and a mandate to make a real difference in the world. Best of all, he wasn't afraid anymore. Now that he knew where his future was taking him he could look back on his days at Psych without even a tremor. There was only one thing that could make his life even better, and that was the love of a beautiful, intelligent woman who would be his partner in the future.

And maybe he was about to have that, too.

He was still having a little trouble believing it. It had just happened a little more than an hour before. He'd put on his best suit for the occasion of his swearing-in, giving himself plenty of time to make sure the end of his tie just kissed the top of his belt buckle, a process that could take anywhere from one minute to an entire workday, when there had been a knock on the door.

"Come on in," he called, assuming it was the room-service waiter come to take his tray away. He'd been too nervous to do more than pick at the food, and normally he would have made sure he was out of the room before letting the tray go, so as not to have to answer questions about whether or not he'd liked his breakfast. But he'd left it out on his ocean-view balcony, and a couple of seagulls had eaten everything except the rind of the decorative melon slice.

The door didn't open, but the knock came again. Gus gave the Windsor knot in his tie a quick tug into position, then walked over and threw open the door.

It took Gus a moment to recognize the woman standing in his doorway, even though he'd seen her every workday since he started at Benson. It must have been because she was wearing a long coat that came down nearly to her ankles. Until this moment Gus had never known Chanterelle to cover any part of her body lower than midthigh.

"I'd like to talk to you for a moment, Gus," she said shyly. "That is, if you're not too busy for me."

"I can't imagine being too busy for you," Gus said.

At least those were the words his brain sent down to his tongue. What actually came out of his mouth sounded more like the distress call of a geriatric harp seal, but she didn't seem to notice.

"Maybe we could walk along the bluff," she said.

Gus glanced out the sliding door to his balcony and saw the palm trees on the terrace bent nearly double in the wind. If it blew any harder Gus would not have been surprised to see one or more of his elementary school teachers fly by, pedaling on bicycles with stolen dogs in the basket.

"I'd love to," he said, and if his tongue couldn't make his meaning clear, he managed to convey his intention by grabbing his room key, stepping into the hallway, and closing the door behind him.

"Not now," she said, looking around as if to see if she'd been followed. "Meet me there in twenty minutes."

Gus passed the requested time span watching an enormous seagull lift the breakfast plate in its beak, then smash it down on the table like a mussel it was trying to shell. Then, with two minutes to spare, he walked quickly through the broad avenues that wound around the resort's whitewashed haciendas. Finally he reached a metal gate, elegantly dusted with rust to show that it dated back to the area's agricultural roots even though it had only stood here since the resort's construction three years ago, and passed through onto a long meadow that ran to the cliffs overlooking the ocean.

Chanterelle was waiting for him on the edge of the cliff, staring out to sea as if waiting for her French soldier to come back and make an honest woman of her. As Gus came up to her she started, then gave him a warm smile.

"You came," she said.

"Of course," he said. "How could I refuse? I'd never get another phone message."

He winced at the stupidity of his joke. The most beautiful woman he'd ever met had asked him to meet her at this, the most romantic place in the world. And what did he do? Act like she was the receptionist and he the boss.

She didn't seem to notice. She took his hand and led him to the edge, although once he had felt the touch of her skin against his he had stopped noticing where he was going.

They stood together and watched the waves pounding against the rock far below. After a moment that Gus would happily have let stretch into eternity, Chanterelle dropped his hand and turned to face him.

"May I ask you a question?" she said shyly, her face cast down to the ground but her eyes peering up at him.

"Anything," Gus said.

"They say," she said, then broke off. "This is stupid. Maybe I should just go back. . . ."

"No, go ahead," he said. If the question was so personal or so difficult she was this hesitant to ask, there was no way he could let the moment slip away. "Anything at all."

She smiled up at him and his heart fluttered. *It's amazing how much prettier her face is when you're not distracted by those legs,* he thought.

"They say that you've got just about no experience in the pharmaceuticals field," she said. "That before you took this job you were some kind of security guard."

If anyone else had said this he would have bristled. From her it was an adorable misunderstanding. "I was a partner in a private-detective firm," he said. "But I was also a salesman for a local pharmaceuticals company."

"I see," she said. "But still it's such a huge thing, to go from that to being president of Benson. It's so impressive."

Gus was even happier he hadn't become defensive at her first question. "I guess I was in the right place at the right time," he said, assuming as much modesty as he could.

"It's got to be more than that," Chanterelle said. "It has to be."

"I hope I bring some fresh perspective to the position," Gus said.

"The very freshest, I'm sure," she said. She turned her eyes back to the ground as if she were searching the ground for a particular blade of grass.

"What's this all about?" Gus said. "I'm sure we didn't come all the way out here just so I could recite my resume."

"It doesn't seem like it would take all that much time, does it?" she said, then colored. "Oh, no, that came out all wrong."

"It's all right," Gus said. "Please go ahead."

"I wanted to talk to you about a job," she said. "Something in the executive suite."

Gus felt mixed feelings flood through him. On the one hand he had hoped that whatever it was she wanted to talk to him about would turn out to be a little more personal than a request for a job. On the other hand, though, if she were an executive, they'd be working closely together every day. She might even get the office next door to his, which wouldn't be too much of a problem since no one had moved into Ecclesine's former space. And a relationship between two highly placed executives would cause far fewer problems than one between the company president and its receptionist.

"It's funny you should mention that," Gus said. "One of my first priorities is to establish an executive-training program for our employees so that we can more easily promote from within when we spot someone with great potential. You'd make an ideal first participant."

None of that was entirely untrue. Although he had never thought of such a thing until this very moment, the trainee program had become Gus' first priority as soon as

Chanterelle suggested she might want an executive position. And since the entire program was designed to bring her into greater proximity to Gus, it would be hard to argue that she was anything but ideal for it.

Gus studied her closely, waiting to see if she'd give him one of those heartbreaking smiles. But she was still studying the greenery at her feet.

"I didn't mean for me," she said. "I meant for my da."

"For Jerry?" All of a sudden the concept of the executive-training program seemed so much less appealing.

"He knows so much about this company," she said. "And he's a hard worker. And everyone loves him."

"That's all true," Gus said. "Do you think he'd like to be, I don't know, manager of information services? Or does he know anything about computers? How about manager of physical information services?"

"I'm serious," she said. If she had stomped her foot on the grass before marching away, it wouldn't have felt out of place. "I mean a position of real authority and responsibility, not some fancy title to make him feel better about what he's been doing for decades."

"I thought he loved doing what he's been doing for decades," Gus said. Why was he arguing with her? Why didn't he just say he'd make Jerry an associate vice president? He had the power now, and what was the point of having power if you couldn't use it to reward those who had helped you on the way up? Especially when their daughter was staring up at you with eyes like the moon, and all you had to do was say yes and she'd fall into your arms. Not that she had made that an explicit part of the deal, but Gus was definitely getting that vibe.

He wanted to say yes. And that was what stopped him. Because he understood the instincts that were driving him toward that answer, and they weren't the instincts of a successful corporate chieftain. He might well decide later that the idea of promoting Jerry was an excellent one. But before he committed himself he wanted to do a little due diligence. The man had been with the company for decades and he'd never been promoted before. Maybe there was a reason for that.

"What do you expect him to do?" Chanterelle said. "Spend his days cursing and his nights weeping? He's a proud man, but fiercely ambitious. Sure, he's got a menial job title, but he's passionate about changing the world. He's never going to ask for what he wants, but that doesn't mean he doesn't want it as much as the next man."

Passionate about changing the world. Gus let those words rattle through his head until they bumped up against the thoughts he'd buried there.

"Just how ambitious is he?" Gus asked tentatively. "I mean, how far would he go to get what he needs?"

"I'm not the right person to ask," Chanterelle said.

"If not you, then who?"

"Bertie Murphy, Casey Reilly, and Daniel Flynn," she said.

"Who are they?"

"They're nobody," she said. "Not anymore. Just three more forgotten men in Shankill Rest Garden."

"Rest Garden," Gus said hopefully. "So they're friends of his in an old folks' home?"

"Very old folks," Chanterelle said with a hint of a smile. "Some of them hundreds of years, all buried together."

"Buried?" Gus said. "I assume they were someone before they were buried."

"Provos," she said gravely.

"What, they rode on train cars?" Gus was completely lost now.

"Not hobos, *Provos*," she snapped, and for a second Gus could have sworn he saw a glint of contempt in those fabulous eyes. "Members of the Provisional IRA."

Now Gus was completely lost. "I've got a 401(k) through

the company," he said. "I didn't know they had other retirement plans."

"In his youth my father was a member of the *Irish Republican Army*," she said, enunciating the last three words carefully enough that Gus would have to realize what the initials referred to. "He and his three mates, Bertie, Casey, and Daniel. In 1969, the year they all turned nineteen, came the rupture."

Gus had an image of all the good people in Ireland being called up to heaven while a handful of others were left behind to do battle with the devil. But that one glint of contempt in Chanterelle's eyes was enough to keep him from asking if this was what she'd meant until she'd given a few more details.

"Ah, yes, the rupture," he said knowingly. "I remember it well. Or I would if I had been born yet."

"Even as a boy, my da believed that the only way to resolve the troubles was through peaceful negotiations," Chanterelle said, eyeing him as if he were about to say something stupid. "But his mates lacked his patience. They bought into the anger of the Provos. They wanted to be part of the violent revolution everyone thought was about to come. But they were just boys. There was no way the Provos would take them on unless they could prove themselves."

Gus started to feel a sense of dread in the pit of his stomach, although he wasn't sure yet exactly why. "So how would you go about proving yourself back then?" he said as casually as he could, as if he thought the tenor of the answer would be determined by his tone of voice.

"How do you ever prove yourself?" Chanterelle said. "If you want to be a thief, you steal something. If you want to be an arsonist, you burn something down. And if you want to be a killer . . ."

"Who did they kill?"

"Simple murder wasn't enough to get them into the Provos," she said. "These people were terrorists. They aimed to use violence to coerce the English into realizing that the price for staying in Ireland was too high for the rewards. So the acts they committed had to be terrible indeed. And if my da's three friends wanted to impress the Provos, whatever they did had to be at least as bad as anything they might have done themselves."

Gus didn't want to hear any more. But he couldn't turn away yet. "What did they do?"

"It's what they planned to do that's important," Chanterelle said. "There was a Protestant nursery school they had to walk past every day. They decided they were going to kill all the children."

Gus was shocked beyond words. "And Jerry knew about this?"

"They told him," she said. "They were so proud of their plan. They wanted him to join them. They could only get their hands on one gun, but they could make as many gasoline bombs as they needed, and Bertie worked for a gardening service, so he could get plenty of machetes for the close work."

"He didn't," Gus said. No matter what suspicions he might have had about the man, there was no way he could have been capable of an atrocity like this.

"How could you even imagine such a thing?" Chanterelle said. "Of course he didn't. He believed in a peaceful future. He believed that the world could be a better place— but only if people were willing to put aside their differences and work together. Massacring a bunch of innocent schoolchildren because their parents happened to belong to the wrong church would hardly advance that goal."

"So, what happened?" Gus said, relieved to hear that much at least.

"I don't know, exactly." Chanterelle turned back to stare out to sea.

"You don't know?" Gus said.

"Not exactly," she said, her voice muffled by the wind blowing off the ocean.

"They didn't kill all the children, did they?"

"I told you, Bertie Murphy, Casey Reilly, and Daniel Flynn all lie in Shankill Rest Garden, and have been there for more than forty years now," she said.

Gus was about to ask another question when the meaning of her words hit him. "He killed them? His own friends?"

"How many times do I have to say this?" she said. "I don't know what happened, exactly. All I do know is that the massacre of the children never happened, my father's three mates lie in Shankill, and Jerry Fellows emigrated to the United States in 1970, where he got a job in the mail room of Benson Pharmaceuticals, a job he's held to this very day. And every day in that job he has done his best to make the world a better place. Is it to atone for what he did in his youth? I don't know and he never talks about it. I only learned this much when he was in the hospital for an appendectomy and he talked when he was coming out of the anesthesia. But I do know he has spent the rest of his life trying to make sure that he leaves the world a better place than he found it. And you would deprive him of the chance to do that?"

Gus ordered his mind not to work. He did not want it to move in the direction it was heading. That wasn't how titans of industry thought. It was strictly the province of detectives. It was murders and criminals and plots and all those things he had walked away from when he'd left Psych. It was the kind of thing that didn't happen in the real world, to real people.

Which meant that this was all some kind of terrible coincidence. Just because Jerry Fellows had come from a violent background didn't mean that he had grown up to be a serial killer. It was possible in the real world to be frustrated with the circumstances of your life without going on a murder spree to even things up.

*This must just be jitters,* Gus thought. He was about to be officially named president of Benson Pharmaceuticals, and the impending responsibility was freaking him out. That was all this was. It was all it could be.

Because if he was making the wrong choice here, if Jerry was everything his detective experience was telling him he was, then Gus would be dead before the morning was over.

# Chapter Thirty-six

This was the greatest moment of Gus' life. He was seated on a raised dais looking out over the resort's vast meeting room, and wherever his eyes fell he saw a member of the Benson Pharmaceuticals family staring up at him with love. Maybe even with a touch of awe.

There in the front row were Ed Vollman and Lena Hollis, who had, judging by the looks on their faces, decided that he was their natural leader. In the back he spotted Arnold from accounting, Lindsey from human resources and Dennis from facilities, all of whom looked like they were thinking back happily on the small ways they had helped him on his road to the top. And there was Jerry Fellows, beaming supportively up at him, his beautiful daughter next to him. What a ludicrous fantasy it was to think Jerry was some kind of terrorist out to take him down, almost as ridiculous as his certainty that Chanterelle had originally asked him out on the cliffs to declare her love. Jerry was the mail guy, she was the beautiful receptionist everyone dreamed about, and that was all they were.

Gus shifted his gaze and saw Shawn smiling up at him from the audience. That made him happier than the rest of it put together. His best friend was here to see him accept the job of a lifetime. For once Gus was glad that Shawn had refused to do what he'd asked him to. This ceremony would have had so much less meaning if Shawn had stayed away from the company. Instead he was one of the flock, who were all waiting to be led by their new shepherd.

And who could blame them? As Gus listened to D-Bob talk about his bold ideas and bright vision, he wished he could look up at himself with that same mixture of love and awe.

"And so," D-Bob said, turning briefly to shoot a warm grin back at him, "I present to you all the new president of Benson Pharmaceuticals, Burton Guster!"

Gus felt himself lifted by the wave of applause and transported to the rostrum. He stood there mutely as his new followers cheered for him.

He had done it. He was the president. All he had to do now was make a short speech, bang the gavel that sat on a stand before him, and his new life would be complete.

His fingers clutched the gavel. "Friends, colleagues," he started. They all looked up at him expectantly.

He had a speech all ready. He'd rehearsed it a dozen times. But now it was gone, leaving only nonsense phrases from old television commercials behind in his brain. He considered starting to talk anyway, hoping that the speech would come back to him, but he couldn't take the risk that when he opened his mouth the only thing that came out would be "Plop, plop, fizz, fizz, oh, what a relief it is."

"My friends and colleagues," he started again, then forced his mouth shut before it could form the words "atsa spicy meatball."

What was wrong with him? Why couldn't he say the words everyone was waiting for?

It wasn't because of what Shawn had told him the last time they'd spoken. He wasn't afraid that he was going to be murdered as soon as he banged the gavel.

Was he?

Gus did a quick inventory of his vital signs. Heart steady, breathing slow and regular, skin cool and dry. If he was terrified, his body was doing one hell of a job of hiding it.

He reached for the gavel again, but his fingers refused to close around it. What was happening to him? Why couldn't he perform this one small act?

He looked out at the audience. They looked back with a mixture of confusion and impatience. Behind him, D-Bob was fidgeting in his seat. He was losing his fans.

Except for Shawn. He was beaming and nodding in encouragement. Did he want Gus to take this job?

Gus felt a stab of betrayal. Shawn wasn't supposed to encourage him to take this job. Shawn was supposed to be fighting against it. That was his duty—to drag Gus back to preadolescence whenever he started to act too much like a grown-up. Sure, Gus had ordered him to stop, but when had Shawn ever done anything he didn't want to do?

That was the difference between Shawn and all the other people in the room. *Look at them out there, gaping up at me like sheep,* he thought. *There's only one reason they're looking at me like that—because their boss told them to.*

And he wouldn't be any different. Sure, he would be the president. But once Gus took this job he would spend the rest of his life doing what was expected of him. That was what it meant to live in the grown-up world. And all the luxuries that came with it, the high-rise apartment and the fancy restaurants and the big office, they were all just markers that could be taken away if Gus didn't behave.

Shawn's world didn't work like that. He did whatever he wanted and didn't care who approved. That was why some people hated him—because he didn't care. He was free.

Gus had been free, too. He'd thought he left that life behind because he was ready for something real. But he'd been lying to himself. What they'd had *was* real. They made their own world and lived in it.

Gus had made a serious mistake with Professor Kitteredge and the consequences had been ugly. He'd tried to tell himself he was atoning for that by moving into the adult world. But really he was just running away. Running away from a life where he had complete freedom and, in consequence, complete responsibility for his actions, to one where he would do what he was told and be relieved of blame. He hadn't been growing up. He was hiding.

Gus looked out at the sheep in front of him and now he was afraid. But he wasn't scared that Jerry Fellows was a serial killer and a terrorist who would kill him the moment he banged that gavel.

He was afraid Jerry wasn't.

Because if Jerry was a murderer, then everything Gus used to know was still true. He was a detective. An outsider. Free.

But if Jerry was just a kindly old mailman, then the world he realized he needed to get back to didn't exist anymore.

Gus' fingers closed around the gavel. He cleared his throat.

"Friends and colleagues," he said. "I know you're all waiting for me to say something."

He looked out over the crowd. This was the moment.

"But first, my friend Shawn would like to say a few words."

# Chapter Thirty-seven

Shawn bounded onto the stage as a confused murmur went through the crowd. Gus could feel D-Bob's eyes boring into his back, but he refused to turn around. He stepped out of Shawn's way and let him take the rostrum.

"I'm sure you're all wondering why I called you here today," Shawn said.

A confused murmur confirmed that the audience was wondering about something, probably whether it was the world that had gone insane or just Gus.

"This is highly inappropriate," D-Bob hissed from behind them.

"I said, I'm sure you're all wondering why I called you here today," Shawn said, raising his arms as if expecting some kind of mass audience response.

The crowd stared at him blankly.

"Technically, I'm the one who called them here today," D-Bob said. "And they all know why they're here. It's our annual employee retreat."

Shawn barely spared a glance back at him.

Gus stepped up next to Shawn, relishing the moment. Over the years, Lassiter had suggested that Shawn and Gus take what he called their "show" on the road. He meant it as a put-down, accusing them of cheap theatrics. But up here on the stage he embraced the insult. Shawn was going to give one of his great performances and Gus felt thrilled to be a part of it.

"Say, Shawn," he said brightly. "Why have you called us all here today?"

"To accept," he said simply.

What the hell did that mean? Gus had known what the next line was supposed to be: *to expose a murderer*. The audience would gasp in collective shock, Shawn would pretend to communicate with the spirits, and quick as boy howdy, Jerry Fellows would fall to his knees confessing his crimes.

Gus took a surreptitious step closer to Shawn and whispered out of the corner of his mouth. "What are you doing?"

"What does it look like I'm doing?"

"I don't have a clue."

"Exactly!" Shawn whispered, then grabbed the microphone from its stand. "My friends, we've got trouble at Benson Pharmaceuticals," he bellowed into the mike. "Trouble with a capital T and that rhymes with P and that stands for . . ."

He held the microphone out to the audience for their collective response. Unfortunately the mike was not sufficiently sensitive to pick up the sound of facial muscles contorting into expressions of confusion.

Finally a voice came from behind them. "Would that be pills?" D-Bob ventured.

"Pills!" Shawn bellowed.

Gus sidled closer to Shawn. "Aren't you supposed to be exposing a killer here?"

"You told me there was no killer," Shawn whispered back. "And that the corporate lifestyle is the only way to go. Who am I to argue with someone of your great wisdom?"

This couldn't be happening. Gus had finally realized

what he wanted out of life and Shawn was hurling it back in his face. He wanted to grab Shawn, to shove him off the stage and out the door. Instead he made a grab for the microphone.

"Let's have a big hand for our former head of security, Shawn Spencer," Gus shouted into the mike before Shawn pulled it away again.

"Yes, pills," Shawn said over the smattering of confused applause. "How long have we been delivering medication through this antiquated form? The basic pill hasn't changed in over a thousand years, and I say it's time to step into the future!"

Shawn held out the microphone to catch the cheers from the crowd, and then yanked it back when it became clear there weren't going to be any.

"Why don't we have computers in pills yet?" Shawn said. "We've got computers in everything else. Why are our phones smart while our pills are still dumb?"

"You're the one who's dumb!" someone yelled from the crowd, and a murmur of assent rippled through the room.

D-Bob rose from his stool and raised his hands for quiet. "The man has ideas," D-Bob said. "Let's hear him out."

Gus stared at his boss, horrified. Shawn didn't have ideas. He was spouting gibberish. How could D-Bob take him seriously?

"Thanks, D," Shawn said. "You may think it's too futuristic to contemplate a pill you can program to fight whatever disease you send it after. In fact, this is based on a technology that's almost fifty years old, one that was hugely promising but was squashed by the traditional pill makers."

To Gus' astonishment, D-Bob looked fascinated. "Tell us about that," D-Bob said.

"You have to understand, they didn't have computers in 1966, so their methods might sound a little primitive today," Shawn said.

"Of course they had comp—" Gus started, but D-Bob shushed him furiously.

"Let the man speak!" D-Bob said.

"But the principle is the same," Shawn said. "The traditional way of doing things is to take one pill that can tackle a particular kind of sickness—headache, stomachache, whatever. But in this other method the scientists sent a tiny spaceship filled with eenie-weenie doctors into the patient's bloodstream. They weren't dumb pills mindlessly attacking the one symptom they were made for. These valiant doctors could look for problems and take care of whatever they found."

"That's *Fantastic Voyage*," Gus sputtered.

"Yes, it is fantastic," D-Bob said. "What a mind this man has."

"It's a movie!"

"There was one trouble with this new technology," Shawn said. "It was really hard to find scientists small enough to fit into a patient's bloodstream. But with today's computer technology, we don't have to worry about that. We should devote this entire company's resources to inventing a machine that will finally make scientists tiny! And that look like Raquel Welch!"

The crowd stared up at him, stunned. But D-Bob was back on his feet, clapping wildly. "Isn't this man incredible?" he shouted to his employees. "Listen to all his ideas! You know, I've never done anything like this before, but I don't think I have a choice."

Gus felt his stomach drop to the floor. He couldn't be sure what was going to happen next, but he knew it wasn't going to be good.

"We were so incredibly lucky that we found Burton Guster to be our new president," D-Bob said. "And now we're even more fortunate. Because I am appointing Shawn Spencer to be Gus' copresident!"

D-Bob thrust his arms in the air for applause. For a long

moment, the silence was so great Gus began to wonder if he'd gone deaf. And then in the front row, a couple of exec-utives started to clap. Slowly the applause rippled through the auditorium as one by one the employees of Benson Pharmaceuticals grabbed for this first chance to suck up to their new boss.

Gus took advantage of the noise to move close enough to Shawn to whisper in his ear. "What's this all about?"

"It's about Psych," Shawn said.

"I left Psych," Gus said.

"You left a detective agency," Shawn said. "You can never leave Psych. Because Psych is you and me. That's why I thought you'd taken this gig as an undercover as-signment. But now I realize you're serious about the whole corporate thing. So Psych is moving to the boardroom."

Gus stared at him. "You'd do that? Seriously?"

"I think we've already seen how seriously I'm going to take it," Shawn said. "But I'm doing it if it's what you really want."

Gus studied Shawn for several seconds, looking for any sign that he wasn't completely sincere. Then he stepped to the front of the stage and raised his hands for quiet. The applause died down quickly.

"I want to thank you all for the warm reception you've given my new copresident," Gus said. "But before we go any further, I think D-Bob should explain what's really been going on the last couple of months." He beckoned D-Bob to join him at the front of the stage.

"What's really been going on," D-Bob said, stretching the syllables out as long as he could while he tried to figure out what he was supposed to say.

"That you never really hired me as an executive," Gus said. "That I am actually a detective working undercover to solve the murders of Sam Masterson, Jim Macoby, Mandy Jansen, and Steve Ecclesine. Although Ecclesine was still alive when we were hired."

"We're throwing that one in for free," Shawn said.

There was a shocked gasp from most of the crowd. But in front, where the other executives sat, there was only a contented murmur and a few exclamations of "that explains it!"

"Umm, right, exactly," D-Bob said. "The man you've known all this time as Burton 'Gus' Guster is actually . . ." He leaned in to whisper to Gus. "What's your name again?"

"Burton Guster," Gus said into the microphone. "But you can all call me Gus. And I'm sure you all know my partner Shawn Spencer, Santa Barbara's premier psychic detective."

Shawn bounded to the front of the stage as if the audience had erupted into cheers instead of another stunned silence. "My friends, we've got trouble right here at Benson Pharmaceuticals," he shouted. "Trouble with a capital M and that rhymes with . . . Well, actually it doesn't rhyme with anything useful right now, but if I come up with something I'll get right back to you."

Jerry Fellowes stood up in the crowd. "Is this really true, Gus?" he said. "That you never had any intention of helping with orphan drugs?"

Gus looked down at the stage, suddenly ashamed of the work he was leaving unfinished. Chanterelle put a comforting arm around her father's shoulder.

"Who cares about the orphan drugs?" Lena Hollis shouted. "What's this about murders?"

"And what's with Santa Barbara's premier psychic detective?" Vollman said. "Did we already run through all the phonies in San Francisco?"

"Other people are much more qualified than I am to take on the orphan drug problem," Gus said. "Like you, Jerry. It's time for you to step up."

"It's funny you should mention that," Shawn said. "Well, not funny in the ha-ha way so much as the terrible, awful, bloody murderous way."

"You can't say my da had anything to do with those deaths!" Chanterelle would have leaped onto the stage if Jerry didn't hold her back in her seat. "He's not a killer."

Shawn cocked his ear heavenward, then turned back to face her. "It's kind of hard to understand, what with the accents coming from the great beyond, but I'm hearing a trio of Irish voices that disagree with you on that count."

Jerry's face flushed. "That was a long time ago," he said. "I'm not that man anymore."

"But you could be," Shawn said. "With the proper encouragement."

"No," Jerry said.

"Just think about it for a minute," Shawn said. "Let's say you were working with one executive who really seemed excited about the whole thing. But every time he was supposed to push the issue with D-Bob, he canceled. And then he got himself roasted. Wouldn't that make you step up?"

"No," Jerry said. "I just deliver the mail."

"Well, what if a new executive managed to talk D-Bob into actually addressing the issue, but Steve Ecclesine was trying to undercut him until someone sabotaged his window and he plunged to his death," Shawn said. "Would that make you step up?"

"Why would it?" Jerry said.

"So I guess Mandy's whole hanging herself in her cheerleader suit after breaking her promise to help didn't motivate you either," Shawn said.

"It broke my heart, is what it did," Jerry said.

"That's pretty much the way I saw it," Shawn said. "My only question is why your daughter couldn't figure that out."

Chanterelle jumped to her feet. "You're crazy," she shouted. "These were all accidents. Why are we listening to this lunatic?"

"Couple of reasons," Gus said. "First, because until I formally submit my resignation, I'm still the president of the company."

"Copresident," Shawn said.

"Copresident," Gus agreed.

"And because we had some friends of ours show your picture around Santa Barbara," Shawn said. "And you were identified several times as the one woman anyone saw Mandy Jansen with in the days before her death."

Gus looked at Shawn, surprised. How long had he known?

"I may have visited Mandy," Chanterelle said.

"Where you used your hypnotism skills," Shawn said. "Although I suspect you might have supplemented your natural powers with some of Benson's finest mood-altering substances. I understand some of them disappear from the bloodstream almost immediately."

"Then there'd be no evidence, would there?" Chanterelle said.

"I suppose even if we had your picture circulated around a certain High Sierra ski resort and you were identified as Sam Masterson's date that day, that wouldn't be evidence, either," Shawn said.

"Did you do that?" Gus said.

"Wouldn't matter if he did," Chanterelle said. "No crime against skiing."

"Unless you happened to give your ski partner a little nudge as he approached a tree at fifty miles per hour," Gus said.

"If two people are skiing together, and one accidentally bumps into the other, that's nothing more than a tragic accident," Chanterelle said.

D-Bob glared down at her. "Even if it's not a crime, this could be a very serious breach of company ethics," he said.

"Then I quit," Chanterelle said.

"Don't be so hasty," D-Bob said. "You are still a valued member of the team."

Gus glared at him. "You are really the worst executive in history," he said.

"All these people your father put his faith in, and they all let him down," Shawn said. "Or they were going to let him down. You thought if you got them out of the way, Jerry would finally have to step up and become the man you needed him to be."

"Whatever," Chanterelle said.

"But if there was a new president and he promised Jerry he'd solve the orphan drugs problem, you knew that would be the end of it," Shawn said. "Because this new president was an idiot who would always say the right thing but never get anything done. And your father would grow old and die, never seeing his dream realized."

"An idiot?" Gus said.

"Go with me here," Shawn said, then turned back to Chanterelle. "Unless, of course, he was so overwhelmed by the position that he killed himself the night of the swearing-in ceremony."

"Wouldn't that be a tragedy?" Chanterelle said.

"It does seem like the kind of thing we'd like to avoid," Shawn said. "So I asked my friends to stop by your room on their way here."

At the back of the room, the doors flew open and six uniformed police officers marched in. Detective Juliet O'Hara followed, holding up a plastic bag that held a piece of hotel stationery.

"Did you find it, Jules?" Shawn said.

"On her desk," O'Hara said. "A suicide note written by Burton Guster." She held up another Baggie, this containing a large plastic bottle. "And enough Benson-brand painkillers to make sure his suicide was successful."

"You were going to kill me?" Gus said.

"It would be more oxygen for the rest of the planet," Chanterelle said.

O'Hara motioned to one of the officers, who went over to Chanterelle and cuffed her hands behind her back.

Jerry looked at her mournfully. "This can't be true," he said. "You can't have done this."

"It was the only way." She was near tears. "You knew it when you killed those three boys to stop the greater evil."

"I've been tortured by that all my life," he said gently. "I don't want the same for you."

"It was your moment of greatness," she said, the tears now flowing freely down her cheek. "When you had the chance to make a real difference in the world and you took it."

"I killed my friends," Jerry said.

"Yes, you did—you yourself," Chanterelle said. "You didn't wait around hoping that someone else was going to act in your place. You saw the need and you did what had to be done."

"At too great a cost," Jerry said.

"At the right cost," Chanterelle said. "You were born to make a difference in this world. You always said so. But you trusted in other people to ensure your legacy. I couldn't let you do that."

"Really?" Shawn said. "All this time you wanted your father to act, so you did what you thought he'd do if he cared enough? I think I see a flaw in that logic."

Jerry took his daughter by the shoulders. "I stayed in this job because it's all I wanted from my life," he said. "I loved my coworkers, even the ones who were weaker than they wanted to be. Did you really kill poor Mandy?"

"She said she was a player, but she was really just a cheerleader," Chanterelle said. "So once she was properly suggestible I had her put on that old uniform to tell the world."

"Just a cheerleader?" O'Hara said. "You mean, like the one who's arresting you for murder?"

She signaled the officer, who led Chanterelle out of the room.

Jerry Fellowes collapsed in his chair and sank his head in his hands. Gus wanted to go to him, but within seconds the old mailman was surrounded by his colleagues, who gathered around to offer him support.

Shawn clapped Gus on the back. "See?" he said. "That's much more fun than a board meeting."

"Except for the part where we destroyed poor Jerry's life," Gus said.

"Because he would be so much happier if his daughter kept on killing people," Shawn said. "Really?"

Gus felt a weight lifting off his shoulders. "I guess it really isn't all about us, is it?" he said.

"Only the good parts," Shawn said.

They were walking toward the exit when a thought hit Gus. "You knew Chanterelle was the killer all along?"

"I don't know that I'd say all along . . ."

"But you knew when you offered to join me as an executive," Gus said. "You knew she was going to murder me."

"It was kind of predictable," Shawn said.

"And if I hadn't chosen to expose the killer here, what were you going to do about it?"

"Take your office," Shawn said. "Now let's go order room service before D-Bob closes our account here."

# Chapter Thirty-eight

"Why do we have to wear these ridiculous getups?" Lassiter said, shrugging into the long, black leather duster. "Blue is the only uniform I've ever wanted."

Shawn and Gus stood with Lassiter and O'Hara outside the mall, each putting on one of the dusters Shawn had borrowed from a local leather-goods shop in exchange for help catching a frequent shoplifter.

"I've always thought you'd look better in orange, Lassie," Shawn said. "But if you want to come along, this is tonight's dress code."

"I don't want to come along," Lassiter said. "How many times do I have to say this whole thing is stupid?"

Gus didn't have an answer for him, although he guessed Lassie had mentioned this at least a dozen times already.

The first had been at the police station, where Shawn and Gus were debriefing the detectives on the undercover operation they'd just completed at Benson Pharmaceuticals.

"I have to say, I'm really impressed," O'Hara said. "I saw Gus in San Francisco a couple of times and I was completely convinced he was for real."

"Not me," Lassiter growled.

"The trick is to convince yourself first," Gus said. "There were actually times when I forgot I wasn't really starting a new life as a corporate chieftain."

"And you were onto Chanterelle all along?" O'Hara said.

Shawn and Gus exchanged a look. "There was a pool of suspects at first," Gus said. "It was Shawn who finally put it all together."

"Only after Gus laid out the entire case," Shawn said. "Although with a slightly different solution."

"It was a joint effort," Gus said.

"Because that's the way we roll," Shawn said.

"So who was your client?" Lassiter said, finishing up his report.

Gus froze. He'd almost convinced himself that he really had been undercover all the time he was at Benson, but the mention of a client reminded him how this had all really started.

"It was Jules, of course," Shawn said. "She asked for help with Mandy Jansen's murder."

"I just meant a consultation," O'Hara said. "I never dreamed you'd go that far."

"No one ever does," Shawn said. "And now there's a little matter of the favor you were going to do in return."

Which was how the four of them ended up on State Street in the middle of the night, wearing dusters.

"I can't believe I'm actually doing this," Lassiter said.

Shawn slapped a rifle into his hands. "You've got to try," he said. "Suspension of disbelief is what it's all about. We ready?"

Gus looked around. Each of them was armed with a rifle. "Let's go," he said.

"Yeah, why not?" O'Hara said.

They moved together as one, stalking down the deserted street.

"That one's mine," Shawn said, pointing into a doorway

at a sleeping homeless man. He raised his gun and fired. The man's chest erupted in red.

"I got one!" Gus said, leveling his rifle at a skinny man in a camo jacket, running across the street. He pulled the trigger and the man fell, a red blotch across his chest.

"It's going to get harder now," Shawn said, pointing at the homeless people scurrying away from them. "They're on the run."

"Yeah, whatever," Lassiter said, getting off a shot at a bearded man asleep on a bus bench and watching him twitch as his chest was covered in red.

"Up to you, Jules," Shawn said.

"Got it." She stepped up to a doorway and with her foot nudged the form sleeping there. "It's over."

The form rolled over and saw the rifle barrel pointing down at him. "Officer?" Frank said in horror. "I thought we were friends."

"Friends don't let friends sleep on the street," O'Hara said. "Rather see you dead. So would Morton."

Frank scurried back in horror as far as he could, then cringed in terror as O'Hara's finger tightened on the trigger.

"Stop! Stop!"

The voice was coming from another doorway. Shawn and Gus whirled, their rifles raised, as a scrawny man with a thick beard and bad sunburn staggered toward them. He wore a filthy Tommy Bahama Hawaiian shirt, now mostly rags, and what were once expensive designer jeans.

"Why shouldn't I take your head off?" Shawn said. "Morton would like that."

The man went pale under his sunburn. "No," he said. "You can't think that way."

"Why not?" Shawn said.

"Because it's not the game," the man said. "It's real! This is all real."

"What's the difference?" Shawn said.

"The game, it's just for play," the man said. "You can't

let it infect you. The stuff you do in there for fun out here has terrible consequences."

"You mean like when you're driving down the street and you speed up to run over a homeless man?" Shawn said.

The man nodded silently.

"Even when you're supposed to be hiding away in your blacksmith's shop, waiting to see if anyone's smart enough to figure out the clue you left in the game," Shawn said.

O'Hara let out a gasp, then looked more closely at the homeless man. "This is Macklin Tanner."

Lassiter looked disgusted. He spoke into the microphone on his sleeve. "Officers Carren, Carol, and Blain. Stand down."

Behind them the three dead homeless men stood up and tried to brush some of the red paint off their clothes before heading over to Lassiter.

"I was going to leave another clue at the barn," Tanner said. "Let them track me down to Bermuda. The first gamer who found me would win a million dollars."

"But when you were still testing it out, you went for a drive to pick up some supplies," Shawn said. "Walon O'Malley was crossing the street in front of you. And suddenly all you could think of was the points you'd score by killing him. After you hit him you were ashamed and terrified. You cut the car you'd killed him with into pieces and hid out down here."

"I wasn't just hiding," Tanner said.

"I know," Shawn said. "You were atoning. Living out the life you had taken."

Tanner nodded, tears streaming down his face. "How did you know?"

"I've spent some time in Darksyde City," Shawn said. "That librarian's a real pain in the ass."

O'Hara took Tanner by the wrists and slipped on the cuffs. "Macklin Tanner, you are under arrest for the hit-and-run death of Walon O'Malley."

She handed him to the three undercover officers and walked with him to a waiting patrol car, reading him his rights as they went. Lassiter shrugged off his duster and let it drop to the ground, then followed.

"That was fun," Shawn said. "What do you want to do next?"

"I don't think Brenda Varda's going to let us back into Darksyde City once we give her the news," Gus said.

"That's okay," Shawn said. "I was pretty much done with *Criminal Genius*."

"You never got to meet Morton," Gus said.

"Criminal geniuses are overrated, anyway," Shawn said. "Once you get up close they're just normal people with bad impulse control."

"Like us, you mean?"

"Exactly," Shawn said. "Hey, I've got an idea. Why don't I ditch you and you try to track me down?"

"That could be fun," Gus said. "Want to give me a hint where you're going?"

"Sure," Shawn said. "If you track me through the San Francisco airport, make sure you save room for dessert."

# Acknowledgments

Like any writer I'd like to claim complete credit for this book. But I have only borrowed these wonderful characters, not only from their originator, Steve Franks, but from the actors who have breathed life into them over the last five years: James Roday, Dulé Hill, Timothy Omundson, Maggie Lawson, Corbin Bernson and Kirsten Nelson.

And I'd like to give a special thanks to my editor, Sandy Harding, for her generosity, her patience, and for the fact that every single suggestion she's ever made has made these books better.

# About the Author

**William Rabkin** is a two-time Edgar-nominated television writer and producer. He has written for numerous mystery shows, including *Psych* and *Monk*, and has served as showrunner on *Diagnosis Murder* and *Martial Law*.

Also available in the new series based on the hit USA Network television show!

# PSYCH
## *A Mind Is a Terrible Thing to Read*

## by WILLIAM RABKIN

After the PSYCH detective agency gets some top-notch publicity, Shawn's high-school nemesis, Dallas Steele, hires him to help choose his investments. Naturally, their predictions turn out to be total busts. And the deceptive Dallas is thrilled that he has completely discredited and humiliated Shawn once and for all—until he's found murdered.

But the police have a suspect—found at the scene with a smoking gun. And she says Shawn took control of her mind and forced her to do it. After all, he is a psychic…

Available wherever books are sold or at
penguin.com

Also available in the new series based on
the hit USA Network television show!

# PSYCH
*Mind Over Magic*

## by WILLIAM RABKIN

When a case takes Shawn and Gus into an exclusive club for
professional magicians, they're treated to a private show by the
hottest act on the Vegas Strip, "Martian Magician" P'tol P'kah.
But when the wizard seemingly dissolves in a tank of water, he
never rematerializes—and in his place there's a corpse.

Eager to keep his golden boy untarnished, the magician's
manager hires Shawn and Gus to uncover the identity of the
dead man and find out what happened to P'tol P'kah. But to do
so, the pair will have to pose as a new mentalist act, and go
undercover in a world populated by magicians, mystics,
Martians—and one murderer...

### And don't miss
*Psych: The Call of the Mild*
*Psych: A Fatal Frame of Mind*

**Available wherever books are sold or at**
**penguin.com**